THE COLD OF SUMMER

SEQUEL TO THE FIRST ETHEREAL

E. L. WILLIAMS

To Sasha,
with love

Em
x ♡

Bramble Leaf
BOOKS

First edition

ISBN: 978-1-8382726-4-7

Cover art by Eclipse Studios

Printed by TJ Books Limited, Padstow

To Stu

* * *

'Another world is not only possible, she is on her way.
On a quiet day, I can hear her breathing.'

— ARUNDHATI ROY

CHAPTER 1

*S*torm took a deep, deliberate breath, filling her lungs with the sweet smell of early-morning summer air and baking bread from the café below. She brushed her fingers against the tassels of the meditation cushion beneath her, coaxing herself slowly back into the real world. She hesitated. There was something else. Something that wanted her attention, but the sound of scrabbling paws on polished floorboards whisked her back into reality. Whatever it was, it would find her again. Next came a soft thud as the spaniel misjudged the opening of the bedroom door, followed by the tell-tale rattle of china.

'You daft dog, I've got to open it first,' Isaac said, laughing from the hallway outside as the china rattled again and the old brass handle on the door turned slowly. She closed her eyes, enjoying the moment.

The door opened, creaking on its hinges, and all at once twenty kilos of over-excited liver-and-white spaniel landed on her lap in a flurry of wags and licks that Storm accepted for the gift they were. 'Where've you been this time?' she asked Hope.

It was Isaac who replied. 'She said she'd been over to Henri's to play with Ludo,' he said, setting the tray on the dressing table. He bent down to kiss Storm on the forehead and then pulled a cushion from the bed onto the floor to join her.

Hope flopped on her back to accept a belly rub, and Storm caught snatches of what she was sharing. Something to do with Henri and Ludo and ... was that a car? Even after all this time, she was still pretty poor at interpreting animal communication, much to Hope's frustration, she didn't doubt. But at least Isaac was positively fluent. The dog wriggled to her feet, shook and, after accepting a final ear rub from Storm, trotted out of the room, tail swishing back and forth in her usual easy wag.

Storm laughed. 'Oh, hello and goodbye then.'

'Apparently, she's off to say farewell to an old friend. A collie, I think,' Isaac said, leaning up to get their coffees, now that the danger of wearing them had passed. 'Something about his people moving to help with fish? I'm guessing it's one of the restoration projects, but she was light on detail.'

'Did you speak to the kids this morning?' Storm asked, snuggling into Isaac's chest as she sipped her coffee.

'Only Finn. Hebe and Fleur have taken their students on a field trip into the Pyrenees to look at the use of adaptogen herbs in magical practice.' He beamed.

'Botany and witchcraft. Chips off the old block, for sure.'

'Finn wants to speak to you though, because, and I quote, "Stormy's so much better on relationship stuff, Dad!"' He rolled his eyes.

'Fifteen going on thirty!' Storm said, thinking back to the

cute five-year-old bespectacled kid she'd met that first fateful day at Isaac's farmhouse. She hadn't dared dream then that she'd have the privilege of helping to raise all three of Isaac's children for the best part of the next decade and get a sister-in-law and nephew thrown into the deal to boot.

'I'm hardly the expert,' she continued. 'I mean, I fell for the first witch to kiss me on the eve of an apocalypse, so I wouldn't say I'm fussy.' She dissolved into giggles as he feigned offence.

'Oh, I see. And here's me thinking it was my wit, good looks and charm that won your heart, but no, you were just desperate!' he said, laughing as he stood and pulled her gently to her feet.

Storm drank him in with her eyes. Ten magical years together. Isaac smiled and tucked a strand of her long chestnut hair behind her ear. 'We don't need to be anywhere for at least a couple of hours,' he said, a smile pulling on the corner of his lips.

Storm ran her fingers through his hair. It was still the same shoulder-length tangle, bleached almost to ash in places by the sun. She kissed him gently, and then, just as she pulled him closer, they heard the exaggerated pounding of feet on floorboards.

Isaac groaned and flopped down on the edge of the bed.

Storm sighed. 'Duty is about to call,' she said, raising her eyebrows.

They heard Veronica's voice from the hallway. 'Are you pair decent?'

'Yes,' they intoned in unison. Storm didn't add that had they been given two more minutes, the answer would have been a very decisive no.

Veronica appeared in the doorway, bouncy blonde curls

framing her cherubic face. She was wearing a pristine white apron over her dress today, which was a delicate lilac chiffon that billowed around her as if it had a life of its own. 'Guess what?' she said, her eyes twinkling. She nodded encouragingly, hurrying them along.

'Oh, let me think, the ascension party has been cancelled because of a worldwide shortage of cucumber for the sandwiches?' Isaac said, rubbing his stubbly chin in mock concentration. 'Or have you just covered so much of Pont Nefoedd in bunting that you've succeeded in blocking out the sun and therefore undoing all our hard work on climate stabilisation over the past decade?'

Veronica cocked her head and arched her eyebrow as she smirked at him. 'I think you'll find that we have the perfect amount of bunting, Mr Smarty Pants, although I may add a few more hundred yards now just to make a point,' she said, laughing. 'Guess again.'

Storm closed her eyes and tuned in. 'Oh!' she said in surprise. 'We have a waker!'

Veronica nodded, her curls bouncing as she clapped her hands together excitedly. 'How wonderful is that on the eve of our tenth Ascension Day?'

'Amazing!' Storm said. She focused on a spot on the floorboards, concentrating. 'Yes, I can feel them now. Oh, how wonderful. Who is it though?' she asked, frowning. 'It feels female, but it's too soon to—'

'It's Jean,' Veronica said, cutting Storm off in her excitement to share the news. 'She woke just a few minutes ago. Gave her granddaughter, Hettie, the fright of her life, apparently. Just sat up in bed and asked if someone wouldn't mind making her a cup of tea. The rest of the family are away up in England working on the forest stuff, but Hettie has told her you'd be along in a bit to explain everything, as per the tradition.'

Storm nodded. 'Of course.'

'I'll let you get organised,' Veronica said. 'Sorry about the timing,' she added with a wink.

CHAPTER 2

When Storm and Isaac stepped into the café, she did a double take. Cordelia's, usually such a relaxed, laid-back hub of the community, looked like it was preparing for a military operation. All the tables had been arranged in long, neat rows, and every single flat surface all but groaned under the weight of dozens of neatly stacked and labelled boxes.

Veronica and chef Jerry, both armed with clipboards and pens, were walking between the rows like a pair of generals inspecting the troops. Storm suppressed a giggle when Isaac pulled a mock horrified face.

She was about to speak when she heard Veronica say to Jerry, 'Asim's sorting that one, aren't you, love?' Then call, 'Asim?' She was met with silence, and without even looking around, she added under her breath, 'He's playing with that puppy again, isn't he?'

Isaac nudged Storm, and they both snorted and gave in to the laugh.

Veronica spun around and spotted them. 'It's not funny,

you pair,' she said. 'We have so much work to do and he's meant to be helping, but every time I turn my back, he's playing with the bloody puppy!'

Storm went over to her friend and gave her a hug. 'The poor love. He waited fifty-two years to get over his pet allergy and then had to wait another ten for a new soul to decide to be born as a puppy somewhere in the vicinity. No wonder he's excited. Bless him,' she said. 'And don't fib, you dote on Logan just as much.'

Veronica sighed. 'I know, he's a little peach – they both are. But that's not going to put food on the table for this party, is it?'

Storm looked pointedly at the rows of boxes and laughed. Veronica tutted, then laughed too.

'How about we take Logan to meet Jean?' Isaac offered. 'He'll meet his first ever waker, and Jean will be able to say that she met a brand-new soul on her Ethereal day.' Storm wrapped her arm around his waist, proud as ever of her peacemaker partner.

'You can ask, but he's already a headstrong little soul,' Veronica said. 'He may well have other ideas, especially if Asim has promised him a ride out on the bike. You'd swear he'd watched *ET*, the way he sits in that basket.'

'We'll ask and he can decide,' Storm said. 'We should only be a few hours with Jean, and I'll see if we can round up some reinforcements for you on the way if you like?'

'You're an angel,' Veronica said, giving her a last squeeze then stepping back to release her. 'Now give me a twirl. I've not seen this get-up in the flesh for a fair few years. When was the last one?'

Storm froze. Her arms were raised at her side, but she was no longer in the mood to show off her ceremonial gown. 'The last dozen or so have all been overseas or out of the area,' she said quietly, 'so I've done them astrally, of course, but I think the last one local enough for me to do in person was …' She paused, the memory as hard as a pebble in her throat.

She saw the realisation dawn on Veronica's face and almost felt Isaac catch his breath behind her. She cleared her throat and said as matter-of-factly as she could manage, 'Sadly, the last one here was Elizabeth.'

There was a moment when the three of them stood in silence, remembering. 'Well, thankfully, there have been a few hundred more over the years that had happier outcomes,' Isaac said, gently taking Storm's fingertips, raising her arm and twirling her as if they were back on the dance floor after their commitment ceremony. She'd worn the same gown then, too. She couldn't bring herself to call it a dress. It was so much more than that. No tailor in the world, old or new, could have created something like this. Isaac joked it had been fashioned by angels, and she often thought he might be right.

Storm felt the fabric, soft as gossamer, caress her bare legs as she turned, felt her heart flutter at the sight of the full skirt, the colour of a freshwater pearl, as it spun. She had found herself wearing the gown on that day in London, standing in the rubble of what had once been a Holland Park mansion, ten long years ago. She had brought the house down upon the Very, the murderous sect that had wanted to sacrifice Lilly, in the mistaken belief that she was the First Ethereal. That they had been prepared to sacrifice all of humanity in their quest to dominate the Earth was still beyond her comprehension. That and the fact that, despite having powerful witches and seers in their ranks, they had been so blind to the connection to the physical and meta-physical worlds. Had they really believed that they could ride out the apocalypse in their luxury bunkers and emerge to claim their Eden once every other human soul had perished?

She knew the answer, of course, but still couldn't reconcile the stupidity of it.

She looked back at her gown. She hadn't been surprised that day to find her tatty jeans and T-shirt replaced by such a work of art, nor had she been surprised by the wings of light that, blessing complete, sat folded neatly on her back. It was the day when everything had changed. But it was also the day when she finally became herself once again.

'Beautiful!' Veronica exclaimed. 'Need a flight check?' she asked, her tone overly bright to compensate for the unwelcome reminder of Elizabeth. Although it had been close to two years ago, the memory was still raw.

Storm felt a flutter at her shoulders as her wings, always hidden until needed, confirmed what she already knew. 'All in working order,' she said. 'Right, let's go cajole a puppy into a field trip and tell Jean that she's now only a decade away from triple figures.'

CHAPTER 3

*L*ogan, a Bernese Mountain Dog built like a small bear cub, had jumped at the chance of an outing, much to poor Asim's disappointment. They had found them in the courtyard playing some sort of game of fetch, although as Logan got a biscuit regardless, Storm was none the wiser as to the rules. What was obvious by the amount of laughing and barking was that they were both enjoying themselves, which was all that mattered.

To his credit, Logan had made a big deal of saying farewell to Asim, licking his cheeks and whining as if they were to be parted for years and not hours, and then, just as they were at the back gate, racing back for a second round of cuddles before finally falling into step beside Isaac and Storm.

Logan had cast a grumpy eye at his dog stroller when Storm collected it from the back gate, but as she'd known would be the case, he had sat on the pavement like a dropped teddy and refused to budge when they were only a handful of shops up the high street.

It was slow going, not just for the weight of the tired

puppy lying happily in his stroller as they walked up the hill, but because everyone knew there was only one reason, or only one good reason, at least, for Storm to wear her ceremonial gown save for Ascension Day. Eyes widened, jaws dropped, and people wasted no time in hurrying over to ask who was awake. Everyone they met wished Jean well, asked that their love be passed on and inquired about her likely attendance at the Ascension Day celebrations. And yet there was a hesitancy there too. There were so few secrets in the new world, so little that went unsaid in a world where love and truth reigned supreme.

'They're bound to wonder,' Isaac said, pulling Storm more closely into his side as they walked, having said their farewells to what she hoped must surely have been the last Pont Nefoedd resident out that afternoon.

'I know,' she sighed, 'wondering is perfectly fine. I just don't want curiosity to tip over into worry. I can already feel the energy levels dipping a fraction.'

'Elizabeth made her choice, Storm. There was nothing you could have done differently to change that,' Isaac said, stopping and turning to face her. He stroked her cheek, and she felt the same rush of energy as she had that first day when he'd kissed her. They had been racing through the secret tunnels under Isaac's farm when the news reached them of Lilly's abduction. Her magic was newly unbound, and she had a cold fury in her belly at the knowledge that it had been Margot, her friend and mentor, who had severed her from her power. She hadn't known how long she could contain her magic. Indeed, she had doubted then whether she could control it at all, returning as it had with a strength that terrified her. But then he'd kissed her, and as she kissed him back, her centre returned.

He held her eyes now, then leaned in and kissed her gently

on the lips, and she felt, just like she had that first day, her equilibrium return.

'Snogging in public now, is it?'

They looked up to see Jack and Lilly strolling towards them, hand in hand, both grinning broadly. Logan chose that moment to wake and started howling to be released from his stroller so that he could meet some more of his none too select club of favourite people.

'I swear you get more Welsh by the day,' Isaac said, slapping Jack playfully on the shoulder before leaning over to kiss Lilly on the cheek. Storm lifted Logan from his stroller, and he barrelled over to Jack the second his paws were on the ground.

'I thought I felt someone stir,' Lilly said, clapping her hands together. 'Oh my, Stormy, you look so stunning. Just like the first day in London.'

Trust Lilly, Storm thought, to only remember the good times. She never once commented on how she had almost been burned alive, or how, as they all stood in the dust of the exploded house, a sniper had made a second attempt on her life. No wonder she had been the first to accept the blessing when the ascension began. Isaac's son, Finn, who had only been five at the time, and new to the delights of toilet humour, had called Lilly 'Number Two' for years as a result, although the teenage Finn blushed scarlet these days when reminded of it.

'Will I rumple you if I hug you?' Lilly asked.

'I think it's part Kevlar, so no,' Storm replied with a smile, and reached over to hug her friend.

'So, is it Jean then?' Lilly asked.

'It is. Remember her eightieth?' Storm said, shaking her head and laughing at the memory of Lilly's face when the sedate afternoon tea she'd been expecting turned, as Storm knew it would, into a gin-fuelled knees-up complete with dancing and impromptu karaoke to old rock songs.

Lilly covered her face briefly with her hands as she giggled into them. 'That was honestly one of the best nights ever! I laughed so much, and my feet were killing me by the end of it – Jean was relentless on the dancing, wasn't she?' Lilly's expression became thoughtful, and she added, 'I remember watching her and thinking that getting old would actually be quite lovely.'

'How are things shaping up in Cordelia's?' Jack asked. He had Logan in his arms and the puppy was nibbling on his necklace, despite Jack's attempts to cover it with his spare hand. 'I take it Asim is back on sandwich duty if you've got Little Legs here?'

Lilly held out her arms to take Logan, who scrabbled in the air to reach her then planted a fat paw either side of her neck and licked her chin until she squirmed.

'Let's just say I think we'll be eating leftovers for weeks,' Storm said, shaking her head ruefully. 'We've reminded them time and time again that nobody really eats in the quantities we did back in the old world when we needed food to sustain us, but there's no telling them. It's like Jerry still thinks we have armies to cater for, and Vee, as you know, is never happier than when she's feeding someone. We've left them to it. They're happy, and it's not like we'll have to worry about waste these days.'

'Will it be a full house?' Lilly asked, giggling while trying to fend off Logan's attempts to wash her ears. She gave up and popped him gently onto the pavement, where he promptly took to pouncing on Jack's shoelaces.

'Looks like we'll have the whole town,' Isaac said, 'so close to two hundred souls in the park tomorrow.'

Storm gave Lilly a meaningful look, remembering how

finding Hope in the park had been the first act of love and selflessness that had brought the young girl, soaked to the skin and shivering, to her door. Neither of them could have known then how monumental that act had been.

'Right,' said Jack, picking up Logan, who had settled on the pavement to chew contentedly on the end of his shoelace. After a last cuddle, he popped him back in the stroller. 'We have detained you long enough.'

Lilly hugged Storm. 'Give our love to Jean, okay?' Then she added quietly in her ear, 'It'll be fine.'

Storm nodded, grateful as ever for the young woman who, in another life, might have been her daughter. 'See you when we get back,' she said, giving Lilly a last squeeze. Then she and Isaac pushed on up the hill, exchanging smiles as they watched Logan marvel at the world in a way only new souls ever could.

When they reached the front gate of Jean's home, a tall three-storey Victorian villa shared by four generations of the Ross family, they stopped. In the old world, the house had belonged to a record producer and his family, but they had gone to Scotland to help decommission the fish farms after the shift. When all but Jean had accepted the blessing immediately, the Ross family had stayed in Pont Nefoedd and chosen a house where they could all live together and take it in turns to be with her when she woke. Storm doubted any of them had thought it would take this long, but if she'd learned anything, it was that souls can't be rushed. Regardless of what anyone else thought, this was the right time for Jean to decide. She felt her stomach clench and her mouth go dry. With an effort, she reminded herself that this wasn't her decision, nor could she influence it in any way. She was here to make an offer – the same offer she'd made to the eight billion human and countless number of animal souls on the day of the great shift.

Storm felt the air stir around her and let out the breath she had been holding. She also reminded herself that she was not alone in this process. Looking up, she saw Cadw land on top of the tall stone gateposts, her head tilted, coal-black feathers lustrous in the morning sun.

'Hello, my friend,' Storm said with a respectful nod.

'Cadw,' said Isaac respectfully.

The crow nodded, then cocked her head in the opposite direction and peered at Logan, who was wriggling in Isaac's arms.

'Logan,' Isaac said. Then, in reply to whatever the bird had said next, he added, 'Yes, new souls are indeed a joy.'

Cadw turned her gaze back to Storm, and with a last nod, took flight. Storm tracked her and saw another six crows had taken up their stations on the roof. They stood in a line, so still they might have been statues. Cadw took her place in the middle, and they all bowed their heads, waiting. Storm's hands felt suddenly clammy, her gown too hot and restrictive, and her breath seemed to have forgotten the way to her lungs.

The touch of Isaac's hand on her shoulder startled her. She spun, and the world seemed to disappear around them. He pulled her gently towards him and planted a slow, lingering kiss on her forehead. Her breath slowed to match his, and when he stepped back, he was smiling as he looked into her eyes. He knew her better than anyone, and in his gaze, she read everything she needed to know. She was ready.

'We'll wait here until you call us,' he said, releasing her hands after a last squeeze.

Taking a deep breath, Storm pushed open the gate and walked up the steps. The front door was already opening.

CHAPTER 4

'*D*o you think Storm is worried about what happened before?' Jack asked, stroking his thumb over Lilly's, as was his habit whenever they held hands.

Lilly sighed. 'I'm sure she is. They used to say, "Heavy is the head that wears the crown," didn't they, but I think in the new world it should be, "Heavy is the heart who bears the wings." I don't think people realise what it is to be the First. Why would they, I suppose? In a world without fear and jealousy and all those other things that made humanity so horrendous in the old world, people just don't seem able to comprehend it now, especially after such a long time.'

'Everyone knows about Elizabeth though,' Jack said, while making the woman's name sound like an insult.

'I don't. Who's Elizabeth?' said a familiar voice from behind them.

'Tim! Michael!' Lilly exclaimed, spinning around to hug them. Michael, who she still thought of as her first boyfriend, at least in this last life, got an extra-long hug. Their relationship might only have lasted a few days before she remembered who Jack was to her, but in falling for Michael, she had also fallen in love with life.

'How you doing, bestie?' she asked when she let him go, craning her neck to look up at him. Still every inch the surfer dude, and now with an equally handsome surfer dude partner.

'We're good, thanks, Lillykins,' he said, grinning down at her.

'When are you two going to give us an excuse for a party?' Jack asked, nudging Tim playfully. It was a well-trodden tease, and Lilly rolled her eyes.

'You pair can talk,' Tim said. 'I don't remember getting an invite to your commitment ceremony. Do you?' he added, turning to Michael, who shook his head theatrically.

'Well, we sort of did that a few hundred lifetimes ago, so ...' Jack trailed off with exaggerated nonchalance.

'Cop out if ever I heard one!' Tim declared. 'Anyway, we may well surprise you one of these days. Listen, I wasn't joking about the Elizabeth thing, by the way. I overheard someone in the bakery whispering about it earlier, too. Have I completely missed something?'

Lilly saw Michael pull a face. 'It was a couple of years ago, before you came home to live. Remember, I told you about the waking that went wrong?' Michael paused, waiting.

'Oh!' said Tim, his eyes widening. 'That was this Elizabeth people are talking about.'

'Yep. One and the same,' Jack said solemnly.

'It was just pure malice on Elizabeth's part. She insisted on a public place to make her decision. Poor Storm assumed, as you would, that it was because she wanted to share a sacred moment with everyone. I'll never forget the horror on Storm's face when, you know ...' Lilly said, remembering how useless she'd felt as she, along with the rest of the town, watched from the river bridge as the awful events unfolded.

'I remember the story now,' Tim said, shaking his head, his eyes on the pavement. 'I just hope Storm doesn't dwell on it.'

'You say that, but I'm sure she does. And today will have brought it all back to her. No matter how many of us told her at the time that it wasn't her fault, she feels responsible for absolutely everything, poor love,' Lilly said, feeling miserable at the thought.

'Jean's no Elizabeth though,' said Michael. 'She'll be fine this time. I'd put money on it. If it still existed.'

'I'm sure it will. Jean is lovely. Will we see you later?' Lilly asked, already feeling brighter. Like Jack, Michael had always had the knack of making her feel grounded and hopeful.

'Oh yes,' said Tim. 'We've got a list of party prep jobs probably as long as you do.'

After saying their goodbyes, Jack and Lilly stood for a moment and watched their friends stride down the hill together, lost in conversation.

'You know,' Jack said, 'I'm glad you picked me, for obvious reasons, but also because if you hadn't, they never would have found each other.'

Lilly looked up at him. 'I bloody love you,' she said, her heart filling to bursting point. Then she reached up and kissed him, feeling the same frisson of excitement that she'd known in every lifetime they'd shared, and in all the between times in the Eternal Forest.

They stood for a few seconds, enjoying the moment until Lilly said, 'Come on, if we get our helpy-helper jobs done at Cordelia's, we'll have the whole evening just for us.' She raised her eyebrow meaningfully.

'Now you're talking! What are we waiting for?' he said as he set off at a jog down the hill, Lilly giggling at his side.

CHAPTER 5

*B*y the time Storm reached the top of the stone steps, she had calmed the butterflies in her stomach. She had welcomed over a thousand wakers since the ascension, as was her duty as the First. Most had been in the days and weeks after the great shift, but there were still a few people dotted around the world who had yet to decide. There was no rush; they had an eternity, after all.

Standing in the doorway, wearing cropped jeans and an oversized black T-shirt knotted at the waist, was Jean's granddaughter, Hettie.

'I hear she gave you quite a fright?' Storm said as she hugged Hettie hello.

'Oh yes. Everyone else is in Windsor for the forests meeting. I stayed to look after Nanna and catch up on the cleaning. I had just turned the hoover off, and she sits up in bed and asks if I'd be a love and make her a cuppa. I proper screamed, Stormy. Top of my lungs job. I frightened the life out of her, bless her.'

Storm laughed, picturing the scene. 'Well, under the

circumstances, I hardly think it's surprising, my lovely. Is she okay now?'

Hettie nodded and made her way up the grand, winding staircase to the first floor. 'A bit confused and, of course, Nanna being Nanna, very impatient to find out what's what, so no change there. Mum, Dad and the others are on their way back, but I know we can't wait.'

Storm remembered back to Jean's eightieth birthday party just before the shift. They had drunk Cordelia's dry, and there had been at least two emergency calls to the off-licence to replenish the gin supplies. It had been the first time she'd seen Lilly really let her hair down, and it had been a joy to behold. She had Jean to thank for that. She'd only just met the young woman but had gone out of her way to make sure Lilly felt like a guest rather than their waitress for the evening. Jean was one of the good guys. Had it not been for the memory of the one who had refused, Storm would have been all but floating up the stairs, eager to welcome an old friend to their beautiful new world.

Hettie stopped in front of the only closed door on the landing, her hand resting on the old brass handle. She turned to look at Storm, chewing at her bottom lip, her eyes searching.

'It'll be okay,' Storm whispered, rubbing the girl's arm and hoping silently that it would be.

Hettie nodded and tried to smile. She raised her eyebrows in question, and Storm said, 'Yes.'

Jean was sitting up in bed in the spacious double-aspect bedroom, gazing out of the large bay window ahead of her. Her hands were wrapped around a mug of tea, a crocheted blanket draped around her shoulders despite the warmth of the day. Her eyes widened when she saw Storm, and she cast from right to left, trying to decide which bedside table to set the mug on. Hettie stepped in to take it from her.

'Duw anwyl!' Jean said, reaching out her hand for Storm's. 'Oh, Stormy, you're a sight for sore, old eyes. What the 'ell have I missed? Eh? Have you seen little Hettie? She's all grown up!'

Storm felt it at once, the soft thrum of an energy signature so pure and gentle that she would have staked her very existence on it. The butterflies in her stomach evaporated and she at last felt able to relax, knowing that Cadw and the rest of the blessing would not be needed today. As if reading her mind, she heard a single caw through the open window and looked up just in time to see the crows fly off into the distance.

She turned her attention quickly back to Jean. 'What have you missed? Well, you'll never catch up on *The Archers*, that's for sure, but as for the rest of it, well, let's just say I'm glad you're sitting down.' Storm scanned the older woman's face, waiting for a sign that would tell her how much she needed to say.

Jean looked away, lost in thought, and Storm did nothing to fill the silence. When at last she looked up and met Storm's eyes, she said, 'I've been asleep for a long time, haven't I?'

Storm nodded.

'To be honest with you, when I first woke up, I thought I was dead for a minute, because everything feels so different. Like being in a dream, all perfect like. But I know it's real. Don't ask me how I know, but I just do. I know, sure as eggs is eggs, that I'm not dreaming, which is why I thought I'd gone.' The words tumbled from Jean's lips with barely a breath between them, the certainty of them masking the question that was obviously uppermost in her mind.

'You're not dead, my lovely,' Storm said, giving Jean's

papery hand a gentle squeeze. 'You are, though, in a sort of in-between state at the moment.'

'Jesus wept, I'm not in limbo, am I?' Jean burst out. 'Don't tell me that nasty young vicar chap was right after all? Oh, I couldn't a'bear him. Horrible man. Horrible,' she added with a shudder.

Storm couldn't stifle the laugh. 'No. Not in the old religious sense, anyway. Let me tell you what happened to the world, the short version anyway, and then you can decide what you'd like to do.'

'It sounds like the bloody *Matrix*,' Jean said with a nervous smile as she leaned back against her pillows. 'No more interruptions though, I promise,' she added, miming zipping up her thin lips and tucking an imaginary key down her cleavage.

Storm bit her lip in an effort to remain serious and began when she felt her composure return. 'The essence of life itself is vibration. Everything and everyone has a frequency, including the Earth herself. It is in the nature of all things to move up that scale of vibration, to constantly evolve, if you like. Towards the end of the 2020s, mystics and physicists arrived at the same horrifying conclusion – for the first time in life's existence, Earth was slipping down the vibrational scale instead of moving up it. While our physical world was imploding thanks to runaway climate change and ecosystem collapse, what was less obvious was that the very fabric of reality was unravelling. As things began to fall apart, the fear levels soared, and so the process ...'

'Speeded up,' Jean offered, then, remembering her self-inflicted vow of silence, pressed her finger to her lips and nodded for Storm to go on.

'Exactly right. Even if by some miracle we'd solved the environmental issues in time, there was the small problem of the energetic collapse. By then, the fear, hatred and downright despair were weighing us down to dangerous levels. We had one hope, and that was the Ethereal.'

At the mention of the name, Jean's eyes widened and filled with tears. She clapped her hands over her mouth. Storm smiled as her own eyes filled in response. She waited.

Jean tipped back her head and blinked furiously, obviously determined not to cry. After a few moments, she pointed a shaky finger at Storm. 'You. You're her. The Ethereal,' she said, her voice trembling. 'I saw you when I was sleeping. Of course I did. Oh, bloody hell, Stormy!'

'The thing is, Jean, I need to ask you ...'

'Oh, hell yes. Yes, with bloody knobs and bows and big bloody bells on, yes!' Jean said, dabbing at her eyes with the end of the bedsheet and smiling so radiantly that it might have lit a small town for a week.

'I still need to explain it to you, so that you're sure. Is that okay?'

Jean nodded enthusiastically and clasped her hands together eagerly.

'Although I didn't know it until the time I was called to do so, my purpose here on Earth was always to decide whether there was enough good, you might say, enough love, left in the world to allow it to ascend to the new frequency. For so long, all I saw in the world outside my little bubble here in Pont Nefoedd was anger, cruelty and hatred. I despaired for the world, and for many years I wanted no part of it. But then – I can fill you in on the details later – amid the darkest times, I realised that even the very worst of humanity is also capable of great love.'

'And that's what made up your mind.' Jean stated it as a fact.

Storm looked at the bedspread as she nodded. 'Yes, that's when my soul decided. That, however, was the easy part. The next task was to issue an invitation to the rest of the living world in the hope that they would ascend to the new vibration too.'

'And they all did?' Jean asked, her face a study in attentiveness.

Storm stood up and walked to the window. This was always the part of the story that she disliked the most, partly because, if she was honest, it was that every soul lost felt like a failure. She looked out of the window and smiled at the sight of Isaac and Logan playing fetch on the road outside.

Shaking her head, she leaned against the windowsill. 'Sadly, no. Some souls decided they liked the world just the way it was. They refused to believe that there was any real danger at all, and when the invitation was issued, they said no.' She had done this enough times now to know the question that always came next, but still she waited for Jean to ask it.

'So, what happened to them then?'

Storm sighed and bowed her head before replying. 'The thing about the new vibration is that only those living things that resonate with it can live within it. Those that refused the blessing, the invitation to the new vibration, were left behind as the Earth ascended.'

'They're dead then?'

'Far from it. They exist just as they did in the old world, but on a lower vibrational plane where there is still fear and hatred and all those other baser emotions. Think of it as another dimension. They're not dead, but unlike us, they can die there, and when they do, their souls return to the highest plane, as all souls do.' Storm paused, searching Jean's face for any sign that she had overwhelmed or confused her.

'Can they come here?' Jean asked, her brow creasing.

Storm shook her head. 'No. It would be like us trying to

live underwater, which, sorry to disappoint you, we're still not able to do.'

'But aside from that, we're living in utopia,' Jean said, her generous smile crinkling the corners of her bright eyes.

'Close, yes. We've still got a lot of work to do to fix the mess we managed to make of the place, but after a decade, we've stabilised the—'

'How long!' Jean's mouth hung open.

'The ascension was ten years ago tomorrow. You've woken just in time for the party, actually, which doesn't surprise me at all, knowing you, Jean,' Storm said, hoping the joke would take some of the sting out.

Jean shook her head. 'Why did I sleep? And why so bloody long?'

Storm went back to sit on the edge of the bed. 'We don't really know for sure. Many did, all across the world. Some for hours, some for weeks, others, like you, for years. We thought at first that it might have been indecision, but almost all decide to become Ethereal. Our best guess now is that it's a combination of healing time and the fact that every soul waits for their perfect moment to reengage with the world.'

Jean nodded, her brow pinched in thought. Then she snapped her head up and asked, 'I'm never ninety, am I?' Before Storm could reply, she added, 'But you don't look ten years older. Is that because of who you are?'

'Now that will be something that will mess with your head a little bit, until you get used to it, anyway,' Storm said, grimacing. 'Ethereals are eternal, and so we choose to appear however we want. Most kids decided to carry on ageing when the ascension happened, but then stopped when they hit a point they liked. Most adults just stopped where they were, some went back a few years, but it's your choice.'

'Bloody hell! If I wasn't decided before, I am now!' Jean laughed, but it turned into a bout of coughing.

When it had subsided, Storm took her hand. 'You're not Ethereal yet, which means you're still susceptible to all of your human ailments, including your bad chest. Are you ready to decide?'

Jean nodded vigorously as she focused on her breathing.

Storm stood and walked to the end of the bed. She closed her eyes, and before the thought could even form in her mind, she felt the skin on her back quicken. Then, all at once, her wings filled the room with the purest white light.

* * *

ISAAC LOOKED UP EXPECTANTLY as Storm opened the front door. 'Well?' he asked, even though he'd have to have been blind not to see the light pouring out of the front bedroom window ten minutes ago.

Storm gave him a double thumbs up and grinned. Logan took that as his cue to try and race up the steps. 'Hang a ding,' Isaac said, catching the puppy in mid-launch, which was no mean feat given the weight of him. 'Ethereal or not, no steps for you until those little puppy bones have grown a bit.'

'There's someone in here who's dying to meet you,' Storm said, tickling Logan's ears. 'Best behaviour, okay?'

'Yeah, right,' Isaac said with a snort as they followed Storm into the house.

CHAPTER 6

*S*torm excused herself and slipped out of the bedroom, leaving Hettie and Isaac to continue answering Jean's many questions while Logan provided the comic entertainment and cuddles. The relief she felt was palpable. While she might have staked money on a happy ending, she would have done the same with Elizabeth too, and on that occasion she had been so very mistaken.

Those who had refused the first blessing had, or so she had thought then, simply left. She had felt each and every soul go, as she had known she would, but she wished them well on their journey and had thought the chapter closed. Elizabeth had proven otherwise.

There had been a long line of wakers that year, and Storm had looked forward to welcoming new Ethereals to their healing world. Elizabeth had given her no indication that she would refuse the blessing, and when she asked to come to town and make her decision in front of the community, Storm had been moved by the woman's desire to share and celebrate such a precious moment with others.

The river bridge had been Elizabeth's choice. Almost everyone had gathered, lining both sides of the old stone bridge, excited and honoured in equal measure. Henri had volunteered himself as chauffeur and had travelled to the city to collect her. Storm remembered his expression as he stepped out of the car. She had briefly wondered why he wasn't smiling. That had been the first sign of what was to come, but she had been so eager to welcome the newcomer, and so innocent of the woman's real motives.

Elizabeth had been a tall, gaunt-looking woman somewhere into her fifties. She had leaned on a stick that was much too short for her, irritably shaking off Henri's offer of assistance. That, Storm thought, had been the next sign, but by then, even if she had understood them, it was too already late.

Storm's heart had hammered as she stood at the middle of the bridge and watched the woman creep towards her. She had glowered at the cheering crowd, curling her lip in response to their applause and shouts of welcome. Had Storm known then? Maybe she had. But the die were cast.

Elizabeth had silenced her even before the first words were out of her mouth. 'Ask me then,' she demanded, her eyes hard as flint and unblinking.

Storm's wings had replied for her, bursting with something that felt like grief from her back. They, like Storm, already knew the answer. She had felt the tears pool in her eyes, and then came the screamed reply.

'Never!' Elizabeth screeched, leaning into Storm's face so that her spittle sprayed her cheeks. Then over and over and over again until the word reverberated around her mind like a pin-less grenade.

Storm heard the cries of anguish from those gathered, felt Isaac's hands on her arm, but she had frozen in place. People were speaking to her, although she couldn't make out what they were saying; others were tugging at her to come away, but she was stuck to the spot as sure as if her feet had sprouted roots. She saw that others were trying to pull Elizabeth away too, but she was swinging her cane, not caring who took a blow from the vicious-looking silver top. All the time, the energies were collapsing around them, disappearing like a watercolour left out in the rain.

Storm knew she had to do something. As the First, it was her job to fix this – to protect the Earth and every Ethereal upon it – but try as she might, she couldn't bring herself to banish the screeching, cursing woman.

The crows had appeared on silent wings from the west. The air had shifted around her, stirred by their flight, and Storm had felt herself able to move again. She had stepped back, almost tripping over her gown in her haste. Elizabeth, still screaming obscenities, had tried to follow, but the crows had quietly circled her, knocking her cane to the floor and then keeping her in place, seemingly impervious to her flailing arms.

Isaac had taken his chance and pulled Storm away, but she had refused to avert her gaze. As she watched, the air around the woman darkened. The screaming stopped and Elizabeth's eyes widened in terror as the crows opened a swirling black void in the air above her head. She looked back to Storm, opened her mouth in a snarl, but then she was gone, pulled into the blackness by what, thanks to Cadw's explanation and Isaac's patient translation, she now knew was the Blessing of Crows. They had done what she had, in that moment, been incapable of doing. They had opened the portal to the lower realm and taken Elizabeth through it. It was by far the kindest thing to do. Storm had known that to have let Elizabeth linger in the Ethereal world would have been akin to leaving a fish gasping for air on the shoreline, but in the moment she had frozen. She would be eternally grateful that nature had provided a failsafe in her friends the crows, and yet their presence was always a reminder of her failure. That the Ethereal world even needed a back-up meant only one thing – as the First, she wasn't good enough.

CHAPTER 7

Storm left Isaac and Logan at Jean's on the pretext of having to do something for Ascension Day. Isaac had smiled his lopsided smile at her. She wasn't lying – she did indeed have lots of things to do for the coming celebration – but she also needed some time to be alone, and Isaac knew her well enough after all these years to notice the signs.

At the gate, Storm turned in the direction of the woods, needing instinctively to be around the old souls that had seen it all in their time. The summer sun was already strong, and it was a relief to enter the shade of the trees. She walked slowly, feeling the vibration of every living thing along the way. She inhaled deeply and rejoiced at the sweetness of the air, and the knowledge that the water in the nearby stream was pure, and that the soil beneath her feet was once again teeming with life.

She thought back to her conversation with Jean. How easily the story of the Ethereals' choice had fallen from her lips. Like a rock, worn smooth in a babbling stream through the telling. It all but slipped out now. It had become the type of fairy tale told to young children before the shift, scrubbed clean of anything upsetting or uncomfortable. She might not have lied about having work to do ahead of Ascension Day, but she had lied by omission. She hadn't confessed to anyone how close she had come to deciding differently. How, as she lay in the rubble of the Holland Park mansion she had just destroyed, she had silently cursed the fact that she'd not been killed in the process. In that moment, she had decided that she had survived only to do her duty as the First.

In that version of reality, so that the angelic and spirit realms weren't sucked into Earth's death spiral, her wings, blackened by the solemnity of their task, would have swept over the world, delivering the only mercy available to her – that of painless death to all of creation. Like the blessing, not all would have accepted, but those that did would be spared the suffering of the Falling. The unravelling of reality and the annihilation of the Earth.

She would find Lilly and then she would begin her grisly final task. But then Lilly had been there, racing towards her, hugging her, and as their hearts had spoken without uttering a word aloud, she had at last understood. All of Lilly's memories had flooded into her, the most recent, and most urgent, racing to the front of the queue. As Lilly had stood in that hideous glass box, waiting to die, she had dropped her empath defences so that she could at least try to understand the motives of her captors. To her amazement, beneath the layers of fear and hatred, she had discovered that they too were moved and motivated by love. And if the Very were capable of love, then there was hope for humanity after all.

The rest had become history. Storm had made her choice with a pure heart, and the angelic and spirit realms and the Earth had been saved. In the ten years since, they had created something close to a paradise, and if the price for that was the weight of responsibility – and self-doubt – then so be it.

When she reached the aqueduct, Storm stopped and leaned against the old stone sides to drink in the view. A white-tailed eagle swooped past, riding a current of air down into the valley below. Laid out before her was the evidence of their work. With the village to the east, everything west, with the exception of a few access roads, had been returned to nature. Fields had become meadows and then forests. Everywhere you looked, nature was busy restoring what humanity had once done its best to obliterate. Storm took one last look, and then, her spirits lifted, she headed for home.

CHAPTER 8

*L*illy, kneeling on the floor in the stock room at Cordelia's, finished labelling the last box of bunting and sat back with a satisfied sigh. They surely had enough now to cover the whole town let alone the marquees that, at that very moment, were being erected in the park.

Ascension Day was always wonderful, but this year felt particularly special as they slipped peacefully into double figures. It felt as though they had more and more to celebrate with each passing day. The climate had stabilised thanks to their global efforts, and thousands of species had surged back from the brink of extinction now that people were taking up just ten per cent of the Earth's land space instead of the ninety per cent in the old world. They still had work to do on the plastic particles that had found their way to the depths of the oceans and the summits of the highest mountain ranges, but science and hard graft were achieving a lot, and for anything truly intractable, they had magic as a back-up plan. Granted, it wasn't quite the Eternal Forest, but Lilly guessed that it was closer now than at any other time in a few thousand years.

'Hey, bunting queen, Vee's dishing out coffee and cake for the workers,' Jack said, leaning around the door. He held out his hand to help Lilly up. 'Even now you can't say no to cake,' he added, grinning.

'Hey, Ethereals might not need much food, but we can still enjoy it,' she quipped, adding, 'And besides, cake is like oxygen.' She planted a noisy kiss on his cheek as she passed him.

While Jerry poured the coffee, Asim was trying, pretty unsuccessfully, Lilly noticed, to make Veronica sit in the one vacant chair left in the café, the others having already been carried up to the park. 'You've been up since four a.m., woman,' he said, his gentle voice on the verge of all-out begging. 'You want to enjoy tomorrow, don't you? Not nod off halfway through. So, park your arse, please, or I'll be forced to withhold your cake.'

Everyone laughed at that, because the idea of Asim denying Vee anything in the known universe was unthinkable.

'Did someone say cake?' came a voice from the back corridor.

'Michael!' Vee exclaimed, taking the opportunity to ignore the proffered chair and instead relieve her nephew of the cake box he was carrying.

'Perfect timing,' Lilly said to Michael, before leaning up to hug him hello. When she let him go, Jack took her place and they did that funny 'man hug' that always made Lilly laugh. Why couldn't some men just hug without all that back-slapping?

'Remy got you on deliveries again?' Asim asked after greeting his nephew with what she considered to be a normal, non-slappy hug.

'Rem's been away all week – Arthur's made all of the cakes for tomorrow, including this one,' Michael said.

Lilly couldn't help herself and let out a little whoop of delight. Her friend Remy made wonderful cakes, but her now teenage son was in a whole other league. 'Is it what I think it might be?' Lilly asked, drumming her steepled fingers together in excitement.

Michael rolled his eyes playfully. 'Yes,' he said with an exaggerated sigh. 'Rosewater and pistachio for his lady of lights.'

Lilly wrinkled her nose at the memory of the toddler Arthur insisting that he could see lights around her head when they'd first met. They'd teased him about it over the years and made sure always to tell his new girlfriends the story just to see him blush. He still called her Lilly Lights, though, so she knew he enjoyed the ribbing.

'And here it is,' Vee said, carrying the unboxed cake in from the kitchen. 'He's outdone himself this time. Look at it!'

All eyes fell on the round, foot-high creation, which was expertly smothered in buttercream, rolled in crushed pistachios and topped with what Lilly knew were sugar icing rose petals crafted to look as though a summer breeze had just sent them tumbling to the ground.

'Oh my, the boy's a bloody genius,' Jerry said, rubbing his chunky hands together in anticipation.

The next ten minutes were completely taken up with cake and coffee. After the usual rounds of appreciative groans at the lightness of the sponge and the delicacy of the flavours, they fell into a contented silence. Asim even managed to steer a distracted Vee to sit down, once her attention was firmly on the cake in her hand.

The bell on the front door sounded just as they were dishing out seconds.

Veronica's head popped up like a meerkat's. 'Hi, Walt,' she

mumbled, pointing her fork at her plate to explain the delay in welcome. 'Want some cake?'

Walt, a tall, scholarly man with thinning grey hair, smiled shyly and pointed at the bookshop end of the café. There was a chorus of 'Hi, Walt', which he acknowledged with a self-conscious wave.

With their second helpings happily savoured, Lilly and Jack gathered up everyone's mugs and plates and took them to the kitchen. When they returned, Walt and Veronica were talking by the door.

'Library's open for everyone now, as you know, so please, just pop over whenever you want. Just let me know if you need a hand. Some of the old buggers didn't get the memo on peace and love in the Ethereal age so are still likely to give you a hard time and pinch your fingers in their bindings,' Veronica said, chuckling.

'Oh yes, be careful, Walt,' Lilly said, joining in. 'One of the sneaky old ones nipped me on the thumb last year, and it really bloomin' hurt.'

'Oh dear,' said Walt, looking nervous. 'These might be enough anyway' – he held up the books he'd picked up from the shop – 'but good to know, just in case.'

'Well, anytime, you know that. Except tomorrow, of course,' Veronica added cheerfully.

Walt smiled, nodded his thanks and headed for the door, then stopped, shook his head and said over his shoulder, 'Ten years and I still feel like a shoplifter for not paying.'

Once they'd waved him off, Lilly rounded on Veronica and clasped both of her hands in hers. 'Right, are you going home to rest now?' she said, trying to sound stern and authoritative. The tilt of Veronica's head told her she'd failed on that front, but Lilly knew she still had a chance if she played her trump card. 'For the good of the community, we need our organiser in chief fresh as a daisy.' She added loudly, 'Don't we, Jack?'

'What?' Jack said a few beats too late, distracted as he'd been by his conversation with Michael. 'I mean, yes?'

Lilly rolled her eyes and Veronica sighed. 'Oh, go on then, Miss Bossy Boots,' she said affectionately. 'Thanks for all your help, Lil, today and over the last few weeks. I mean it, you've been wonderful as always.'

Lilly beamed and shrugged. 'I've loved every minute. It's going to be the best yet, I just know it. And we'll have Jean this year too, and Logan. It'll be an Ascension Day we'll never forget.'

CHAPTER 9

*B*y the time Lilly and Jack reached the top of the hill, the sun was slipping slowly behind the mountain. Lilly remembered how bare it had looked when the conifers had been felled all those years ago to make way for the replanting of a native broadleaf forest. Although in tree terms it was still little more than a toddler, it was at last how nature had intended it before humans had put profit before all else. The fields on the lower reaches, once a sea of yellow rape seed stretching all the way to the horizon at this time of year, were now a hotchpotch of glorious colour.

As the human population plummeted and food became a pleasure, not a necessity, what had once been agricultural land was returned to nature and to the animals that had previously been farmed for their flesh. To see them now, living freely and contentedly, was something that never ceased to gladden Lilly's heart. Many of those animals who had chosen to stay needed support in the early days as they too adjusted to the Ethereal age. Isaac and other shepherds had revelled in the opportunity to steer their charges, not to the life beyond to escape pain and suffering but to a life on Earth that they could at long last enjoy to the full.

'I'm assuming you don't want any dinner,' Jack said as they turned into their street of neat Victorian cottages. There had been a debate early on about the logic of demolishing the new houses built on the outskirts in favour of the less spacious, less energy-efficient properties in the old town. It hadn't lasted long. The old houses had been retrofitted for cosiness in winter and the hastily built rabbit hutch newer builds had been carefully deconstructed and the land returned to nature.

Lilly snorted and rubbed her stomach. 'I don't think I'll need dinner for about a week,' she said, pushing open the small green front gate that led to their cottage. The front garden was a riot of colour. Henri had helped her plant it. They had used the box of a jigsaw entitled 'English Cottage Garden' as inspiration. The bees buzzed in the foxgloves and a cloud of butterflies took to the air from the buddleia as they walked up the tiled path and pushed open the front door.

They were met first by the sound of a strangled meow. Anchor sat at the foot of the stairs, feet buttoned up and tail flicking back and forth.

'I'm sorry, Anc. Did you get lonesome?' Lilly said. 'We were a bit longer than we thought.'

Anchor followed them into the sitting room and climbed onto the arm of the sofa. From there, he launched himself onto Jack's shoulder. Lilly could barely reconcile the image of the hissing, spitting hellcat who, all those years ago, had sought to keep Jack as far away from her as felinely possible. To see them now, you'd think they'd been best friends all their lives. She'd even asked Isaac to try and extract an explanation. Anchor had just said that he had known that Jack wanted Lilly to go home to the Eternal Forest and that Lilly had wanted to stay living on Earth. He'd never allowed himself to be drawn on how he knew. His only answer was, 'Cats know these things', and with that they'd had to content themselves. Once it was clear that neither Jack nor Lilly planned on leaving, Anchor had abandoned his objections and made the first steps towards reconciliation. The rest was part history, part bromance.

Later that night, lying curled into Jack in their bed, Lilly thought about all of the lives they had shared together. She remembered them all now, but none could hold a candle to this one. They were living in paradise and, she thought just before she drifted into a dreamless sleep, she couldn't be happier.

CHAPTER 10

*S*torm gave up on sleep just after dawn. Once the sun was up, she reasoned, it was okay to join it. Sliding out of bed so as not to wake Isaac, she grabbed her dressing gown and padded barefoot into the kitchen. She missed Hope's wagging tail and wondered how she was enjoying her trip with Ludo.

She spooned coffee into the cafetière then filled the whistling kettle. Thinking better of it, she muttered a quick spell and poured the boiling water over the grounds. She allowed the coffee to brew naturally. For some reason, magic spoiled some things that nature decided should happen in their own good time. As she waited, her mind drifted to her first bad night's sleep in years. It wasn't as if she'd been plagued by nightmares, but there was something nibbling at the edges of her contentment.

Henri was making his big announcement today, but that, like Jean's waking, was a cause for celebration, not for this sense of – what exactly? She couldn't name it. It was a shadow on an otherwise cloudless, sunny day. She plunged her coffee, chose the biggest mug they had and went down to the courtyard.

The sound of birdsong and the buzzing of early bees greeted her as she pulled open the back door. The smell of sweet peas, honeysuckle, jasmine and roses washed over her on a breeze that, although not yet warm, held the promise of a summer's day. Without warning, her mind drifted back to that day in London, replaying the scene of devastation around them. The dust falling like grey snow. The grand old house she'd turned into rubble with her fury. Birds falling from a sky dominated by a gigantic hammerhead cloud, attended by blood-red lightning. She forced the pictures from her mind and reminded herself that they had not just survived but thrived. So much had been transformed and restored since that hateful day, herself included. The Earth flourished once again, and those that had threatened it were gone forever.

A cloud scudded across the sun, carried on a sudden gust of chill wind. It cast a fleeting shadow across her face, and she shivered as gooseflesh rose on her bare legs. She heard a crow caw and looked up to see a bird she didn't know perched on the open back gate. Not one of the seven she'd seen at Jean's. She tried to concentrate and tune in. Not here to announce another waker but not here by accident either, she thought. She smiled and raised her hand in greeting, and it cawed again in reply. She was about to speak when a voice from the doorway said sleepily, 'I thought you were up with the larks, but I see it was actually a crow.' Isaac chuckled before raising his hand and saying, 'Hello, friend,' to the bird.

Storm smiled up at him and rolled her eyes. 'Morning, my love,' she said. When she glanced back to the gate, the crow had vanished, taking with it, for reasons she couldn't put into words, another small piece of her contentment.

'Want some breakfast to go with that bucket of coffee?' Isaac asked, yawning.

Storm shook her head. 'Not today. I'm leaving space for the mountain of food we'll be expected to eat later. Did the crow say anything?'

Isaac frowned and inclined his head towards the gate. 'What? Just now?'

'Yes, the one that was just here,' she said, noticing, and not liking, the note of irritation in her own voice.

If he heard it, Isaac chose to ignore it. 'Nope, not a dicky bird. Just doing the rounds, I suspect,' he said, yawning again. 'I'll leave you to your morning meditation then, my love.' He blew her a kiss before heading back upstairs. The sound of his feet heavy on the old wooden stairs delivered a strange sense of comfort.

Storm's mind returned to the crow. If there had been something important, surely they would have waited? Or said something to Isaac? She sighed. One bad night's sleep and she was letting her imagination run away with her. She put down her coffee, closed her eyes and slipped into her morning meditation. When she opened her eyes again an hour later, her sense of disquiet hadn't lifted as she had hoped it might. She sighed and told herself off for being a worrier. She had never been a fan of public speaking, so decided that was all it was – good old-fashioned nerves. After picking a handful of sweet peas for the kitchen table, she headed back upstairs to prepare for her favourite day of the year.

*a*scension Day began just after dawn for Veronica. She knew her friends were only being kind instructing her to rest, but the truth of it was that she loved this day and didn't want to miss a second of it. Granted, the preparations took months of work, but the day itself was always a delight, and everyone would be talking about it for weeks afterwards. She loved how the community came together to celebrate, not just the saving of the world as they knew it but their evolution into what many had always hoped humanity to be capable of becoming.

Veronica missed nothing about the old world. Borders, money, possessions, religion, politics; all those things became instantly irrelevant after the shift. Without fear to drive them, people simply abandoned everything that didn't serve their higher good and focused instead on love. Love for themselves, each other and everyone around them. Without fear, there was no anger, no fuel to ignite hatred of the other – and because everyone was equal, there was no longer any sense of otherness. Everyone was trusted. Everyone was loved, and most importantly, everyone knew it.

She found Asim in the kitchen, trying and failing to keep Logan quiet as they rough and tumbled on the rug. Unnoticed, she watched them play, enjoying the simple pleasure each was taking from the game. The kettle whistled and Asim leapt up to silence it.

'It's okay, love, I'm up already,' she said, greeting him with a hug.

'Happy Ascension Day, my love,' he said over her shoulder as he held her.

'Happy Ascension Day, my wonderful man,' she replied, just as Logan woofed and planted his fat paws on the back of her knees.

'You too, sweetie pie,' she said, crouching to plant a kiss on his soft head and ruffle both his ears. 'You're in for a treat today! Loads of people to see, lots of food, stories, music and dancing probably until dawn.'

'Right then, my lovely, sit yourself down. I've got cinnamon toast ready to warm, fruit in the fridge, and tea is coming up. No arguments – it's tradition.'

Veronica had no intention of arguing. She let herself be gently guided to one of the chairs at the breakfast bar, her husband's soft hand on her back. After what had felt like a lifetime of dinners for one in their vast house while Asim travelled on business, she had savoured every moment of the last ten years they'd been able to spend together. When they had travelled, taking advantage of the elegant new solar ships and trains, they'd done so together, taking their time and savouring the experiences along the way.

As her mind wandered through her checklist for the day, she resisted the urge to ask him again about the satellite links. Storm's Ascension Day address would be beamed to every community in the world, as it had been from the very first anniversary. She knew Asim and his team of technical helpers would have it all under control, so she buttoned her lip and instead sat and delighted in the sight of her husband burning cinnamon toast while trying to fend off a nagging puppy.

CHAPTER 12

*I*t felt strange to Storm to be putting on the ceremonial gown two days in a row. Standing in front of the Cheval mirror in the bedroom, she ran her hands lightly over the fabric, wondering for what must have been the millionth time what it could be made of.

She loved wearing it, of course she did, felt blessed every day to be the First, the symbol of what they had all chosen to become, and yet … Her train of thought was broken by the sound of scrabbling paws on polished floorboards. Whipping around, she sank to her knees just in time to wrap Hope, a blur of liver-and-white fur attached to a frantically wagging tail, into her arms.

'Oh, baby girl! It's so wonderful to see you,' she said as she tried to catch snatches of images Hope was flinging her way, a download of her trip with Ludo, she guessed, but she was gabbling too quickly for Storm to keep up. She might be the First, but Isaac was the animal communicator in this family. Storm laughed. 'Well, I'm guessing you had a wonderful time.'

'I think that, my dear, is a given,' said a deep, familiar voice from the doorway.

Hope woofed playfully in response and then trotted out of the room, tail still wagging.

'Henri!' Storm cried, getting to her feet. She crossed the room and enveloped him in a hug. 'It's so wonderful to see you. And thanks so much for driving them.'

Henri waved away the thanks. 'Complete pleasure. It was such a joy to see them all so happy.'

He paused and took a step back to examine her, his palm pressed to his chest. 'My goodness. You look truly spectacular.'

Storm felt her cheeks colour. 'Thanks. You all prepared for later?'

Henri's smile broke into a broad grin. He bit his lower lip and nodded. 'We're all set, but the wait is sheer torture, dear girl. Torture.'

Storm clasped her hands together. 'Oh, Hen, I'm so excited for you. I can imagine how hard it is to wait though. Just a few hours more and you can tell the world.'

He wiggled his eyebrows at her, and she laughed. 'Now, is there anything you need me to do?'

'I'm all set, thanks, my lovely, but you might want to ask the boss. She has a clipboard of jobs looking for good homes.'

Henri put his hand to his heart and tilted his head. 'Then I shall seek out the fair lady Veronica and offer up my humble services in the hope that I may be able to provide some assistance,' he said in his best Royal Shakespeare Company voice.

Storm laughed. 'Careful, she'll have you doing a turn on the stage if she gets wind of your thespian talents. It's not too late for her to shoehorn in another one-man play, you know.'

Henri chuckled, and Storm watched as he strode down the corridor. In just a few hours he'd be joining her on the stage to make his big announcement. Her heart leapt in anticipation. Glancing at the bedside clock, she went to her wardrobe and pulled out her most comfortable shoes. Being Ethereal didn't quite make you immune to sore feet, and today was a day for comfort over style when it came to footwear. She pulled a face at the sight of the once-white trainers in her hand. One too many forest walks with the dogs had left them covered in a thin but stubborn veil of brown mud, made all the grubbier in contrast to her gown. She closed her eyes and whispered the spell. She felt the molecules in the air around her rearrange themselves, and when she opened her eyes, all traces of the mud had vanished and the trainers were so bright they all but shone.

Storm felt as though she was walking on air as she padded down the corridor and felt quietly smug for adding an instruction for comfort to the cleaning spell. Judging by the racket emanating from downstairs, the troops had arrived to transport the food up the hill to the park. The air rang with the sound of laughter and the good-natured banter of friends and neighbours. If excitement could be measured on a scale, Storm thought, they must surely all be around the level of a four-year-old on Christmas Eve after way too much sugar.

What happened next was so unexpected that Storm lost her footing on the top of the stairs. One minute she was confidently putting one foot in front of the other, the next she was surrounded by darkness and falling. Her magic flared instinctively to protect her and held her suspended over the stairs. Just moments later, the light returned and Storm was able to plant her feet and steady herself.

Unable to process what had just occurred, she lowered herself to sit on the stairs. Her breath was short and rapid. Her hands, when she held them out to inspect them, were trembling. She tried to clear her mind, but even when she had regained her calm, all she could see was the briefest of flashes. It was as if the picture had been wiped while the paint was still wet. Just a blur of dark greens, swirling together in darkness and confusion. She felt her magic stir in her belly, felt the cold flood of it through her veins. She swallowed hard. The sound of a foot on the squeaky bottom step snapped her out of herself. Whatever it was, she'd deal with it. Right now, though, they had a party to throw.

CHAPTER 13

The park looked like a scene from a fairy tale when Lilly and Jack arrived with their consignment of food.

'Wow,' Jack said as he stood, open-mouthed, at the gate. 'They've seriously outdone themselves this year.'

Lilly grinned. 'I think someone might have gone a bit OTT with the magical decoration though, don't you think?'

The sight before them was something to behold. The miles of pretty pastel bunting she'd been prepared for, but the other changes took her breath away.

Where there had once been bowling green-variety grass, two-thirds of the park was now a knee-high wildflower meadow. A network of meandering paths led to picnic tables covered in pretty tablecloths, jugs of bright summer flowers at their centres and plump pastel-coloured cushions on the chairs. A circus tent decorated in shades of pink, lilac, lemon and pale blue sat next to the wood. Through its opened doors, Lilly could see the delicate glow of fairy lights that would provide the backdrop to the evening's dancing. There were at least a dozen smaller tents too. Some for shows, others for refreshments, face painting, commemorative photographs and artworks. There were probably others as well, but Lilly's mind was already whirling.

Scanning left, she saw an open-air stage, complete with lighting rigs that wouldn't have looked out of place at the Glastonbury Festival. Never having been to a festival in the old world, she had no idea if people had sat on bales of hay, but she imagined they did.

In the distance was … She blinked, then screwed her eyes closed. When she opened them again, she realised that no, her brain hadn't been playing tricks on her. At the far end of the park, where there had once been a lake, there was now a sandy beach. 'Are they actual waves?' she asked incredulously. 'We have a beach. With real waves.'

Jack shook his head and laughed. 'Well, that's what you get when the town is home to two uber-powerful witches! Come on, let's get these delivered and we can see what else they've magicked up overnight,' he said, heading down the path.

With their consignment safely delivered, they wandered around the field looking for something to do or someone to help, but with only an hour before kick-off, it looked to be all under control.

'Well, we tried,' Lilly said. 'It looks like everyone's just super organised this year.'

'Vee was clear on our orders, so I suppose there's nothing for it – we're going to just have to clock off and begin enjoying our day. Happy Ascension Day, Lil,' Jack said, taking her in his arms.

Reaching up to kiss him, she said, 'Happy Ascension Day, my love.'

'Best one yet?' he asked, holding her gaze, eyebrows raised.

'Best one ever,' she replied, laughing, then kissed him again, just for luck.

'Lilly!' When she spun around to see who had called her, Lilly saw her friend Hettie waving at her from a bistro table set up in front of one of the innumerable cake stalls. Beside her was – Lilly caught her breath – Jean!

Ten minutes later, most of which had been taken up with hugs and happy tears, they were all settled around the small table, chatting excitedly about the day's coming events.

'Tell the truth, bach, I've spent the last twenty-four hours wondering if I'm still bloody dreaming,' Jean said to Lilly. 'I mean, it feels like home, course it does, but it's all so, so wonderful. And some bits are ...' She gestured in the direction of the new beach and shook her head. 'I'm half expecting Willy Wonka to appear and offer me a tour of the chocolate factory!' She laughed at her own joke.

'Jean, do you mind me asking what you remember of your rest?' Jack asked cautiously, taking a forkful of angel cake. Lilly smiled; he always ate the pink layer first.

'Course not, lovely boy,' Jean said, patting his arm. 'This is going to sound weird now, but it was like I was remembering all the times I'd been alive before. It wasn't like I was living the lives, you understand, but, I dunno, like they were in some giant photo album that I was going through. Reminiscing like. Some took no time at all to look at, and others took ages. And then when I was done, I woke up gasping for a cuppa tea.'

'What I don't get,' Hettie said, 'is why some people slept in the first place. I felt the blessing and just said yes. And all my old lives were just sort of there, like I'd known about them all along.'

Lilly shrugged. 'I suppose everyone is different. And as Storm always says—'

'The timing is always perfect,' Hettie, Jean and Jack all said in unison.

'My money is on the fact that Nanna just waited until we'd done all of the hard restoration and re-wilding work before making her grand reappearance,' Hettie said, rolling her eyes and leaning away from Jean, anticipating a poke in the ribs for her joke.

'Bloody cheek,' Jean said, feigning an indignant air.

After a few moments, she added, 'One thing I've noticed though – where's all the little children?'

'That's definitely one of the only downsides of the new world,' Jack said. 'There are some children still being born, but there aren't that many because kids are the souls who decide to start again. Because there's no death anymore, just a relocation of spirit from one realm to the next, and because everyone can basically choose whether or not to age, most people have just chosen to stay as they are and enjoy the new world as adults. And of course, we have had our hands full cleaning things up, which has occupied just about everyone.'

'I think we're different now too,' Lilly said. 'Back in the old world, people had children because they wanted a family or because they wanted to experience being a parent. Some even had kids because they were scared of growing old with nobody to support them. It's different now because we're all family and everyone looks after everyone else. Plus, everyone remembers being a parent in at least one of their other lives, so I suppose it's just not as important as it used to be.' She shrugged.

'Not to mention the fact that there are no accidental conceptions these days either,' Hettie added.

Lilly looked around the park and sighed. 'I miss them though. There's something lovely about their innocence. I'm sure once people tire of being immortal, more will choose to forget for a while and try being kids again just for the sheer joy of it. That's why we've all been so cock-a-hoop over Logan, I think. A new soul is just such a delight.'

Jean nodded but said nothing. They sat in silence for a while, eating their cakes and watching the world go by.

'And is anyone going to tell me who this Elizabeth is, or was?' Jean asked, putting down her cup and looking at each of them in turn. Hettie lowered her head immediately, leaving Lilly and Jack to exchange an anxious look.

With a shrug of resignation, Lilly said, 'That's probably a story for Storm to fill you in on, but let's just say that not everyone made the choice to become Ethereal as quickly or as graciously as you did, Jean.'

The older woman frowned and was about to ask more when, to Lilly's great relief, Jean's eldest daughter, Sandra, came racing towards them, a look somewhere between disbelief and elation on her face.

Lilly and Jack took their cue. 'We'll leave you to it,' Lilly said, but she doubted Jean even heard her.

CHAPTER 14

$\mathcal{J}$ saac could feel Storm trembling ever so slightly as they climbed the hill, his arm looped through hers. He doubted anyone else would have noticed, not even Veronica or Lilly, but it was there, just the merest hint of apprehension that reminded him that the role of leader was still, even after all this time, uncomfortable for her.

Storm had accepted her destiny without complaint from that first fateful day in London. Hers was a burden that few people appreciated. To be the First was, in many ways, to also be the last. The last person on Earth who, for the sake of keeping a balance between the high and low energies, needed to remember fear. He squeezed her arm in his and she smiled at him. Her brave smile, he noticed. How he loved this woman.

They had been together since that first day. It had been the last day of the old world. Since then, she had become not only his partner but also mother to his children, Finn, Hebe and Fleur, and favourite aunt to his nephew, William. Storm and his sister, Katharine, had formed a strong bond, and it had all been so effortless. He couldn't remember them even discussing it. It was as if everyone just knew from day one that they would be a family from that moment on. No longer needing the isolation of Isaac's farmhouse, they had all moved into an old house not far from Veronica and Asim's. The children grew and, aside from Storm's official duties, they lived a happy, normal but magical life.

He and Storm had only recently moved back to Cordelia's, craving the noise and chaos that their now empty nest no longer provided. Hebe and Fleur were in France teaching magic, and Katharine and William were in Norway working on the Global Archive Project. That Finn had wanted to join his cousin and aunt had come as a surprise, but Storm and Isaac had done their best to hide their disappointment. Despite the great shift, it was hard to let go of old thinking, and fifteen still seemed so young to be out in the world, even chaperoned by Isaac's kick-ass sister. That they couldn't make it back for today had been another disappointment, but he understood their need to walk their own path and, Ethereal or not, he'd vowed never to stand in their way.

The crowds lined the path as they entered the park, cheering, clapping, whistling and waving. Isaac felt Storm relax slightly as she waved back at the happy faces of their friends and neighbours and welcomed the visitors who had made the journey to Pont Nefoedd to be part of the day. The crowd was at least four people deep in places. A sea of laughing, smiling faces.

Isaac startled at one face in the crowd. A young man, standing at the back but tall enough to be seen above everyone else. It couldn't be. Someone slapped him playfully on the shoulder; Isaac turned to say hello, and when he turned back, the young man was gone.

'Everything okay?' Storm whispered.

'Fine. I just thought I saw someone from a long time ago, that's all. It couldn't have been, though,' Isaac said.

'You never know,' Storm replied breezily, 'people have come from all over. Maybe it was your friend after all.'

Isaac gave a non-committal nod. Now was not the time to bring up the past, or mention that if it had been the young man he thought it was, he had not called Isaac a friend for a very long time.

They followed the path through the wildflowers to the big top, the community falling in behind them, their excited chatter and laughter a warm, reassuring wave at their backs.

Once inside, Isaac walked with Storm to the foot of the stage steps, kissed her and scanned the tent for Lilly and Jack. Henri was sitting in the front row with Veronica and Asim. While Logan and Hope rolled around playing on the floor, Ludo sat next to Henri in the chair, like a sentry on the night watch. Isaac tickled the old dog's ears as he passed and gave Henri the thumbs-up sign. Henri nodded nervously in response. This, Isaac knew, was going to be the highlight of an already magical day.

Lilly beamed and clapped her hands together excitedly as Isaac took his seat next to her. Anchor was wrapped around her neck like a scarf, his eyes fixed on the stage, tail swishing like a metronome. He nodded hello to Jack. Lilly already looked like she was going to burst with happiness. Man, she was going to go off the scale when she heard Henri's news. He couldn't wait.

'Where are Michael and Tim?' Isaac asked.

'Up the back sitting with their families,' Lilly said.

Isaac turned in his seat, craning his neck. When he caught sight of them, he waved, and half the tent waved back. That was one of the things he loved most about the new world – everyone was a friend. He scanned the rest of the tent but could see no sign of the young man he thought he'd seen earlier. He'd obviously been mistaken.

When every seat was filled, the house lights dimmed and the tiny drone cameras that would beam Storm's address around the world hovered into place. The spotlight clicked on, illuminating her on the stage. Isaac was torn between the desire to cheer right there and then just at the sight of her and the impulse to sweep her up in his arms and carry her home to safety, where she'd not have to endure the trial of public speaking. He settled on just beaming love in her direction.

'Welcome, my dear friends,' she said, smiling and opening her arms wide. Her voice was soft but betrayed none of the fear Isaac knew she would be feeling. 'Welcome to our tenth Ascension Day!' Predictably, the crowd went crazy, and judging from the huge screens around the sides of the tent, the uproar wasn't confined to Pont Nefoedd. The whole world seemed to be cheering, and Isaac felt his heart swell with joy.

'A decade of peace. A decade of love. A new world. Without fear, violence or hatred. Where the lion really does lie down with the lamb,' Storm continued once the cheering had finally subsided.

'My friends, each and every one of you made a choice on that fateful day when the future of the world hung by the thinnest of threads. You chose love, and what we enjoy today is as a result of that choice. Of your choice. The choice to ascend and evolve into what, deep down, we always knew ourselves capable of being.'

'We have achieved so much over the last ten years. Our planet is at last healing, our animal friends are finally free and equal souls.' At that, one of the dogs barked, and everyone laughed.

'And, by working together, as one global community of Ethereals, we have begun to undo the damage wrought on our precious planet by the ways of the old world. We have much more to do, of course, but as we celebrate this momentous milestone in our history, I want to thank you from the very depths of my heart for choosing love.'

Storm bowed her head, and Isaac felt the crowd catch and hold their breath in anticipation. It was likely only seconds that felt like long minutes, but then, all at once, there they were. Her wings, so vast today that they filled the entire stage, exploded in a flash of light so bright that even he felt the force push him back into his seat. There was a collective gasp from the crowd, and then they went wild once more. Magical, glittery ticker tape rained down from above her as tiny, silent fireworks whizzed and spun stars around her then shot out over the audience.

Lilly was the first on her feet, cheering, whistling and jumping up and down, but in a heartbeat so was everyone else. On the screens, Isaac could see the world go nuts in celebration, and he knew his face would be sore from smiling come the evening.

He scanned the tent, enjoying the sight of so many people joined in an act of such joyous celebration of life. He became vaguely aware of Anchor growling, but dismissed it. Why would Anc be growling amidst such a celebration? Then Lilly nudged his arm. Before he could tear his eyes away from the stage, she grabbed at his sleeve.

'Look,' she hissed in his ear, all traces of exuberance gone.

When Isaac looked at her blankly, she added urgently, 'Can't you see it? Storm. Look!'

Isaac snapped his gaze to the stage. Storm was still standing there, her wings outstretched, the inexhaustible ticker tape and fireworks still doing their thing. Drones hovered all around, beaming the footage across the world. She was still smiling. Anchor escalated his rumbling growl. Whatever it was that Lilly and the cat could see, it wasn't visible to him. Isaac turned to say as much, but then he saw it. The shadow was small, no bigger than a man's fist, but it was hovering directly over Storm's heart. He studied her face and suddenly saw the glamour.

'Shit,' he muttered under his breath to Lilly.

'What do we do? I don't think anyone else has noticed,' Lilly said in his ear.

Isaac didn't have time to think of a plan or even respond, because at that moment, Storm folded her wings, and when the crowd quietened, she spoke.

'Friends, before we turn to the important business of celebration, I would like you to welcome our dear friend Henri to the stage to make a very special announcement.' Her voice was just as strong and as calm as it had been before.

Isaac took his cue, slipping out of his seat and walking as casually as he could to the front of the stage. Henri was already mounting the steps. After embracing Henri and yielding the stage to him, Storm walked calmly down to stand next to Isaac.

He had been shaping the spell in his mind since he'd left his seat, and now, with her trembling hand held firmly in his, he focused on sharing his energy with her. It flowed eagerly from his hand to Storm's, like water to someone dying of thirst. Always so independent and self-contained, the fact that she was accepting it so readily spoke volumes. He longed to pull her aside and ask what on Earth was going on, but the eyes of the world were on them. It was at times like these he really envied the animals their telepathic abilities. After a few seconds, he felt the trembling subside, although he could still feel the glamour in place around her, shielding everyone from seeing what was really going on underneath it.

Henri cleared his throat and the applause drifted away. 'I

won't keep you long, dear ones. I know that standing between good people and feast is a recipe for absolute disaster.' The crowd responded with a good-natured laugh.

'I will cut to the chase,' he said, his voice betraying just the hint of nerves. 'It is my absolute delight to announce that my darling wife, Dot, who many of you know passed into spirit some thirteen years ago …' He paused, took a deep breath and concluded, 'has decided to return to us.'

Isaac watched as Henri opened and closed his mouth, unable to continue above the roar of delight from the crowd. Returners were even rarer than wakers, and that someone so much loved and admired in life should choose to come back to them was, without doubt, the news of the century. Isaac's own eyes filled with tears as he saw Henri pull out his handkerchief and mop his eyes.

When at last there was quiet again, Henri said, his voice a little shakier than before, 'As you can imagine, my darling wife has had much to occupy her in spirit since she left us, even more so following the shift, but her work now complete, I think she's finally got fed up of me cluttering up the astral plane with visits. She also mentioned something about missing cake.' Everyone roared with laughter, and Henri beamed.

'So without further ado …' He held out his arm stage right and added, his voice cracking, 'May I present my darling wife, Dot.'

Although Isaac had met Dot numerous times in spirit, seeing her in the flesh made him momentarily forget the incident with Storm. Wearing a brightly coloured floral summer dress in shades of purple, belted at the waist, Dot was every bit the archetypal vicar's wife. Her short silver-grey hair was perfectly set into soft curls that framed her pink apple cheeks. She had what Isaac's mother had always called 'grandma bosoms', so large that any fretful baby was instantly lulled to sleep when cradled against them. She hurried across the stage to Henri, her cardiganed arms outstretched and eager. Ludo sprang from his seat and raced up onto the stage to complete the reunion. The ticker tape and fireworks rained down upon them once more, and Isaac knew there wouldn't be a dry eye in the house.

Storm squeezed his hand as if to leave, but Isaac held on gently for a few seconds more, focusing on offering as much of his energy as he could muster. When she met his eye, he saw first the broad, delighted smile of the glamour, but then, as if peering through a smoked mirror, he saw Storm's real expression beneath. Even without magic, she was doing her best to put on a brave face, but he could still read the anxiety in her eyes. She pulled her hand slowly from his, then kissed him lightly on the lips before taking the steps back up to the stage.

CHAPTER 15

Storm had hoped that Dot and Henri would provide enough of a distraction for her to slip away with Isaac unseen, but she was out of luck. While people waited their turn to congratulate the couple, they also lined up to quiz Storm about the spiritual elements of soul returns. Their list of questions seemed inexhaustible. She had no idea how much longer she could retain the glamour, and Isaac's injection of energy, while welcomed, was waning quickly. He had offered her more, but she had refused. One of them depleted was bad enough. She felt her back slicken with sweat at the effort of maintaining the spell. Her vision began to blur at the edges, and she wondered how much longer her increasingly unsteady legs might be able to keep her upright. Just as she feared all might be revealed, she saw Jack and Lilly pushing their way politely through the crowd.

'Storm,' Jack said brightly, holding his mobile to his shoulder. 'Sorry, but we have to borrow you for a few minutes for some official business.' He held up the phone to the gathered crowd by way of explanation.

Feeling the relief flood through her, Storm, still holding tightly to Isaac's hand, followed Jack and Lilly into the backstage area. As soon as the door closed behind them, Lilly grabbed the nearest chair and Isaac steered Storm towards it.

She sank gratefully onto it, letting the glamour slip at last. She knew she felt rough, but by the expressions on her friends' faces, she looked even worse than she felt. Isaac held the back of his hand to her forehead as he might a sick child's.

'What happened in there?' Lilly asked, kneeling in front of her and taking both of Storm's hands. 'We saw a shadow hovering near you. Are you hurt?'

Storm shook her head, as much to try and clear her thoughts as to confirm that, physically at least, she was unharmed. She took a deep breath and closed her eyes, trying to piece together what had happened on the stage.

'Whatever it was, it's gone now. I'm depleted from the effort of maintaining the glamour for so long.' She paused, then added more quietly, 'And from maintaining the equilibrium.' She searched their faces to check that they understood her meaning.

Jack was the first to speak. 'Whoa, what? You mean the balance dipped?' His voice was a hoarse whisper, and he glanced over his shoulder at the door as he spoke.

Storm nodded.

'I don't get it. What are you saying?' Lilly asked, looking first at Jack, then Isaac, then back to Storm.

'It's probably nothing,' Storm said, mustering a level of reassurance into her voice that she didn't entirely feel. 'As you know, as the First, part of my role is to maintain the energies at our new frequency. Any low-vibration energy that comes into our world needs to be cancelled out with a higher vibration to maintain the balance. That's all I was doing.' She tried for a nonchalant tone, but even to her own ears it sounded false.

'The shadow me and Lil saw was some sort of low energy?' Isaac asked.

Storm shrugged. 'It might have been, or it might have been my own energy dipping as a result of the glamour spell. You two are pretty attuned to me, so maybe that's why you picked it up.'

'I didn't see it,' said Jack, 'and by the looks of the crowd, nobody else noticed it either.'

'Anchor did too. In fact, I think he saw it first, because he started growling. Then I saw it,' Lilly said.

Storm forced a smile. 'Clever cat. Stop looking so worried, the lot of you. I very much doubt that it's anything to bother about. It was just an energy flux that picked a really bad moment to show up. Had I been serving coffees in the café it wouldn't have mattered a jot, but I had to resort to the glamour given the circumstances – I didn't want to spark global panic on Ascension Day by looking a bit shaky round the edges.'

They each looked as unconvinced as she felt, but by some sort of silent agreement, it was decided that the matter would be parked at least until the end of the day.

CHAPTER 16

'Anything?' Jack asked as he sat down on the hay bale next to Lilly and handed her a fresh glass of beer. The bonfire they were sitting around was one of many that had been lit at dusk but were now burned down to just a mound of glowing embers.

'Nope,' she said, tearing her eyes away from Storm, who was swaying back and forth with Isaac on the dance floor to a slow song. 'I'm beginning to wonder whether I imagined it,' she added with a yawn.

'Well, you, Anc and Isaac imagined it then, if that was the case,' Jack said, chinking his beer glass against hers. 'Maybe what she said was right though, about the energy fluctuations and stuff. I mean, I bet there's loads we don't know about what it means to be the First. She might have to deal with this sort of thing all the time, but she's hardly the type to go moaning about stuff, is she? Maybe it was just bad luck, like she said, that she got walloped by something today when the eyes of the world were watching.'

Lilly nodded slowly, then turned and rested her palm against his cheek. She studied his face, his beautiful, handsome, wonderful face, and wondered, not for the first time, how she'd managed to live the first twenty years of this life without remembering how deeply in love with him she'd always been. She knew that had the tables been turned, there was no way she'd have been able to endure even a day, let alone two decades.

He kissed her on the nose and made her giggle.

'You're a wise man, you know?'

'Well, it has been said,' he said, puffing out his chest and making a face.

'Dot is just as amazing as I knew she would be,' Lilly said, squinting through the darkness to the little islands of light around the various refreshment and entertainment tents to try and catch a glimpse of Pont Nefoedd's one and only returnee. The crowds had dwindled considerably in the last hour, as fatigue finally overwhelmed the desire to eat and drink and celebrate the paradise that was the new Ethereal age. 'I can't see them though.'

'No. They've gone. I saw them in the beer tent. Dot looked dead on her feet.'

Lilly raised an amused eyebrow at him and held his confused gaze until the penny at last dropped.

'Oh hell. Yes. Unfortunate turn of phrase on my part.' He grimaced. 'As I was saying, Dot looked a bit tired, first day back and everything, so they were heading home to the vicarage. Actually, they asked if we'd pop over tomorrow.' He took another swig, and Lilly wondered when he would have remembered to tell her if the subject hadn't come up. She sighed and leaned her head on his shoulder.

'Anc, Ludo and Hope went with them too,' Jack added.

'Thank you very much and good night!' the PA boomed, and Lilly looked to the stage, where the band members were already heading for the wings. Putting their beers hastily on the floor, they both clapped somewhat belatedly. Jack stuck his fingers in his mouth and whistled loudly.

'Bet you never get stuck for a cab in the city,' Veronica said, appearing from the darkness and sitting down with a groan on the adjacent bale. 'You know, I might ask for some whistling lessons. I've always wanted to be able to do that.'

Jack grinned at her. 'Anything for you, Vee, you know that. Asim still here?'

Veronica shook her head. 'Logan flaked out, so he took him back to Henri's, or I should say, Henri and Dot's,' she said, wrinkling her nose in delight. 'I think he was glad of the excuse, to be honest.'

'I forgot you're staying there tonight too,' Lilly said. 'By the sounds of it, they'll have a houseful.'

'Just like old times. Dot will love that, first night back or not. That house was always the heart of the community back in the day, and she was never happier than when she had someone to feed and fuss over – the more the merrier.'

'Please, no more talk of food!' Isaac said as he and Storm joined the group. 'We've been dancing half the night to try and burn off the calories, and my feet are seriously bloody killing me now.'

Everyone laughed. As much at the idea that the perma-toned Isaac had ever had to worry about calories as at the use of the arcane word. The correlation between food, health and physical appearance had vanished with the ascension.

With their glasses refreshed and the fire magically stoked and rejuvenated to drive away the approaching coolness of the small hours, they sat and picked over the highlights of the day.

Lilly wondered whether Storm had confided in Veronica about what had happened on the stage, but as she'd barely let Storm out of her sight all day, she doubted there had been the opportunity.

Watching her now, relaxed and radiant in the glow of the fire, it was easier to believe that Jack was right. Maybe it had just been one of those things. Even that thought left her feeling that she'd somehow missed an opportunity to support her friend. Jack was right about something else too – there were probably lots of things that Storm had to shoulder alone. Being the First, the poster child for the entire new world, the beacon of love and peace in the Ethereal age ... well, ascended or not, it couldn't be easy. Lilly chided herself for not taking more time to ask Storm how she could help her.

Lilly felt something shift in the air around her. The sensation was familiar but distant, like a song half remembered from childhood. Her breath hitched high in her chest as if the rest of her lungs had shut down for the night. She closed her eyes and tried to focus, but her hands were already trembling, the back of her neck suddenly damp with a cold sweat.

Everyone else was laughing as Jack recounted his many surfing wipeouts at the park's temporary beach that afternoon. Lilly opened her eyes just in time to see the fox hurtle into their midst, wild-eyed, chest heaving and looking as if all the devils of hell were chasing her. Everyone fell silent at once.

Lilly sank to her knees and laid a gentle hand on the vixen's back, understanding at once what the animal was feeling. Storm manifested a shallow bowl of water and, kneeling to join Lilly, placed it in front of the shaking fox.

'Take your time, there's no rush,' she said quietly. The hiss and snap of the fire and the faraway chirrup of the crickets were the only sounds to be heard above the fox's rasping breath.

After taking a long drink, she sat and looked directly at Storm, then at Isaac. It had been Isaac who had first heard the animals after the shift, and while others were very slowly trying to learn, he was still by far the most adept at reading and interpreting the visual language used by all of the non-human Ethereals.

Lilly felt her sense of disquiet grow into something far darker. She had tried all day to put it aside and focus on the joy of the occasion, but it hadn't gone away entirely. Now she realised that it had merely been waiting in the shadows.

'That can't be,' Isaac said patiently to the fox. 'Violence is beyond us all now. Could you have been mistaken, perhaps?' His words were measured for maximum gentleness, but they still elicited an anguished howl from the vixen, who paced back and forth in front of him, frustration pouring off her in waves of emotion. That, at least, Lilly could feel and understand.

'Forgive me, of course you're not mistaken. I'm sorry, my friend, but as you can imagine, this is news that, well ...' Isaac paused, momentarily lost for words. He rubbed his forehead. 'What I mean to say is that what you speak of, it's just not possible. In the old world, yes, but not now – none of us is capable of such ...' He left the sentence hanging in the air, unsure of how to complete it.

'Will you rest here with us until first light?' Isaac asked the fox. 'Then we'll come with you and see for ourselves.'

The vixen considered the question, then in reply, she turned three times in a tight circle before slumping down in front of the fire, her tail over her eyes. Lilly doubted the poor creature would be able to sleep; even with her empathy shield hauled out of the quiet part of her mind where it had languished unneeded for so long, she could still feel the weight of the creature's terror.

'Isaac?' Storm asked at last, her voice pinched and tight.

Isaac was silent for a long moment. When at last he spoke, there was a slight tremor in his voice. 'Someone is hunting,' he said. 'Our friend here just found a body in the woods.'

CHAPTER 17

There was silence around the fire for a long time. Storm watched as stray embers floated and danced up into the dark skies as if they still hadn't a care in the world. She tracked them as they disappeared into the fading night, and tried to collect her thoughts. She knew the others were waiting for her. Waiting for the First to speak, to offer some reassurance, some great wisdom from the light of the new world. That she could give neither felt like a knife in her heart.

The signs had been there, hadn't they? The bad night's sleep. Nearly falling on the stairs. Then the attack on the stage. She needed to call it what she had feared it was at the time. She hadn't wanted to believe it, but as the saying went, wishing doesn't make it so.

She stood up and faced her friends. Lilly was sitting on the grass next to the vixen, leaning against Jack's legs as he stroked her hair and she, in turn, stroked the fox. Isaac had taken a seat next to Veronica. She'd not found the moment to tell Vee what had happened on the stage, hadn't wanted to ruin her special day, but she realised now that she'd have to.

She would likely get a rollicking for the delay too. That would need to wait though. They needed a plan.

Storm took a deep breath, then said, 'We have no reason whatsoever to doubt what our vixen friend saw in the woods. So at first light, Isaac and I will go and see for ourselves.' She held up her hand to cut off Jack's protests even before he'd managed the first syllable. 'I need to see for myself, and I need Isaac's communication skills,' she added by way of mollification. 'I wish I could say that this, like the shadow on the stage, was just an energy shift, but in my heart I now think it is something rather more than that.'

'What bloody shadow?' Veronica demanded, her eyes wide and fixed on Storm.

'I'll fill you in later, Vee, I promise. I thought it was nothing at the time, but now I think differently.'

Veronica raised her eyebrows and pursed her lips. Storm winced inwardly.

'I wanted to believe it was nothing. I was going to tell you tomorrow, obviously, but today didn't feel like the right moment.'

Somewhat consoled, Veronica softened a little. 'I think I should enact the protocol for the library,' she said, rummaging in her huge handbag for her phone.

'I think that's a sensible precaution,' Isaac said. He looked at Storm, and she could almost hear the question in his mind.

She answered it out loud. 'For everything else, let's not panic people until we know what we're dealing with. The last thing we need is for people to become afraid – that will just drag down the vibration level and make any problem we do have ten times worse.'

'It'll make them vulnerable too,' Lilly said quietly, not taking her eyes off the sleeping vixen.

'It'll be dawn soon,' Jack said, nodding in the direction of St

Teilo's, where the patch of sky around the bell tower was beginning to lighten.

'Let her rest a little longer,' Lilly said, stroking the vixen's back. A thin line of amber eye appeared, then closed again.

Veronica stood up. 'I'll go and sort us out some tea then.'

Knowing that her friend was always happiest when she was busy, especially during periods of stress, Storm joined her. 'I'll help you,' she said. She'd take the opportunity to fill Vee in on what had happened earlier on in the day too.

They had taken only a dozen or so steps away from the fire when Storm buckled under the force of what felt like a hammer blow to her solar plexus. Along with the physical pain came a sense of fear and dread that she'd not encountered in a very, very long time. She was dimly aware of Lilly crying out, strong, familiar arms around her, and then there was nothing but blackness.

CHAPTER 18

*S*torm woke in an unfamiliar room. She stretched out her hand tentatively and felt thick cotton sheets beneath her. The room was dark but for the edges of the heavy brocade curtains at the window. She felt a soft paw on her cheek, and then a familiar weight on her chest. Anchor.

'Hey, my lovely boy,' she said, her voice hoarse. She reached out to stroke his head. The purring began in earnest, followed swiftly by some gentler than usual head bumps.

Storm frowned. This wasn't Lilly and Jack's cottage, she knew that much. Even in the half light, she could see that the room was much too big. There was something familiar about it though. The sheets smelled faintly of lavender and there were other smells, beeswax, woodsmoke, baking. She tried to concentrate, but the effort of trying to locate herself made her head spin.

Anchor settled on her chest, and she focused on his purring and her own breathing until the room stopped wheeling around her.

'The vicarage,' she whispered, and, as if to confirm the

point, Anchor got up and sat next to her, feet buttoned together, still purring. Storm levered herself up to sitting, expecting her head to swim again and relieved when it didn't. She was still wearing her ceremonial gown, and she wondered if whoever had put her to bed had just given up trying to figure out how to get her out of it.

A soft knock at the door preceded a far louder complaint from old hinges. Lilly's face appeared, backlit by sunlight that darted across the polished floorboards. 'You're awake,' she said with a sigh of relief. Crossing the room, she perched on the side of the bed and took Storm's hand gingerly. 'How are you feeling?'

'I'm fine,' Storm answered automatically, but then checked herself. Was she fine? She didn't feel unwell. Wasn't light-headed, but there was something that didn't feel quite right. As she couldn't explain it, she decided to wait until she could. Anchor let out a loud yowl from beside her as if calling her on the omission. 'At least, I think I'm fine. Mostly fine,' she conceded. 'What am I doing here though?'

As she said the words it all came flooding back to her. While she'd remembered fainting at the park, the rest, until now, had been decidedly fuzzy. It was like the memories were wedding guests all searching for their names on the table settings. 'Oh no, what time is it?' she said, flinging back the covers and swinging her legs out of the bed.

'Wait,' Lilly said, jumping up to put a steadying hand on her friend's shoulder. 'It's just after eight in the morning. Isaac and Jack went with the vixen at first light to see what she found. We won't know anything until they get back.' The words tumbled out at twice Lilly's normal speed.

After a breath, Storm nodded and sat on the edge of the bed, feeling a little redundant. Anchor rubbed his side along her waist, and she scooped him up for a cuddle. It had been his choice to live mostly with Lilly and Jack since they'd moved back into the flat. He had told Isaac that he preferred the garden and the peace and quiet that was always hard to find at Cordelia's. Storm missed him terribly, gobbling up his visits and every last cuddle he'd allow her. He rubbed his head under her chin and purred loudly.

Lilly stood up and went to the wardrobe. 'I nipped back to yours to get you something to wear,' she said, pulling out a long white floaty shirt and Storm's favourite pair of jeans. She held up a small overnight bag. 'I put undies and stuff in here. I stuck your flip-flops in too.'

Storm felt her eyes swim with unexpected tears. She tried to banish them before Lilly noticed, never a winner with an empath in the room.

'Hey,' Lilly said, hurrying back to the bed and wrapping her arm around Storm. 'Whatever it is, we'll deal with it.'

Storm nodded. She didn't trust her voice or her emotions to say much else.

'Or is it because I brought the wrong jeans?' Lilly added playfully.

Storm let out a slightly gurgling laugh and took the neatly folded handkerchief that Lilly fished out of her pocket and handed to her. She blew her nose, wiped her face and eyes and took a deep breath. The smile on her lips felt forced, and she chided herself for giving in to tears.

'I'll let you get dressed,' Lilly said. 'Then we can talk about it all over coffee and muffins. Dot's been baking since dawn.'

CHAPTER 19

$\mathcal{J}$ ack pushed another low branch from his path. The forest was thick here, forcing them into single file behind the vixen. Their plan to set off straight from the park at first light had been disrupted by Storm's collapse. Isaac had somehow managed to catch her before she hit the ground, but when, after ten minutes, it was clear that she wouldn't be coming round anytime soon, they had taken her to the vicarage. Isaac had carried Storm. Lilly had carried the still exhausted vixen.

Dot and Henri, woken by Vee's frantic call, had been waiting on the doorstep when they reached the front gate. Mesmerised moths had circled silently around the coach lights either side of the door, and aside from the slow tick of the grandfather clock in the hallway, the only noises had been footsteps and the sigh of meadow grasses and flowers that lined the front path, moving in the chill breeze.

Isaac hadn't wanted to leave her. Jack understood that only too well. Even now, after all these years, the memory of being away from Lilly picked at him like a splinter. He had no idea what was happening, but his gut told him that it wasn't anything good.

Jack and Lilly had retreated to the kitchen when Isaac had carried Storm upstairs to the only unoccupied spare room, Dot leading the way and Veronica close behind. He'd put the kettle on just for something to do, but their coffees had cooled in their hands as they sat huddled into one another around the old scrub table. The vixen had curled herself into a tight ball on the old armchair by the back door, and it had looked to Jack as though she had finally relaxed enough to sleep.

It had been another couple of hours before Dot apparently succeeded in persuading Isaac that Storm would be safe in their care. Jack had only known her for a few hours, but he already understood what she had meant to everyone. Isaac had appeared in the kitchen, bleary-eyed and looking as if he'd aged a few years in the space of a few hours.

Back in the woods, Jack felt his gut twist the moment they entered the clearing. His body reacted to the sight of the butchered deer even before his eyes could get the message to his brain. Whoever killed the doe had hacked off her head and discarded it on top of a large pile of guts. Jack knew that her terrified eyes would haunt his nightmares for an eternity.

Isaac was crouched on his knees, his head in his hands. Jack scanned around for the vixen. She had stopped short of the clearing and was stood further along the path, her head bowed. He went to her and dropped to his knees. She leaned into his leg and, unable to find any words, he simply laid his hand on her side.

After some long moments, Isaac joined them. After clearing his throat, he said, 'We'll need to bury her remains, but not here, of course – the land has been desecrated.' He nodded in the direction of the clearing without looking at it, but when Jack did, being careful not to dwell on the remains of the doe, he noticed what he'd missed. He stood up and braced himself to approach the scene again. The whole area was lifeless. It looked as if every single living thing had pulled itself away from the horror of what had occurred there. There was not a blade of grass or a tuft of moss to be seen. Jack stalked around the perimeter. Even the trees that ringed the clearing looked to be half dead, with only the branches that pointed away from the scene still clinging to a few leaves.

When he returned to Isaac, the vixen was gone. 'I asked her to warn the others,' Isaac said, his eyes only meeting Jack's for an instant before scanning the thick woodland once again. 'She wanted to,' he added before Jack could ask the question. He'd only known the fox a few hours, but he admired her courage. To have stumbled across such carnage would have been horrific for an ascended animal who had long since abandoned the need to hunt and consume others in order to survive. 'She'll come back to us again if she's frightened. She promised.'

Jack pulled out his phone to check the map co-ordinates. He gestured with it towards Isaac. 'I'll make a note of the location so that we can come back with what we need,' he said, feeling safer in the realms of practicality than diving into the question he knew would be foremost in Isaac's mind as well as his own.

A loud crack sent Jack instinctively to the forest floor. It had been a decade since he'd last heard the sound, but that it was a gunshot was unmistakable. He looked up to see that Isaac had hit the ground too. He stared back at Jack, his eyes wide in question. Jack nodded to confirm that he was unhurt before crawling to join him. Both men scanned the forest around them. Jack could feel his heart beating a tattoo against his ribs. He wondered if Isaac was feeling the same thing.

The man appeared as if out of nowhere, crashing through

the trees at a blind run. Isaac was the first on his feet and was already racing after him by the time Jack had scrambled to standing. He was heading west, into the newer, replanted parts of the forest which weren't as dense as the more ancient areas, but it was still hard to keep up with him. Dressed in khakis, he was hard to spot. Jack might have lost sight of him completely, but just then, his cap snagged on a branch and the man's bone-white hair became a beacon against the gloom that seemed to be closing in behind him.

As they approached the old forestry road, a sickening thought occurred to Jack. He tried to call out to Isaac, but he was too far ahead. Surely he'd realise the danger too. Jack pumped his legs as hard as he could and reached the road just in time to see the running man pause. To his left stretched a long, dusty downhill trail sandwiched between a sheer wall of earth and rock and the crisp, bright nothingness of the mountain's edge.

Jack groaned as he saw the man turn right and sprint up the hill and into the mouth of the most ancient part of the wood. Now that he was out in the open, Jack saw the rifle slung across his back and the hunting knife sheathed at his hip. He remembered the doe's pitiful eyes and gritted his teeth. Even so, they had to warn him. He pushed himself on, his leg muscles burning. The man disappeared into the trees.

'Stop!' Jack hollered, cupping his hand around his mouth to make his voice carry. 'It's not safe!'

He heard the scream and instantly knew they were too late. He ran into the wood and found Isaac standing at the edge of the aptly named Dead Man's Drop. When the mountain had been farmed for fast-growing pines, this topmost part of the track had been fenced off with hazard signs. Too steep for the machines that harvested the trees, the forestry owners had allowed native trees to flourish. That they had successfully done so right to the mountain's edge was what had given rise to its name.

'I called out to him, but either he couldn't hear me or ...' Isaac dragged his hands through his hair and kicked out angrily at loose stone as he cursed under his breath.

Before Jack could respond, they heard a groan. Racing to the lip of the mountain, they peered cautiously over the edge. By some miracle, the hunter was caught on a wide, grassy ridge some twenty feet below them. One leg looked to be bent at an unnatural angle, but he was coughing and, therefore, was at least still breathing. Relief flooded through Jack, and he and Isaac exchanged the briefest of smiles before focusing on how to reach the casualty.

CHAPTER 20

*I*saac had won the argument about who would climb down to the ledge. As the hunter was armed, and as Isaac was the only one with recent combat training, Jack had had to defer to his logic. Listing military experiences from past lives had quickly proved to be futile.

Isaac thought of his climbing kit neatly packed in the spare room back at the flat and cursed himself for not having it with him now. That they even had a rope was a minor miracle, though. He'd found it in the backpack he'd borrowed from the vicarage. He'd only taken the pack because Dot had insisted that they take water and energy bars with them, just in case. He'd have to thank Henri when they got back for his levels of boy scout preparedness.

The descent was easy enough, and as Isaac approached the ledge, his mind was focused on the practicalities of rescuing the injured hunter. They'd need a stretcher and a full mountain rescue team, for sure. It would probably be easiest if the man remained unconscious.

Once on the ledge, Isaac noticed that what he'd taken to be

a flat platform of bare rock was actually grass. Or at least it had been. All the vegetation was now blackened and curling around the wheezing, unconscious hunter. Forcing himself to focus, Isaac assessed the situation. The unnatural angle of the man's left leg and the steadily growing patch of blood staining the front of his combat trousers was odds on a compound fracture. What other injuries he might have sustained remained to be seen.

'Hello, my friend. My name is Isaac and I'm here to help you.'

Isaac jumped back as the hunter suddenly lurched forward onto his elbow and thrust a large hunting knife in his rescuer's direction. 'Stay where you are,' he snarled, blood spraying from his curled lips. 'I don't need your kind of help.' He coughed, and with the knife still firmly held, leaned over and retched. Isaac watched as pools of bright red, syrupy blood pooled on the floor beside him.

Isaac studied him. In old-world terms, he looked to be in his sixties, but his body was hard and muscled, his pecs and even his abdominals visibly flexing under his tight khaki T-shirt. This man was all granite. Isaac's eyes snagged on something incongruous strapped across the hunter's breastbone. It was a large flat silver disc adorned with what might have been sigils, although it was hard to see clearly.

When at last the hunter looked up, his skin had taken on a chalky greyness that had Isaac mentally calculating how quickly they could scramble the helicopter.

Isaac risked a step forward, but the man gave a raspy, rattling cough, then said, 'Get the fuck away from me, you mongrel. You're not even human.' He spat a huge globule of blood, obviously aiming for Isaac's boot but missing by metres. 'This world doesn't belong to the likes of you,' he said with a sneer, his lips peeling back to reveal bloodied teeth.

'We're taking back what's ours. I'm just sorry I won't be around to see that witch whore leader of yours burn for what she's done. Tell her we're coming for her.' Setting his cold, unblinking stare on Isaac, he spat on the ground beside him, and in one determined move, dropped the knife, grabbed the disc and ripped it off his chest.

The light appeared first in place of the hunter's eyes, and Isaac's immediate thought was that he had somehow weaponised himself and was about to attack. With no cover on the ledge, the only option was retreat, but almost before he could fully process the thought, the pale blue light poured from the hunter's nose, ears and then his open mouth. He might have been screaming. He certainly looked to be contorting in pain. The light tracked slowly down his neck and chest. When it reached the place where the disc had been, there was a great flash so bright that Isaac had to shield his eyes.

Isaac lowered his hand just in time to see a portal open up above the man's head. It was so dark, it looked to be fathomless. The hunter was still screaming, his head thrown up now, his eyes transfixed by the portal. Then, in an instant, everything that had once constituted the body of the hunter was sucked into the blackness. The portal shrank, and when it was the size of a penny, it vanished.

CHAPTER 21

'What the hell just happened?' Jack yelled from the top of the ridge. Though he'd seen it with his own eyes, he was still having trouble processing. He couldn't hear what had been said, but the hatred on the hunter's face was hard to miss. You forgot that, Jack realised. After a decade of love and peace in the world, it was an unwelcome reminder of how things used to be. How fear and hatred had ruled the lives of so many, blighted the lives of countless others, and had nearly brought an end to life itself.

Isaac didn't reply. He stood staring at the spot where the hunter had vanished.

'Isaac!' Jack shouted, louder this time.

Snapping his head up, Isaac stared open-mouthed at Jack, then back to the spot where the man had disappeared. Jack checked the anchor for the rope and then flicked the end towards Isaac.

'Let's move,' Jack said, deciding that direct instruction was probably what would bring his friend back to the present moment. Isaac responded at once, climbing mutely up to the path. When he reached the top, he sat on a rock and put his head in his hands.

'You alright, mate?' Jack asked, resting his hand on the other man's shoulder.

Isaac exhaled a long breath and nodded. 'Just about. Yeah.'

'Was that what I think it was?' Jack asked.

'Yep. We have a major fucking problem, Jack.'

CHAPTER 22

$\mathcal{B}$y the time Jack and Isaac made it to the lower forestry road, they had been over the morning's events almost a dozen times. Jack had watched Isaac closely and was relieved to see his friend's usual demeanour return the further they got from the scene of the accident. As they rounded the last bend, they could see Lilly and Veronica walking to meet them.

When Jack caught sight of Lilly, he let out the breath that had somehow lodged in his chest back on the ridge. Just seeing her seemed to tip his world back on its rightful axis. She broke into a run, her arms flung wide, something close to panic shadowing her beautiful face.

She all but collided with him, wrapping her long arms around him and squeezing tight. 'What the hell happened?' she said when she stepped away, searching first his face and then Isaac's. 'We felt it, whatever it was. It was like a shock wave of horribleness.'

'Storm?' Isaac asked.

'She's awake, has been for a few hours,' Veronica said as she joined them. 'We all felt it, whatever it was, but Stormy took the brunt of it. She's okay,' she added hastily, her hand on Isaac's arm. 'She was caught off guard and came over a bit faint, but she's fine now. Just worried about you pair. Henri and Dot are with her.'

'Okay. Good,' Isaac said, the relief washing over his face.

They walked on in determined silence for a few moments. Veronica spoke first. 'They're back, aren't they?' she asked, not breaking her stride and not looking at any of them. 'They found a way to cheat the shift,' she said, her voice thin, barely audible.

Jack and Isaac exchanged a look. Jack shrugged. There was no way they could sugar-coat this for anyone. Isaac took a deep breath and said simply, 'Yes. The Very are back.'

Veronica nodded and pursed her lips together but said nothing more. When she dabbed at her eyes with the sleeve of her cardigan, Lilly slipped free of Jack's arm to link hers through Veronica's as they marched on in silence.

Isaac slowed his pace, and Jack followed suit. When the two women were out of earshot, Isaac said, 'I don't know how to tell her.'

Jack nodded. He knew exactly what Isaac meant. Maybe like Vee, Storm had already guessed that the Very were back, but would she know that she seemed to have become their public enemy number one? Even without the events in London, as the First, she'd be the obvious target anyway. What difference did a little personally motivated hatred make?

'Just tell her what happened. Same way you told me. I doubt you'll be telling her anything she doesn't already know anyway,' Jack said, stopping to put his hand on his friend's shoulder. 'She's stronger than all of us put together, you know that.' He tried to smile, but he knew his attempts to reassure Isaac sounded a little hollow.

After a moment, Isaac said, 'You're right, but I wish she didn't have to be. She never wanted all this. She just wanted a normal life, but she carries it all, you know?'

'Wasn't there a myth about a goddess who swallowed all sorrows?' Jack asked.

Isaac snorted. 'That'd be apt, wouldn't it? And just like Stormy too, if she thought it would save the rest of us.'

They walked in silence, picking up their pace when the vicarage came into sight. When Isaac spoke again, it was almost a whisper. 'They're coming for her, Jack.'

Jack's heart pinched at the fear in his friend's voice. He swallowed hard. 'I know, mate. But we're not going to let that happen, I promise,' he said. Exactly how he was going to keep that promise, he had no idea.

CHAPTER 23

Storm sat on the old bench in the vicarage garden, Ludo and Hope like sentries at her feet, tense and watchful. Under usual circumstances, they'd be playing, snoozing or begging for tickles, but today they were all business. They sat facing the garden, their eyes on the perimeter. Anchor sat next to her, mirroring the dogs' posture. That alone would have been signal enough that something was wrong in their perfect world, but Storm could feel the change in every atom of her being.

'Mind if I join you, my dear?' Henri asked from the back doorstep.

Storm felt the knot around her insides loosen its grip ever so slightly at the sound of his voice. She smiled in reply. Anchor relinquished his spot at Storm's side to let Henri sit down, but repositioned himself on the arm of the bench next to her.

'I see you're already well protected,' Henri said, giving Hope's head a rub and winking at Ludo when he turned briefly to wag at his human friend.

Storm reached out to stroke both dogs. They acknowledged the contact with a wag each, but still they did not turn
their attention from their watching. Storm felt the meaning of
it catch in her heart like a thorn. Anchor moved to her lap,
sitting with his back to her, his fat tail twitching as he
continued his vigil.

'Well protected indeed,' she managed, although it was with
some effort that she kept her voice strong. She thought back
to Lilly's kidnapping, how Hope had been so brutally kicked
as she tried to defend her friend. Storm had seen it in her
mind ever since she'd been told. She closed her eyes now to
block out the thought.

'We may, of course, be overreacting,' Henri said. Storm
knew it was a question, and she wished she could offer some
reassurance. Henri had lived so long without his beloved Dot,
and now, less than twenty-four hours after her return, they
were staring once again into the abyss. So much for her belief
that the timing of things was always perfect.

'We'll know more once Isaac and Jack get back,' she said.
She tried to smile at him, but had to look away when she saw
the hope in his eyes. She couldn't lie to him, and yet she
couldn't bear to break his heart either. Playing for time
seemed like the only option.

Henri let out a long, resigned sigh. 'I'm sorry, my dear, that
was unfair of me.'

Storm made to reply, but he cut her off with a gentle raise
of his hand. 'No. Don't take that on too by letting me off the
hook. I laid the weight of hope and expectation at your feet,
and as ever, you picked it up, ready to carry it for me. We both
know my hope is likely misplaced. We can all feel the shift in
the air. I'm sorry, dear heart.' He patted her knee.

Unable to find the words, Storm leaned into him and

rested her head on his shoulder. Henri stroked her hair, and they sat in silence for a while.

'Whatever this is, you know we'll overcome it, don't you?' Henri said. 'We saved the world, remember? We did it once and we'll bloody well do it again. You mark my words.'

Storm smiled. She didn't dare think what would have happened without Henri back then. His visions had been the catalyst for their quest to find the Ethereal, but it had been his conviction that had really mattered. That had always been bone deep, and she loved him for it. That they had been looking for her all along was the source of endless amusement, of course. The punchline to what might have been a joke had the stakes not been so astronomical. If she'd had a pound for every time someone had asked her if she *really* hadn't known that she was the First Ethereal, she'd be a rich woman. Funny how sayings stuck, she thought. Everyone was rich now that money was no more.

'You, me and the Scooby Gang forever,' she said, smiling.

They both laughed. Then Storm pecked him on the cheek.

'What was that for?' he asked, looking delighted.

She shrugged. 'Just for being you.'

The dogs leapt to their feet, heads cocked, bodies tense. Storm felt her breath catch, but just a beat later, she too could hear what had alerted them. Isaac and Jack were back.

CHAPTER 24

*S*torm resisted the urge to follow Henri into the house. She wanted nothing more than to feel Isaac's arms around her, but she was also acutely aware of the need to lead by example. Everyone would look to her for their cue, and she needed to keep the energies as high as was Ethereally possible. From where she sat on the bench, she could hear the noise levels escalate as the large vicarage kitchen filled with the voices of those she loved most in the world. She swallowed the lump in her throat as she registered their hushed and anxious tones. It reminded her of funerals in the old days. Everyone trying so desperately to be normal and keep it together while staggering under the weight of their grief. She focused on the other noises instead. Chair legs scraped against old quarry tiles, the huge copper kettle being filled, the clink of crockery. Nothing, not even a crisis of global proportion, would be permitted to happen in the vicarage without tea.

Bracing herself, Storm took a deep breath and stood up. She scooped Anchor into her arms, and with Hope and Ludo at her heels, she went into the kitchen. The look of relief on

Isaac's face was palpable. He rushed towards her, and when he folded her into his arms, Anchor sandwiched between them, she could feel the fear in him. She leaned her head on his chest and wrapped her free arm around his broad back, trying to distract herself with the sensation of well-defined muscle under her fingertips.

Unable to delay the moment any longer, Storm pulled back and looked up into Isaac's eyes. He tried to smile, but she knew him too well. She reached up, her hand to his cheek. 'It's not going to happen,' she said, holding his gaze. 'Okay?' She stayed stock still until he nodded, then reached up to kiss him gently on the lips.

'Right, my lovelies,' she said, turning to the room, 'who's not got a cuppa yet?'

Ten minutes later, Henri, Dot, Isaac, Lilly, Jack and Veronica were all settled around the huge old kitchen table. Storm had persuaded Ludo and Hope to rest, and while Ludo lay stretched out in his bed by the Aga, the spaniel was curled, cat-like, on the old armchair in the corner.

With mugs filled, all eyes turned to look at Storm. She straightened her back and began. 'Before we get into it, I want to say a proper welcome home to our darling Dot.'

Dot, sitting at the end of the table nearest the Aga, next to Henri, beamed. 'We have missed you so much, my dear friend,' Storm said. 'That you're back with us now is, I think, probably the most potent symbol of the Ethereal age. What we used to . call heaven is closer than ever to our life on Earth. What's more, it's no longer a one-way ticket but a two-way door. Welcome home, darling.'

Henri hugged his wife close as everyone raised their mugs to toast her, and she mouthed, 'Thank you,' to each of them. Such a Dot thing, Storm thought, trying hard to stay out of the limelight. With the energy levels if not exactly raised but at least not as flat as they were, Storm asked the question she guessed they were all dreading.

Looking from Jack to Isaac and back again, she said, 'Are they back?'

The two men exchanged a look, but it was Isaac who answered. After clearing his throat, he said, 'They're back, my love. We're pretty sure they've used magic to protect themselves from the shift.'

Before he could say any more, Storm said matter-of-factly, 'They're coming for me then.'

Even to her own ears, her voice sounded remarkably calm, although it was far from how she felt.

Isaac looked away, and the seconds stretched into what felt like an eternity. She knew he was trying to compose himself, and she hated having to ask, but they needed the facts and the only way to get to them was to get the difficult emotional stuff out of the way first.

She was about to ask again when he looked up, held her eyes and said with an effort, 'Yes, my love. I'm pretty sure they are.'

Storm had braced for the answer and so managed not to miss a beat. 'To be expected. Okay, tell me everything from the beginning,' she said briskly.

When Isaac finished recounting the events of the morning, there was complete silence in the room. Storm felt the weight of it pressing against her, as if the walls themselves were closing in, intent on crushing her. She felt the tell-tale prickle at her shoulder blades as her wings readied themselves to leap to her defence. She closed her eyes and, with an effort of will, stilled them, whispering to them in her mind as she might have calmed a spooked horse. She often wondered why, when wings were so obviously associated with birds, hers always brought with them a sense of the equine.

Hope whined from her seat in the armchair, and Storm looked up to see five pairs of human eyes and two pairs of canine ones staring at her. When she met Lilly's eyes, the younger woman's face crumpled into tears.

Storm stopped herself from running to comfort her friend, although it took an enormous effort. 'Enough,' she whispered, holding up her palms. 'This is not the time to give in to fear. We can none of us afford to board that runaway train. So, no tears, my darling,' she said, nodding to Lilly, 'and no panic. That's what they'll want. The more we fear, the more the vibration will drop and the stronger they'll be here. Our best defence is to keep our energy up and our frequency high enough to make this a hostile environment for these low lives.'

Everyone nodded, except Henri. 'Henri?' Storm said.

'You're right – of course you're right, my dear. It's just that …' He rubbed his chin, not making eye contact. 'It's just that they'll still be able to come after us, won't they? If they're using magic to protect themselves against the high frequencies, then they can still exist here. And they can still do us harm. Can't they?'

Storm swallowed before she answered. Her throat felt scratchy and dry, but she didn't reach for the water jug on the table. They were depending on her. The entire world was depending on her, and it felt as if even an admission to thirst might somehow shatter something fragile. Yet, she could not lie. Especially not to these people she loved so dearly.

She pulled out a chair and sat at the table. She closed her eyes as she conjured a protection spell, her memory taking her back to the first and last time she'd done so. Back then, it was to protect her friends in the garden of a Holland Park mansion that she was about to obliterate. An act she hadn't planned on surviving. Today, there was no danger of falling masonry or untested magic, but the threat somehow felt even greater. She couldn't put a force field around their hearts, no matter how much she wished it, but she could keep the shock to the energy levels from plummeting – for the time they were together, at least.

When she opened her eyes a few seconds later, she said, 'They can. Hurt us, that is.' Looking at Veronica, she said, 'We'll need to ask the library, but I'm fairly certain that their presence can send us back to the brink of damnation.' Storm's heart ached as she watched the anguished faces of her friends, but she pressed on. They needed to know.

'We are in a bind. In the new world, we gain strength from love and kindness. Every Ethereal chose love and rejected fear. That's how we made the world and that's how we've sustained it, by keeping the vibration high. But the Very chose fear. Admittedly, dressed up as tradition, authority, natural selection and divine choice, or whatever other fairy story allowed them to feel entitled to their power. They will now use violence because that is their nature, and by them doing so, we will fear and inadvertently lower the vibration for them.' Storm gave a rueful half-laugh. 'We will feed their vibration and weaken our own.'

The room was silent until Jack pushed back his chair, the wooden legs scraping on the old tiles. Storm watched him pace, his hands raking through his hair. 'There must be something we can do,' he said. 'I mean, we can't just sit here waiting for them to come and attack us.'

'We don't even know how many of them are out there. And what if they're not just here? The Very had factions all over the world. What if this is some kind of organised awakening?' Veronica said, tipping her head back and blinking furiously in what Storm knew would be a vain attempt to stop herself from crying.

'But the opposite might be true too,' Lilly offered, trying to smile and nod everyone into agreement. 'I mean, this could have been just one man, right? A sole survivor who's now dead, angels rest him, but who can at least pose no further threat.'

Storm wanted so much to agree, to shrug and smile and say something comforting, but it couldn't be. 'We can hope, of course we can, and we must. But we also have to prepare ourselves. Isaac, I think we should speak to Katharine, see if any of her old military pals ascended. They might have some ideas. Vee, can we get Asim on the case with surveillance drones and security? I'm assuming the library is back under lock and key?'

Veronica said, 'Asim went back to enact the emergency protocol and check everything in the early hours.'

'Henri, Dot, we'll need to find a way of warning the town without frightening them. I've no idea how, but I'd love your ideas.'

'What about you?' Lilly asked. 'They said they were coming for you. We need to get you somewhere safe. The library is bomb proof, isn't it? Or the bunker at Isaac's old farm?'

Storm weighed up the consequences of telling the truth and answered with a half-truth instead. Forcing herself to smile, she said, 'Both great ideas, Lil. Can you and Jack grab some maps?'

'I'd better call my sister and tell her to get the animals somewhere safe. And we'll need to tell Michael,' Veronica said. 'Isaac, if you give me the co-ordinates for the doe, I'm sure they'll be able to recover her remains too.'

'Wait.' Storm held up her hands as everyone made to stand. 'Before we disperse, I need each of you to give me something that you can wear at all times. I only need it for a moment.'

'You're giving us a shield like the one the hunter had?' Jack asked.

Storm paused. 'We need to keep our vibration levels high,' she said, then held out her hands.

Henri and Dot handed over their wedding rings. Isaac his watch. Veronica, the pale amethyst pendant that had been her mother's. After a moment's hesitation, where Lilly seemed to be deciding between her small heart-shaped gold necklace and the plain silver band she wore on her left hand, she handed Storm the ring. 'Less easy to lose,' she said with a shrug.

'Can you do this without me taking it off?' Jack asked, holding up his left arm and pointing to the braided black fabric bracelet he'd worn since the day they'd all returned from London. Storm smiled, knowing that within the tightly wound cloth were strands of Lilly's hair woven with his own.

'Of course,' she said. Storm went to stand next to Jack and, holding the thin fabric between her thumb and forefinger, charged it. She heard Jack suck in a breath. 'Sorry. Bit of a head rush?'

Jack gave a slightly breathless 'Yep' before exhaling loudly as Storm let go and stepped away. 'That's some mighty fine mojo you've got there,' he said, examining the bracelet as if it might give some sort of clue to what had just happened. Storm looked away.

'Please, my darlings, keep these items on from now on. They can't leave your person for any reason. Not even for a second. Is that clear?' she asked, conscious that she sounded unusually bossy and hating it.

When everyone nodded, she forced a smile that she knew fooled precisely no one.

$\mathcal{V}$eronica hovered by the back door, waiting for Storm to say her goodbyes. Hope and Ludo had obviously appointed themselves her personal bodyguards as they flanked her every step. Anchor had at least been persuaded from her shoulder and was now stationed in the kitchen window, keeping watch. Storm reached up to kiss Isaac, her hands on each side of his face, their eyes locked. He held her cheek, stroked it with his thumb while holding her close. It brought a lump to Veronica's throat. There had been a time when she feared her friend would never find love again. What she and Nick shared had been wonderful, but though she'd never say it aloud, not even now, there was something almost elemental about the love Storm shared with Isaac.

'Is Storm coming with you to the library?' Lilly asked, breaking Veronica's train of thought.

'Oh, Lil, you made me jump. Er, yes.'

After scooping up Anchor, Storm joined them. To Veronica's relief, at that exact same moment, Jack called to Lilly to tell her that her phone was ringing in her bag.

Once outside, Veronica all but felt the tension leave Storm's body. She reached over and squeezed her arm. 'Probably not the time to tell her,' Veronica said as she headed for the car.

'Tell her what?'

Veronica stopped and looked at Storm, who, she thought, was doing a spectacularly bad job of feigning ignorance. 'To tell her that you can't hide. That the First can't be cut off from the flow of the world without consequences.'

She saw Storm suck in a breath, but not wanting to push the issue, continued on to the car, the dogs still at Storm's side. They didn't speak again until they were on the road out of the village. 'She'll figure it out soon enough,' Storm said quietly, leaning her head against the window. 'She's a smart cookie, our Lil.'

'She is, but …' Veronica let her words trail off, unsure how to articulate what she needed to say next. 'I'm just worried about you and—'

Storm cut her off with a hand on her arm. 'I knew there would be repercussions, Vee. I killed people in that house. Had it not been for me—'

'The whole fucking world would have gone up in smoke!' Veronica surprised herself with the force of her anger. Hope whined from the back seat, sensing the change in atmosphere. 'No, worse, actually. We would have all been sucked into some sort of low-vibrational dimension where, I dare say, burning slowly to death would have felt like a long weekend in bloody Butlins. No way, lady! No way are you going to carry that guilt for those monsters. Have you forgotten why you blew them all to smithereens? Have you?'

She was on a roll now, her mouth forming words before her brain could kick in and censor her. 'They were about to burn our Lil alive, and had they realised that you were the

First Ethereal and not her, then it would have been you in that oven! I thank the angels that I wasn't there to see it, but I've pictured it in my nightmares more times than I care to recall. So no, you give those sodding bastards not one iota of your thought. You saved the world, for fuck's sake!' Her voice cracked, and she was relieved to see the gates of the house as they rounded the last bend. She bit her lip, determined not to cry. She pulled into the drive and waited for the security drones to sweep the car. The sight of the locked gates that had stood permanently open since the shift was a stark and sickening reminder of how much life had changed in such a short space of time. Was it really just yesterday that her biggest headache was whether there'd be enough bunting for the party? The gates slid open and Veronica pressed the accelerator, wanting the safety of her library and the comforting sight of her husband.

She glanced at Storm. She was sitting with her head leaning back on the headrest, her eyes closed, lips pressed into a line and fat tears sliding down her cheek. Veronica reached for Storm's hand and held it.

When she spoke, Storm's voice was barely a whisper. 'There's nothing we can do, Vee. They will come for me, and if we fight, they'll win.'

'Then we'll just have to hide you and suffer the consequences,' Veronica said, even though she knew in her heart that that wasn't an option either. It all felt so hopeless.

Storm was already shaking her head. 'You know I can't hide, not properly anyway. If my vibration is absent or even just muted for any length of time, then things will begin to unravel and that will just play into their hands. The odd hour off the grid here, maybe, but the odd hour won't be enough. These bastards have already waited ten years. They'll bide their time.'

Veronica parked as close to the front steps as she could. She had her hand on the car door handle when Storm said quietly, 'The only option I have is to run. If I keep moving, then I at least give everyone else a chance.'

Veronica felt a chill snake down her spine. She turned in her seat to face Storm. 'Oh no you don't. No way,' she said, shaking her head so vigorously her blonde curls bounced about her cheeks. 'There is no way on this green Earth that any one of us would let you do that. Besides, you're the First! Where could you go where nobody knew you? Eh? And it wouldn't work anyway. Think, Stormy! I studied them, remember? My mother, angels keep her, studied them for donkey's years. These people are some of the very worst of humanity. They're not going to play by the rules. They're not going to be sportsmanlike about it. Remember, half of this lot hunted animals for fun! They loved nothing more than ripping some poor, exhausted creature apart after a long chase. No. You will not be prey for the likes of those monsters, and if you run, they'll just snatch someone you love as bait to get you back.'

Storm opened her mouth but closed it again without saying a word. Veronica saw fresh tears well in her friend's eyes and bit her lip to halt her own.

'Tea, cake and an hour on the couch to recharge your batteries. No arguments. I'll see what the library has to say, and we can take it from there. Agreed?' she asked, eyebrows arched.

After what felt like an age, Storm sighed and nodded her assent.

CHAPTER 26

*L*illy dried the last of the dishes while gazing out of the window at the vicarage garden. So many of the plants in their own cottage garden started life here. Henri had helped them transform the small rectangle of space at the back of the house from astro-turfed plastic wasteland into a thriving haven teeming with life. As only two of the cottages in the row of six were occupied full time – the others the community maintained for visitors – they had decided early on to take down parts of the dividing walls to provide better access for wildlife. It had been even more important then, back when the world, although saved energetically, was still recovering from the ravages of human abuse.

Henri had shared his grandmother's stories from the war years as they worked, and they'd chatted about the parallels and marvelled at the goodness in humanity when fear was banished and love and kindness allowed to reign supreme. All over the world, those who had chosen to stay were focused on nature's recovery, and now, balance restored, most things just took care of themselves. She still liked to garden though,

helping nature along where she could, keeping out of the way
when needed to. The thought of all this being threatened
again, of all the animals ending up like the poor doe on the
mountain, was just unbearable.

'Penny for them,' Dot said brightly as she bustled into the
room.

Lilly jumped at the sound, and the sugar bowl she'd been
drying fell into the old ceramic sink and shattered. 'No!' she
cried, staring despondently at the pieces.

Dot hurried over and put her hand on Lilly's shoulder. 'It's
only an old bowl, sweetheart, don't fret. We've got dozens in
the cupboard.'

Maybe it was the touch or Dot's wonderfully warm smile,
but Lilly felt the tears that she'd been trying to hold at bay all
day finally spill down her cheeks.

Dot held out her arms. 'Oh, cariad, come here.'

Lilly let herself cry, and once she began, she found it hard
to stop. She cried for Storm and the threat to the world. She
cried for her friends and the murdered doe, and she even
cried for the hunter who had died in the forest. It had been
such a long time since she'd cried that the sensation felt alien
to her. For her first twenty years, tears had been an almost
daily occurrence, but since the shift, since finding Jack again,
her life was perfect. She had a family, a place to belong and the
joy that came from seeing a world filled with love and kindness. A world where even death had been vanquished. That
was what she'd firmly and joyously believed until today.

Dot rubbed slow circles on Lilly's back. 'It's all been a bit
much, hasn't it, sweets. Bit much to say the least. You let it all
out.'

Lilly wanted to pull herself together, but the larger part of
her just needed the comfort. She was used to feeling the
energy of others, but there was something physically

comforting about Dot, too. She was like a warm eiderdown on a winter's night and, Lilly thought, she smelled like Christmas – chocolate, cinnamon and oranges. The thought made her smile, and at last, the tears stopped. She gave Dot a last squeeze and stepped back, patting her pockets for a hankie.

'Thank you,' she said after blowing her nose. 'You give the best cwtches.'

Dot beamed, the action erasing some of the worry from her round face and making her eyes twinkle. 'You know what they say, anyone can hug, but only the Welsh can cwtch. I suppose I have the physique for it,' she said, pointing to her ample bosom. 'There wasn't a fretful baby in the village that I couldn't soothe to sleep back in the day.'

'Is it strange? Being back, I mean,' Lilly asked.

Dot pulled out a chair and sat down at the table. 'Yes and no. In some ways it's like no time has passed at all, but so much has changed since I was alive.' She rolled her eyes. 'And I keep using the wrong words. I mean, I know now that I was always alive, I was just alive somewhere that wasn't here, but I suppose old habits, even in speech, die hard.' She smiled, and Lilly pulled out the chair next to her.

'Do you mind me asking why you came back?'

'Of course I don't mind. I don't think the answer is very exciting though, so please don't be disappointed.' Dot chuckled. 'Time doesn't really work in the same way as it does there, as you well know, so it doesn't feel like I've been dead' – she mimed quote marks in the air around the last word – 'for thirteen years. I was just busy reflecting and exploring, relearning things that I'd forgotten when I was here, catching up with old friends and, of course, keeping an eye on my Henri from afar. We all felt the great shift, of course, and it was cause for such celebration. Every soul, incarnate or not, felt it, and it was such an almighty relief. If you think the afterlife is free from stress, think again. Watching the corporeal world slide towards the Falling was horrendous. We didn't have perfect knowledge, of course – the universe still keeps some of her secrets close – but it was pretty clear that if Earth fell, then we'd be gone too. I was so proud of you all.'

'Well, it might not have happened at all if you'd not written Henri that letter,' Lilly said.

'Ah, the letter. That was the easy bit. I think I was just the hand that held the pen. No, it was the dreams that wore me out. It took such a lot of practice to reach him, and when I did, it was so hard to be clear. Walking into someone's dream, as I quickly discovered, is like turning up at a party where everyone else is as drunk as a skunk and you're the one trying to have a sensible conversation. But I had to try something, especially once I realised how much time had passed. The energies hit a sort of tipping point, and suddenly it was urgent.'

'Did you know Storm was the Ethereal?'

'No,' Dot said. 'I knew she was important in some way, but I think her identity was probably the universe's best-kept secret. It was a secret even from herself, after all. I suppose it had to be that way or else the decision would never have been pure. I can't imagine anyone being able to carry the weight of that responsibility otherwise. Can you imagine? Make the wrong choice and damn all of creation to hell.' Dot shuddered, her eyes screwed shut against the thought.

'Is that why you're back now?' Lilly asked.

Dot nodded. 'I think so. You have to admit that the timing is a bit odd.'

'One last mission.'

Dot cocked her head in question.

'Back in the forest, before this last life, I woke up from a dream and I just knew that I had something important to do. I told Jack I needed one last life. One last mission. He wasn't happy, bless him, but he agreed to be my guide in spirit.' Lilly had never forgotten the pain on his face that day and would never be able to comprehend how he'd watched over her for twenty years, knowing that she remembered nothing of their love and their myriad lifetimes together.

'Poor Jack,' Dot said. 'That must have been so tough for him.'

'He's probably the strongest person I know – after Storm,' Lilly said. 'I bet Henri was overjoyed to have you back.'

Dot's face lit up. 'And even that's an understatement. He had visited, of course. His years as a shepherd gave him a head start when it came to slipping through the realms after the shift, but as you know, there's nothing quite like Earth. I knew he was committed to the reparation project, so wouldn't be joining me for a long time, but we were okay with that. Nothing like visiting rights to the hereafter to help heal your heart. Then I told him about my decision and, well, you can imagine.'

Lilly clapped her hands together, caught up in the joy of Dot's story and the bow wave of love that she felt wash over her. Then she remembered that Dot's grand return had been marred by death and the promise of destruction. The hunter's dying words rang in her ears. 'Tell her we're coming for her.' Try as she might, Lilly couldn't contain her fear. Had it not been for Storm, she would have been murdered at the hands of the Very, burned to death in their mistaken belief that it was Lilly who was the First Ethereal and that killing her would save their wretched idea of the world. They'd realised their mistake too late and now they meant to try again.

'She'll have to hide,' Lilly said, getting to her feet. 'That's the only way we can keep her safe. We have to keep her energy off the grid so they can't track her. She can go to one of the magical bunkers. Isaac's is probably the safest, although if she stays at the library, then at least the books could help. We'd need to stock it, of course, food, water and stuff, and then figure out some sort of watch to make sure they didn't launch an attack, but if we ...' Lilly stopped her pacing and snapped her head up when the weight of the silence in the room registered. Dot was looking at her with an expression of such sadness. She was biting her lip as if literally trying to hold back the words that were desperate to escape. She held Lilly's gaze, as if willing her to hear what was sitting heavy and unspoken in the air. Lilly frowned. Her mind felt like a frustrated bee trying and failing to find the entrance to the hive. Then at last the penny dropped into place. She closed her eyes against the realisation, but it was no good.

'I'm an idiot,' she said, her head dropping to her chest. 'She can't even hide.'

Dot got up and came to stand in front of her. 'Firstly, you're not an idiot. You're a wonderful friend who's trying to keep our Stormy safe. But you're right. She can't hide – physically or magically. Physically because her energy signal is so strong it would be like trying to hide an elephant in an ant's tea party.'

'And magically because without the frequency of The First, we'd lose everything anyway,' Lilly said miserably.

Dot nodded. 'Our Stormy is, for all intents and purposes, the tuning fork to which all reality on Earth resonates now. Take away that vibration, even through magical means and with the best of intentions, and ...' Dot shrugged. 'We're done for.'

CHAPTER 27

*R*eluctantly surrendering to Vee's orders to rest, Storm had lain down on the old, battered couch in the sunroom, the dogs at her side, Anchor curled into her chest. She had always loved this room, filled as it was with what had to be a few hundred house plants. They took up every inch of space. Some sat in pots on the floor, others on the purpose-built shelving that lined the room, while still more hung suspended from the glass ceiling. She smiled at the memory of Asim and Isaac sitting at the kitchen table making their plans for the room. Having rejected the use of magic as 'cheating', the botanist and the techie had designed what they claimed to be the perfect plant room habitat. There seemed to be a sensor for just about everything, light, shade, humidity, soil nutrient levels, and an entire network of tiny pipes and lights designed to cater for the plants' every need. Integral to the plan were the couch and the three other meditation spots dotted around the room – Isaac had been adamant that the plants needed more than tech to sustain them; they needed love, attention and appreciation too. No one on Earth would argue with that logic. Until now, of course. The thought snapped Storm from her memories and put paid to any ideas of further compliance. Vee would no doubt give her 'the look', but she'd done her best to rest.

'Don't let on that you helped me with the cake, okay? We don't want to worry her,' Storm said to the dogs as she stood up. 'You rest up here. I'm safe in the house, I promise.' Ludo and Hope exchanged a look, appeared to come to an agreement and settled down. Anchor, however, followed her.

Storm found Vee in the library. It felt strange to go through the old security routine after so many years. After the shift, Asim and Veronica had operated an open-house policy so that anyone could visit the library. Some of the seriously old tomes had been a bit huffy at first, but most had come around after a few years. Most of the books had welcomed visitors with the enthusiasm of new teachers in a classroom full of eager students. They'd practically flung themselves at visitors and seemed genuinely delighted to be sharing their ancient wisdom far and wide. With the return of the Very, they could no longer take any risks. When the last security door slid away to admit Storm, she felt the tension in the air, as if every volume was whispering its worries to its neighbour.

Veronica was at the large reading table, glasses perched on the end of her nose. As she read one book, she was absent-mindedly stroking the cover of another, as one might a nervous animal. She glanced up, looking a little startled, then raised her eyebrows in disapproval. There was that look, Storm thought.

Storm held up her hands in placation. 'I know, I know. I tried, Vee, I really did, and I do feel a bit more rested, I promise, but we need a plan. They're unlikely to hang about now that they know, and I need to understand how we keep everybody safe.'

Veronica chewed her lip, but after a few seconds, sat back and tossed her glasses onto the table. Storm smiled despite the situation. In a perfect world, with perfect health and perfect vision, Vee still found it impossible to read a book without her glasses. Some habits just didn't need to be broken.

She took a seat, and Anchor hopped silently onto the reading table.

'It's as we suspected. If we fight, we lower the vibration. If we run, they'll find us. If we wait ...' Vee pinched the bridge of her nose and screwed her eyes closed. 'Sick, evil, bastard people. Who in their right mind could want to destroy paradise?'

Storm reached out to rub her friend's hand. 'We'll find a way.'

'Henri!' Asim bellowed as he burst into the room, Ludo, Hope and Logan at his heel. 'They shot Henri!'

CHAPTER 28

*T*he drive to the vicarage felt like one of the longest of Storm's life. Veronica had always been a skilful driver, but today she would have given the pros a run for their money, flooring the accelerator all the way as Storm conjured a spell to gently clear the country roads of any soul who may be crossing.

The information had been scant. Dot had called to say that Henri had been shot while he was in the garden. He was insisting it was only a flesh wound, but Storm knew his capacity for understatement.

'You know it might be a trap,' Asim said from the back seat, where he sat sandwiched between the animals. 'They might be trying to flush you out.'

Storm turned to look at him. He was such a gentle man. Back before the shift, Storm had often caught herself wondering how such a sweet soul could have built such a phenomenally successful global IT security business. Quick to smile, slow to anger and softly spoken, he was living proof that sometimes the good guys really did come out on top.

'I know, lovely, but we have to take the risk. I can shield us from the car to the house, but,' she added, looking at Veronica, 'probably best to get as close as possible.' To Asim she said, 'I'll go in first just in case and cover you from the door.'

Storm's phone burst into life, the ring impossibly loud in the confines of the car. Seeing that it was Isaac, she answered via the hands-free so that they could all hear.

'Me and Jack have done a sweep of the area. Looks like whoever it was took the shot from the churchyard. We found a bullet casing,' Isaac said, his voice tight and clipped, sounding every inch the close-protection police officer he had once been.

'That must have taken some finding,' Asim said.

Isaac snorted. 'Sadly not, mate. The sniper left the casing on top of a headstone. They wanted us to know it was them. Anyway, we'll do another sweep. Cover the area for you just to be on the safe side.'

'Thanks, my love. We're minutes away now,' Storm said.

Storm was out of the car and through the kitchen door of the vicarage even before Veronica had properly stopped, leaving a protective tunnel of energy in her wake to shield her friends. She could feel her magic, usually such a gentle presence, coursing through her body on high alert, her wings scratching at her shoulder blades, impatient for release.

She found Dot, Henri and Lilly at the kitchen table and only had time to acknowledge Michael and Tim with the briefest of nods before Veronica, Asim and the animals burst into the room. Seconds later, Jack and Isaac arrived.

'Show me, please,' Storm said, crossing the room to stand next to Henri. Ludo had already beaten her to it and was busy licking Henri's free hand.

Henri tickled the old dog's ears as he rolled his eyes at

Storm. 'My dear girl. It is, I promise you, a mere flesh wound. Whoever it was intended to send a message, not bump me off.'

Storm stood her ground and, after a few moments, saw Henri's shoulders slump in resignation. He nodded, and Lilly carefully removed the tape securing the dressing, then peeled it off to reveal a long horizontal wound. It was already healing, but the fact that Henri could have been hurt at all made Storm's knees go weak.

'Luckily, these fine chaps had stopped by to check in on us, so Dr Tim was on hand to patch the old duffer up,' Henri said, trying for lightness. Nobody else made a sound.

Tim cleared his throat. 'It's a surface wound alright, but I can imagine it still hurt like hell. It'll heal quickly enough. We all mend a lot quicker these days, but you're under doctor's orders to rest while that happens, okay? This would be a shock back in the old world, but now, when violence shouldn't technically be possible, well, it will need some time.' He held his hand out to Lilly, who gave back the gauze pad and bandage for Tim to replace.

Henri sighed, his eyes trained on the floor, but Storm saw the slight tremble in his hand. Her wings all but screamed at her back. The need to vanquish this threat to her friends, to her world, made her blood simmer close to boiling point. She pushed down the other thought, the need to make whoever did this to Henri pay.

Jack was the first to break the silence that had settled over the room like a rockslide. 'Well, we now know that there was more than one of them. We also know they're trying to make their presence known. The earth in the churchyard was all scorched where the sniper sat, just like what happened to the grass around the hunter on the mountain, so they must have an effect on the immediate area around them regardless of their woo-woo pendants.'

'I think that's probably what the entire world would look like if they came back,' Lilly said in a small, quiet voice. The room was silent for a long minute, then she added, 'Wait, does this mean people can die again? I mean, for ten years it wasn't possible to injure someone through violence, but in two days we've seen a doe murdered and now Henri shot. What does this mean for spirit?'

Storm didn't trust herself to speak immediately, so focused on straightening her spine and squaring her shoulders. She scanned the room. The fear was coming off them in waves, and even if she hadn't been able to read the vibration, their faces told her everything she needed to know. She took a deep breath.

'I think that's a reasonable assumption, Lil,' she said softly, 'but we're going to do everything Ethereally possible to protect our world.'

When Lilly's wide, frightened eyes met hers, she swallowed down the lump in her throat and addressed the room.

'Okay, so we can assume that they have a witch amongst their number,' Storm said, grateful that glamours could be used on the voice as well as the appearance.

'And we can assume that whoever it is is pretty powerful,' Isaac chipped in, 'but it's hard to believe that one of our own refused the blessing in favour of the Very when coercion wasn't in the mix.'

'It's hard to believe because we don't want to believe it, but we can't rule it out as an option,' Tim said.

'Does it need to be current magic though?' Jack asked. 'I mean, magic doesn't have a sell-by date, right? It doesn't go off, so maybe they got a witch to magic those amulet things before the shift. Maybe they don't have a super witch on the team with them now.'

'That's a fair point,' Storm said. 'I like that idea a hell of a lot more than thinking that another witch sided with them, but there's a trap in there, too. I think we at least need to entertain the possibility that it might be historic, but let's not be blinkered by what we hope to be true.'

'If we identify the witch, would that help us figure out how to break whatever spells they used?' Dot asked.

Isaac and Storm both said 'Yes' at the same time. She found his eyes, and he winked at her. Under normal circumstances, he would have said, 'Snap! Make a wish.' She did anyway.

'Do you think Margot could have done it?' Lilly asked, her eyes fixed on the kitchen table. 'You know, before ...'

Storm knew Lilly couldn't bring herself to finish the sentence. *Before the Very shot her in the throat and she died in my arms*, Storm thought. She smiled at Lilly to reassure her. 'Let's go get your girl.' That had been the last thing Margot had said to Storm. Seconds later, Margot, the friend and mentor who had once been closer than her own mother, was gone, cut down by bullets that had been meant for Storm.

'It's certainly possible. Or she may well know who they have amongst their ranks,' Storm conceded, although the thought made her sick to her stomach.

Michael raised his hand before saying with a shrug, 'Well, can someone just go ask her?'

Henri let out a snort of laughter. 'Bloody brilliant!' he said, clapping his hands together and then wincing. 'You've done it again, my boy!' he went on, using his good hand to waggle an approving finger in Michael's direction. 'You have a glorious knack, young man, for asking just the right question at just the right time. You did the same back when we were looking for the journals, do you remember?'

Michael smiled and gave a self-conscious shrug, but looked pleased with himself.

Storm felt the first stirrings of something like optimism

deep in her core. She nodded slowly, still processing the idea, but he was right. If it had been Margot, then the simplest and quickest way to know was to go into spirit and ask her. She'd not heard from Margot since the shift, but that wasn't unusual, as many of those who had passed before the ascension had pursued other paths unrelated to their last incarnation on Earth. Others, like Dot, were just busy doing other things. The thought of seeing her old friend again, alive and well, made her heart swell, and it was all she could do to control her wings as they strained excitedly at her back. The thought was quickly shadowed by the realisation that, of course, she couldn't go herself. The disappointment brought a sudden lump to her throat. She swallowed hard and cleared her throat, but it seemed as if everyone else was already one step ahead. As she opened her mouth to speak, everyone said in unison, 'I'll go.' She smiled. And now they had a room full of wishes.

CHAPTER 29

hile Storm had been touched by the en masse volunteering, after ten minutes of increasingly more vigorous argument, the volume creeping ever higher as her beloved friends made their respective cases for why they should be the ones to put themselves in mortal danger, she had had enough. Her head pounded in a way that it hadn't done since before the shift, and when she made to stand, her legs felt almost too weak to hold her. She stood anyway, willing her energy into place to steady herself. The effort made her vision swim, and she had to force herself to stay calm. She could feel Isaac's eyes on her, but she daren't turn her head.

'Enough,' she said, her voice calm, and more measured than she felt. The room fell instantly into a tense silence.

'Thank you. You are, by far, the most wonderful souls I know, and I am grateful to you all for volunteering, but my sense is that it isn't as straightforward as we think. Vee, as keeper, perhaps you could tell us what the library has to say about walking between the realms, then we can hear from Isaac and Henri. As Soul Shepherds in the old world, they'll know a thing or two about the practicalities. Then Dot, as someone recently returned, we'd love to hear from you.'

'Well, I'll confer with the library when I get home, of course,' Vee said, 'but from what I understand, we can think of the spirit world as being divided roughly into two. The high vibration and the low, with us here on the ascended Earth sandwiched in the middle, but thanks to the shift, far closer to the higher realm than ever before. Forgive me for telling you all something you already know, but I like stories to start at the beginning. Those who refused the blessing at the ascension rejected the chance to attune to the higher vibration of the Earth – they slipped into the lower realm. Those that accepted the blessing ascended with the Earth and became Ethereal. But two-thirds of souls, remembering their true nature at the point of ascension, went straight to spirit to continue their journeys in the higher realms. Everyone with me so far?' She smiled tentatively as she scanned the faces around the table, and Storm smiled encouragingly in return.

'Is this where we get heaven and hell from, Auntie Vee?' Michael asked.

'Sort of, although religion put a load of old toffee around the concept, of course, in order to frighten the masses into compliance. Ironically, in the process, they kept humanity locked into fear for millennia, preventing the enlightenment they all claimed was their goal.' She shook her head irritably and added, 'Bloody idiots.'

Henri huffed. 'Religion is one thing nobody misses from the old world, that's for sure.' Which was met with an answering murmur of agreement from the room.

Veronica continued, 'In terms of physics, we're just talking about frequencies. People either choose love and go high or choose fear and go low. That fundamental choice determines their reality. Don't get me started on why anyone would choose the latter, but sadly, they do. Then, once in the lower realm, they're stuck in a downward cycle of energy, and that really must feel like hell, I'm sure. I'm not talking demons and pitch forks, though – it'll be different for everyone depending on their experience. As they say, hell is a place of our making. The realms are kept apart in order to preserve the integrity of frequencies. We're seeing first-hand the havoc that low-frequency humans are having on the new Ethereal world, and that's why we keep our visits to the higher realms to a minimum. We are pretty close to spirit now in terms of vibration, but we still bring down the average when we visit in Ethereal form, which is part of the reason shepherds' – Veronica nodded at Isaac and Henri – 'back in the day did their work astrally.'

'Is that because we're still a bit human?' Lilly asked.

'Precisely,' Henri chipped in, raising his eyebrows in question to Veronica. She gestured for him to continue.

'As a Soul Shepherd, we had to walk between all three realms. Isaac, dear boy, please jump in if I get this wrong, won't you, but our job was to see animal souls safely into the higher realm where they all naturally belong, but some were so traumatised at the point of slaughter, so imprinted on the energy of their human tormentors, that they'd either just linger on Earth or sometimes they'd even head in the other direction. That was always the most dangerous part of the calling, as we would have to follow them into the lower realm and coax them back to the light. We'd have mere seconds to do so as the risk of getting trapped ourselves was so great.'

'Trapped how?' Lilly asked.

Henri gestured to Isaac to pick up the story.

'Misery loves company, for one, so there are the other souls who, given half a chance, want to keep you there. They're not the biggest issue, though. The biggest risk is from the desire to stay.'

'Stay?' Jack snorted, incredulous.

'Being there is a lot like being depressed. You know the feeling when you're so low you can't be bothered anymore? When everything is grey and pointless and you just want to lie down and sleep? Well, that's how it starts, and very quickly it gets ahold of you and wild horses couldn't motivate you to move.' Isaac shook his head as if trying to dislodge whatever unwelcome memory had settled there.

'So nobody has ever come back from there?' Lilly asked tentatively, scanning from Isaac to Henri and back again.

It was Veronica who answered with a shake of her head. 'There's an old tale about a seer who could walk between all the realms unscathed, but the details are pretty sketchy. But if we're talking about Margot, then we don't need to worry about the lower realm at all. Every sense I have is telling me she ascended, but I can check the register when I get home.' When Veronica was met with a room full of questioning expressions, she said, 'Yes, the library keeps a log of souls. It appeared just after the shift. It's small enough to fit in a coat pocket, and yet, give it a name, any name, and it will tell you which realm they're in. It's …' She pulled a face and turned her palms up as she shrugged. 'Bonkers. I always wondered why we had it, but all becomes clear now, I suppose.'

It took another hour of debate before they had finally decided on who would look for Margot. Tim had forbidden Henri from going anywhere while he was still healing, and Veronica, Isaac, Tim and Asim were all ruled out because their skills would likely be needed in an emergency. Storm had quickly stepped in to prevent Dot from throwing her hat into the ring, suggesting that Henri needed her, and that her direct and recent experience of the afterlife was contribution enough.

'The three amigos it is then,' Lilly said, giving Jack and then Michael a decisive nod. 'When do we leave?'

CHAPTER 30

*I*t had taken an effort to persuade the newly christened 'three amigos' that they couldn't, and shouldn't, leave for the spirit world right away. There was the library to consult, briefings to be held and the small matter of training three new Ethereals on how to walk between the worlds.

'I need to brief the town, and then,' Storm said with a sigh, 'the world. If the Very are here, we have to entertain the possibility that they might be elsewhere too.'

'But won't that play into their hands, Stormy? If we put the word out now that there are madmen on the loose, then the energy levels will plummet. For all we know, that's what they're banking on,' Dot said, her hands wringing the tea towel she'd been using to dry the mugs.

Storm nodded slowly. 'That's a risk, certainly, but I'm not sure what choice we have. We can't leave souls exposed. We already know that they're hunting for food, so who knows what else they'll do.' She got up to pace around the kitchen.

'With any luck, it's just me they want, but we can't rule that out.'

'The hunter looked like an old military type, either by profession or aspiration, so maybe we need to think in those terms,' Isaac said, rubbing the stubble on his chin in the way he did when he was thinking.

'Katharine then,' Storm said, feeling like she was reading his mind. If anyone could still remember the old ways of the military, it was Isaac's sister, who had served with the British Army in their special projects team, the blacks ops unit tasked with keeping an eye on the magical community.

'Read my mind,' Isaac replied.

'Okay, so we need to reach Katharine and ask for a view of likely tactics, but I think we can assume that we're all targets. As much as we miss them, it's probably lucky that the kids are away too, otherwise they might be targeted as leverage. Assuming, that is, that they know the details about our connection. The magic school where Hebe and Fleur teach used to be like Fort Knox, I know, but what about Finn, William and Katharine? How secure is their site?'

'I called Katharine this morning, right after we found the doe. They're safe. They're spending most of their time in the underground archive anyway, and she said she'd briefed the girls. Knowing them, I'm sure they would have already picked up on something in the ether,' Isaac said, worry creasing his forehead.

Henri's shooting might have been a warning, but Storm wasn't about to take the risk that they'd stop at that. Her magic roiled in her stomach at the thought of the kids or anyone else being hurt – or worse.

'We'll need to consult the library, so why don't we all stay at ours. At least we have some bricks-and-mortar security plus assorted gadgetry that I'm sure my beloved can reinstate,'

Veronica said, patting Asim's hand affectionately. 'Then there's the library itself, which is bomb proof and magically protected.'

'Bomb proof!' Storm said, her eyes wide. 'I should have guessed.'

'My dear Stormy, it always pays to be prepared for all eventualities,' Asim replied, smiling. 'It's also flood and fire-proof,' he added, his shy smile widening into a satisfied grin.

Storm felt the knot of anxiety loosen ever so slightly. 'Okay, we have a plan. We'll move to Vee and Asim's for now. Isaac will speak to Katharine, and from there, we'll decide on whether to brief the town. I'm guessing that if anything had been picked up overseas, I would have heard about it by now, so I'll hold off calling the global co-ordinators.'

'Best wait until we're home before making any call,' Asim cautioned, looking at Isaac. 'I'd like to run some checks first – just to make sure that our communications are not being intercepted.'

'Good point. It feels like an age since we've had to think like this,' Storm said with a sigh. What she didn't add was how depressingly easy it seemed to be to slip back into fear and mistrust.

'Right. I suppose we should gather anything we think we'll need and aim to set off as soon as we can. We're losing the light already and I'd prefer not to travel in the dark,' Storm said, eyeing the setting sun through the window.

'Do we have enough vehicles?' Jack asked, scanning the room as he counted heads.

'We came in the van,' Tim said, 'so you take that.' He turned to Michael. 'I should probably check on my parents and help get the animals inside – yours too. But I can come over later.'

Storm saw the disappointment on Michael's face and his attempt to mask it. But by the looks of it, it didn't fool Tim for a second – he pulled Michael into his arms and held him. There was a lot to be said, Storm thought, for falling for the boy next door – even if the next door in question was a farmhouse half a mile away.

'No. I'd be happier knowing you were there, keeping an eye on the family,' Michael said. 'I'll call you when we're back.'

After hugging goodbye, Tim turned to Jack. 'Can I borrow your bike, mate?'

'Course. It's at the cottage. Helmet's in the hallway.' As an afterthought, Jack added, 'Tim, can you lock all the doors when you leave?'

His words settled on the room like smog. That doors needed to be locked, home and hearth protected, was almost more shocking, Storm thought, than everything they'd been discussing.

'We have Erma here too,' Henri said. 'About time the old girl was pressed into service again. Not quite our grand tour, my love,' he said, addressing Dot, 'but another chapter in our adventure certainly.'

Storm thought of the old motor home and remembered the party they'd had to wish Dot and Henri bon voyage on their grand tour of old friends and favourite haunts. Most of the village had turned out to wish them well. She'd had no idea then that the next time she'd see her dear friend Dot she'd be in the hospice, their time together rapidly diminishing.

The memory seemed to have resurfaced in Henri too, because he stood abruptly, his chair scraping along the tiles. 'Right. We'll need spare clothes, I dare say. We have plenty in the cupboards on the landing. You never know when someone might drop by on their travels.'

Dot's expression was wistful rather than sad, but if she, too, was remembering those times, she didn't let on. 'Where are your old journals, Hen darling?' she asked, stopping him in his tracks halfway to the hall.

'I've got them,' Lilly said. 'They're at our house. I was studying them a few months ago.' She gasped and put a hand to her mouth. 'I've got a book from the library too, Vee, on magical writing,' she added, sounding horrified. 'But books shouldn't be out of the library now. What if the Very get hold of it!'

Veronica held up her hand. 'You weren't to know, lovely. I dare say there are dozens out there with friends and neighbours. The books have some tricks to keep themselves safe if they're in danger, don't you worry. Dot is on to something, though. We should probably pick up Henri's journals on the way just in case there's something pertinent hidden in them. We can fetch the library book while we're there.'

'We have a plan,' Storm said. 'Let's do it.'

Within seconds, the room was a hive of activity.

CHAPTER 31

*H*alf an hour later, they were ready to leave, standing in the kitchen with assorted boxes and bags on the floor. Only Asim remained seated, his eyes glued to his tablet. The sound of Isaac's boots on the stairs caused everyone to look expectantly at the door. He emerged, binoculars in hand.

'All clear on the visual and the thermal scan, but that's not to say they're not there, just out of range,' Isaac reported. 'Let's make it quick. Storm, you're with Henri and Jack in Erma, the motor home. Lilly and Michael, you're with me in the van with the animals, and in the car we've got Vee, Dot and Asim.'

'All systems suggest the house is clear,' Asim said, rolling up his tablet and getting to his feet in one fluid movement.

'Time to go,' Isaac said.

Storm felt a chill flash across her skin, quick as frost. She snapped to attention when she realised someone was calling her name.

'You okay, babe?' Isaac was standing in front of her, concern in his eyes.

'As well as can be expected, yes,' she replied, trying to reassure him. 'Be safe, my love,' she added, reaching up to hold his cheek in her hand. He held her hand in place and turned his head to kiss her palm.

'I will if you will,' he said, stepping closer to kiss her lightly on the lips. 'Come on, we need to move.'

Storm nodded. They were the only ones left in the kitchen. She wanted to speak but found that she didn't have the words. Instead, she leaned up and kissed him again, before turning for the door.

The sun was slipping behind the mountains by the time the convoy emerged from the vicarage. Once on Church Road, the van, with Michael at the wheel, peeled off to collect the books from the cottage. Storm waved as they turned off, her throat dry. With Jack at the wheel of the motor home, they followed Vee's white sports car down the hill. Storm remembered Erma's rattly old diesel engine, back in the dark old days when people couldn't have cared less about the air and the climate. What a stupid species they had been, Storm thought.

There was never much traffic on the roads in the new world. There were so few people compared to the old world, for one thing, but the rhythm of life was so much different too. Living in a community meant you didn't pop to the shops when you ran out of bread; you went to your neighbour instead. People lived close together now, abandoning whole swathes of the world so that nature could reclaim it. Even so, the streets, as well as the roads, felt eerily empty as they made their way through the town. Cordelia's was in darkness, and Storm found herself muttering a quick spell to lock the doors. Two shops later, after worrying that one of her neighbours may be inside looking to pick up a book or some food, she quickly unlocked them again.

When they reached the bottom of the hill, Vee's car turned left, following the line of the river to the bridge and the A-road that was by far the fastest route to the house. Jack turned right towards the mountain road that would eventually take them to the second of Pont Nefoedd's bridges, two miles upstream.

Storm looked out of the passenger window, her eyes on the darkening river shrinking away beneath them. The sun was setting much more quickly than they'd expected, and she couldn't shake the feeling that this trip was their first big mistake. When the river disappeared from view, lost to the valley below, Storm closed her eyes and tried to organise her thoughts and separate intuition from plain old fear. She could feel something hovering at the corners of her mind, like a shy newcomer at a party, unwilling to step into the room and speak.

'Everything okay, dear heart?' Henri asked from the bench seat beside her.

Storm open her eyes. They had all been silent since setting off, as if, by some unspoken pact, it would ensure the safety of their journey. 'Yes. Fine,' she fibbed. It was almost dark now, and Henri's and Jack's faces were in shadow. There were no streetlights on the mountain road, never had been, even in the old world, as it had fallen out of use when the new A-road was built. They'd chosen this route precisely for that reason, but now, as the shadows won the battle with the dying light, it didn't seem like such a good idea.

They slipped back into silence, and it was only as they rounded the last bend and the old bridge came into sight at the bottom of the hill that Storm realised she'd been barely remembering to breathe. She told herself off, not that it ever did any good. No matter how many times she told herself that, as the First, she needed to be beyond such feelings, she found it impossible to just switch off her emotions. Not for the first time, she wondered what it would have been like these past ten years to have been a regular Ethereal. To have lived in love and joy, without the burden of fear or responsibility.

Erma all but glided down the hill, taking the bends with the grace of a grand old dame used to dancing in high heels. Beyond the crash barrier, Storm could once again see the river below them. The lights from the old bridge, soft yellow orbs in the distance, seemed to call them on.

'We're on the homeward stretch. Not long now and we'll be eating tea and crumpets in the library,' Henri said playfully.

Jack sucked in a breath. 'Not bloody likely, mate. Can you imagine Vee's face if we got butter on a book?'

They all laughed, clearly picturing the precise look on Vee's face at any such indiscretion and the not-so-ladylike words that would surely follow.

'Fair play, butter would be bad. Maybe we could suggest crisps instead? Or a few flaky pastries?' Jack added, all innocence.

'Or maybe some jam doughnuts, if we promised faithfully to be ever so careful and—' Henri didn't finish his sentence because at that moment, Storm felt his weight, barely restrained by his seatbelt, slam into her side as Erma bounced off the crash barrier, metal screaming against metal. Jack was pulling at the wheel, steering them frantically back from the edge.

'What the hell?' Storm shrieked.

'Bullet,' Jack said, pointing to a narrow plume of what looked to be steam disappearing into the night from Erma's bonnet.

'Hold on,' Jack said as he pressed the accelerator. 'We need to get off the mountain. They're going to have us over the edge.'

Another bullet slammed into the motor home. This one turned the windscreen into a mosaic of opaque glass. Henri punched it with his good arm, and it crumbled and fell into the cab. Jack picked up speed. The bridge was so close, and beyond it the flat, dark forest road that might at least offer them some cover.

As if waking from a dream, Storm did what she should have done from the off: she covered Erma in a protective bubble. As they neared the mouth of the bridge, the energy field rippled six, maybe seven times in quick succession. 'They're still firing then,' Jack said. 'Nice try, suckers.'

The realisation hit Storm like a hammer. What a fool. She sighed and covered her eyes with her hands as she groaned. 'Idiot!' she said to herself.

'You had no choice, my dear,' Henri said, shouting to make himself heard over the noise of the wind.

'What? What did I miss?' Jack yelled.

'Now they know for sure who's in the car,' Henri replied.

They didn't see what hit them. First they were in the air, and then they were in the water.

CHAPTER 32

'They should have been here before us,' Isaac said to Lilly from the front steps of Veronica and Asim's home. 'It's two minutes to your place from the vicarage. Chasing that obstinate, bloody library book around the place delayed us by twenty-six minutes, but their route, even though it was longer on the mountain road, should have only taken fifteen minutes, sixteen at the most, which means …'

Lilly put her hand on Isaac's arm. 'I get the maths. I'm worried too, but the signal is poor on that side of the mountain. Once they're out of any black spot, we can call them and find out why they're delayed. Erma is pretty ancient, remember – new engine or not, they've probably had to push her up steep bits,' she said, trying to reassure him and herself. 'Look, if anything has happened to them—'

The rest of Lilly's words were lost as she felt a hammer blow of emotion slam into her chest. She bent double, bile racing into her mouth and her lungs screaming for air. The fear and panic were crippling, unlike anything she'd ever experienced. Even at her most sensitive and vulnerable before the shift, nothing had ever felt quite like this. She was dimly aware of Isaac's hands on her arms, steadying her. She heard him asking over and over what was wrong, his voice rising into urgency, but she couldn't answer. It was like she was underwater. Then there was another voice in the background. Shouting, screaming for them to get inside. She felt herself being half carried, half dragged across the steps. She tried to help, tried to make her legs hold her weight and move her forward, but like her voice, they seemed lost to her. Then came the explosion. The force of it knocked her to the floor, taking what little air she had left in her lungs with it. She lay there on the steps, her ears ringing, as a hail of what might have been earth and stones or bullets rained down upon her. She didn't care, because right then she was pretty certain that Jack, Storm and Henri were all already dead.

CHAPTER 33

The first thing Lilly became aware of was a deep, resonant purring. Next was the weight on her chest, which was shifting right to left and back again, taking light and shadow with it. It took her a few moments to put the pieces together, but Anchor beat her to it by reaching out one of his huge ginger paws and patting her tentatively on the cheek.

Reality flooded back to her, and for a moment she was tempted to feign sleep, but Anchor had always been wise to that one. He leaned forward to bop his head against her chin, and as the tears slid from Lilly's still closed eyes, he redoubled his purring and rubbed them away with his whiskery cheek.

Lilly had been dimly aware of the sound of claws on polished floors skittering out of the room, and a few moments later, Veronica came in. Lilly didn't need to open her eyes to know; the smell of her delicate perfume was always enough.

'Oh, sweetheart, you're awake,' Vee said, taking Lilly's hand in hers.

Lilly felt the cry escape from somewhere beneath her ribs and make a break for freedom. It burst out of her, part wail, part scream, before dissolving into uncontrollable sobs. Anchor moved to her lap to allow Vee to hold her, while she cried herself back into an exhausted sleep.

When she woke again, she was lying on her side. Anchor was curled into the hollow of her neck and seemed to be asleep. When she stirred, planning to slide out of bed without disturbing him, he snapped into wakefulness, like a night watchman caught snoozing on the job. 'It's okay,' she whispered. Her lips and tongue felt too big for her mouth, making her own voice sound strange in her still ringing ears.

Anchor studied her face for a second, headbutted her chin once for good measure and then jumped down. He paused by the door while she peeled herself off the bed, noticing as she did everything that was battered and bruised. At least nothing appeared to be broken, which she supposed was something.

'Isaac!' she said, the realisation dawning that she might not be the only one injured. Anchor answered her with a strangled-sounding meow before disappearing. Pushing herself off the bed, Lilly felt the floor rise up to meet her. She sat back down for a second, and when she tried again, the floor stayed where it was meant to be. It felt like every muscle in her body was screaming, but it was her back that hurt the most. Gritting her teeth against it, she walked as quickly as her pain-riddled body would allow.

She was grateful that they'd put her in one of the downstairs guest rooms, as she doubted she could have negotiated stairs, especially not the sweeping marble variety that sat at the heart of Veronica and Asim's enormous house. Once in the hallway, she followed the sound of raised voices coming from the kitchen. Everyone was speaking together, making it impossible to discern one from the other. She was pretty sure she would have recognised Jack's voice amongst a crowd of thousands, though – but with a realisation that made her almost physically sick, she knew he wasn't in the kitchen.

Everyone stopped talking when she appeared. She scanned the room and found Isaac sitting at the breakfast bar, his left eye covered in a thick dressing and a bandage hanging loosely from his half-covered head. Relief flooded through Lilly. She was now pretty sure that Isaac had saved her life. While she was almost certain she no longer wanted life without Jack in it, she was still grateful.

Isaac tried to get up, but Dot put a hand on his shoulder and, when he slumped back into his seat, took the opportunity to re-wind the bandage he had presumably been trying to take off. Michael crossed the room and hugged her as if she were made of glass. When he stepped back, he kept his arm around her shoulders and guided her to the breakfast bar, then when lifting her leg onto the high bar chair made her wince, he helped her up. Dot stroked her back, then busied herself with the first aid box. Veronica put a large mug of black coffee in front of her and Asim gave her a smile so sad that she thought her heart would break afresh. But it was when Isaac looked at her she knew for sure. His unbandaged eye was red and bloodshot, and when it met Lilly's, it pooled with tears. She held out her arms, and they held each other as they cried. Her nausea returned, the weight of the grief in the room almost overwhelming her. She knew she should shield herself, do the thing that Jack had drummed into her since she was a child, but part of her wanted to be engulfed in someone else's pain. Maybe if it became too much, it would take her completely.

They might have stayed like that all day if Anchor hadn't jumped onto the breakfast bar and, with a deliberate paw, knocked Lilly's mug onto the floor just as Hope, Ludo and even little Logan burst into a barking frenzy.

'What happened?' Lilly asked. 'It felt like an explosion.'

'They fired a mortar into the grounds. We think ostensibly to destroy the helicopter – they succeeded there,' Asim said from the floor as he mopped up the spilled coffee. Anchor perched next to Lilly and watched unapologetically. When he stood up, Asim used his free hand to tickle Anchor under the chin. 'Were we getting too maudlin for you, Anc? Clever so-and-so.' Anchor narrowed his eyes and pulled away.

'So they don't want us escaping,' Lilly said flatly.

'Looks that way,' Asim replied from the sink, where he was washing his hands. 'I'd reactivated the security net around the house and grounds, but we only had a few seconds' warning. That they have artillery like that is, well …' He broke off, obviously not wanting to finish the sentence.

'But why don't they just fire at the house? If they can do it once, why haven't they done it again? Get it over with,' Lilly asked. Asim's eyes went first to Veronica, then Michael and Dot. Isaac sniffed and put his head in his hands.

'I can no longer sense Storm's energy,' Isaac said, his voice breaking. 'Looks like they achieved their mission already.'

Lilly shook her head. 'Nor can I,' she mumbled, her voice hitching as she struggled not to cry.

Anchor rubbed his head across her chin, then headbutted her, first gently, then a little more persistently. She ignored him as the tears fell.

Lilly squeezed her eyes shut and felt the comforting, familiar weight of others' pain pull her into blackness. Like a predator dragging a fresh kill into a dark cave, she was ready to surrender to it. That's when Anchor bit her hand.

'What the—?' she screamed, jumping out of the chair, the

pain of the bite, which was only really a nip, nowhere near as wounding as the pain of the betrayal. Anchor slashed his enormous tail back and forth across the countertop, his eyes narrowed to amber slits. She'd never seen him look so angry, and his energy was rolling off him like a tidal wave of fury.

'Isaac?' Lilly asked, hoping their resident communicator could fill in the blanks.

Isaac shrugged and shook his head, not willing to try. Anchor let out a furious yowl, and the dogs kicked off again with angry, vicious-sounding growls interspersed between ferocious barks. Lilly had only once heard Hope growl, on the day the Very had grabbed her off the street. As for Ludo and Logan, she had doubted them even capable.

'Ludo?' Dot asked, clearly as perplexed as everyone else as to this sudden turn of events.

Isaac looked up and scanned the room. To Lilly, he seemed like a man waking from a dream – or, more appropriately, a nightmare. He glanced at the dogs, who were standing shoulder to shoulder in a straight line. Then he cocked his head, as if listening. The dogs went quiet but stood stiff as boards, eyes staring. Anchor stalked across the counter to sit in front of Isaac. His tail had slowed to a gentle swish, and she was grateful to see that his eyes were back to normal.

Lilly felt her pulse pounding in her ears. Was there hope after all? She reached out to Jack in her mind, but there was still nothing. Just an endless black void where the love of her life should be. She got the same response when she tried to sense Storm and Henri. Just nothingness. The equivalent of cosmic static. Like the signal was missing – or jammed.

When Isaac's lips curled into the faintest of smiles, Lilly let out the breath she'd been holding. 'What? What are they saying?'

Isaac reached out to Anchor and the cat all but sprang into his arms, purring with what Lilly could only assume was relief. 'Well, after telling us off for the pity party, they're saying quite clearly that while we may not sense them, they most certainly still can.'

CHAPTER 34

*T*he river lost no time in deluging the cab of the motor home. Without the windscreen, there was nothing to slow the shock of the cold, dark water. Storm barely had time to draw a breath before it surrounded them. The force of the water was the second shock, the river seemingly in two minds about whether it wanted to drag them to its depths or haul them downstream. She fumbled for the seat belts, popping hers and Henri's. When she reached for his arm, she found he wasn't moving. She hoped Jack had done his own as she knew they had just seconds to escape the cab. A hand on her left arm told her that Jack was already out and there to help her with Henri. As she grabbed a handful of Henri's jacket and pushed off from the seat, she was struck by the sickening realisation that they'd likely be shot, or worse, the moment they surfaced. They had to have been tracking her energy signal, and so the only way out was to buy them some time, whatever the cost.

Her lungs were screaming for air by the time she surfaced. Henri was still sandwiched between her and Jack, his head

lolling in unconsciousness. Jack pressed his ear against the
older man's nose and, after a moment, nodded at Storm. At
least he was still breathing.

Storm poured every ounce of her strength into battling the
current. Catching her breath, she looked around. The light
from the bridge did little more than cast a pretty glow over
the rushing water, and the sun was all but set behind the
mountain. Storm remembered that the bank underneath the
bridge was low and shallow. She'd seen people fishing there
back when such barbarity was the norm. 'Bridge,' she splut-
tered. Jack nodded once, and together, they began battling
their way upstream.

The crack of automatic gunfire made them both freeze,
but then came whoops of delight from the bridge.

'Take that, you filthy bitch!'

Storm looked up to see two men silhouetted above them,
one high-fiving the other.

'Boss'll be pissed she didn't get to burn her, though,' said
the second man wryly. 'Have you done another scan, to be
sure?'

The first man sighed. 'What? Floating bodies full of lead
not enough for you?'

When the second man didn't reply, he pulled something
out of his pocket. After a few seconds he said, 'All clear. Ding
dong, the witch is most definitely dead. Come on, I want a
beer.'

As the throaty roar of a retreating diesel engine split the
night, Storm and Isaac swam for the bank, fighting the current
and pulling Henri along between them. As Storm's foot finally
touched the rocky bottom, Henri jerked into alertness. They
collapsed onto the stones and stayed there, unspeaking until
the sounds of their ragged breaths and fits of coughing had
subsided. Henri was the first to push himself up to sitting. 'I

think I must have taken a bang to the head,' he said matter-of-factly, touching his fingers to his temple gingerly.

Storm and Jack both sat up. Storm raised her finger, about to conjure a light, but stopped herself just in time. 'Sorry, magic's off limits for a while,' she said. 'Are you bleeding, Hen?'

Henri peered at his fingers, but the light was all but gone. 'I think so,' he said, 'but I don't think it's bad. Maybe just a passing stone in the water or a bit of wood. I feel a bit foggy, but no headache yet, so that's good. We'd better move before they come back.'

'I don't think they'll be looking for us. Not for a while anyway,' Storm said.

'How come they didn't see us? I didn't have time to cloak us,' Jack asked. 'And what was with the whole boo-ya bullshit about killing the witch?'

Storm took a deep breath. Half of this would be easy to explain, half of it not so much. 'I realised as soon as we were in the water that they'd pick us off the second we surfaced. They must have been tracking my energy signal or something. Asim's tech confirmed we weren't being bugged or spied on by drones, so that's the only other thing that makes sense. So I projected a glamour of the three of us coming up for air. That's what the goons shot at. Then they saw our bullet-ridden bodies float away downstream.'

'Hence the high fives,' Jack said contemptuously. 'Sick fucks.'

'But if they're tracking your energy, my dear, surely that wouldn't work for long?' Henri asked, his voice raspy.

Storm waited a beat before answering. 'I had to cloak us completely. I wasn't even sure it was possible, but it was the only way. As far as the world is concerned, we're no longer in it.'

'Wait, what?' Jack had been whispering, but his voice rose to close to a shout.

'It was the only way, Jack. We're still in the world, our world, it's just that our energy can't be detected.'

'But that means ...' Jack's voice was suddenly hoarse.

'Oh dear lord,' Henri said. 'My darling Dot.'

'I'm sorry, but it really was the only way to get us to safety.' Storm knew that although she'd been trying for assertive, she sounded close to pleading.

Even in the twilight under the bridge, Storm could see the horror on her friends' faces. 'But the animals can. They're more sensitive, so I didn't exclude their frequency. With any luck, our furry friends will have filled in the others long before there's any drama about our untimely demise,' she added quickly.

Jack huffed out a long breath. 'Wait, the Very will expect things to start unravelling without you, won't they? They'll be waiting for the energies to plummet so they can reappear without their medallion things.'

'The cloaking will show a dip in the energy, and I doubt they'll expect it to be instant, so I'm guessing we have a few hours before they figure out their mistake.'

Although Storm would have felt safer going through the woods for speed, they chose to walk along the road. They stood at the end of the bridge, staring into what looked to be a wall of solid blackness. This road was so beautiful in the daylight. The forest stretched either side of the winding country road for mile after mile, the trees' canopies knitting together to create the impression of an arboreal tunnel. However, it didn't look so inviting on a moonless night. Especially without the benefit of a torch or the option of a witch's light.

'Should we hold hands?' Henri joked.

The soft glow from the bridge gave just enough light for Storm to see that the wound on his head had dried into a jagged line of crusted blood. But at least it had stopped bleeding, she thought.

A snort made them all jump and spin around. Standing behind them were a stag and a white doe. Storm bowed her head in welcome. 'My friends. "Thank you" seems inadequate.'

The stag snorted again, and the doe dipped her head in acknowledgement, then walked into the darkness, her white coat seemingly shining like the moon itself.

'The world is full of magic things,' began Henri, resting his hand lightly for a moment on Storm's shoulder.

'Patiently waiting for our senses to grow sharper,' Jack concluded.

The stag walked ahead to join the doe, and for a glorious mile or more, Storm focused only on the sound of their hooves on the tarmac and the light of their guide.

When the gates of Veronica and Asim's home came into view, Storm almost cried out with relief. They took it in turns to thank the deer. Even in the Ethereal age, manners were important, and deer were sticklers for proper etiquette. She knew that news of the killing would have already spread like wildfire, but she implored them to be careful all the same. Storm punched in the access code, crossing her fingers that nobody had bothered to change it since before the shift. After an agonising few seconds, she heard a motor kick into life and the gates opened.

Storm turned, but the deer had already gone. Then came the unmistakable sound of feet sprinting on gravel. She heard her name being called, although the voice was a half shout, half cry. And all at once, there he was, running towards her, Lilly and Dot either side of him and the dogs at their heels, barking joyfully.

CHAPTER 35

*D*awn was breaking by the time the story of the bridge attack had been told, retold, dissected and analysed. They had abandoned the kitchen for the lounge and its long, sumptuous cream sofas that were all the better for snuggling up to their loved ones.

Henri's head wound had been tenderly cleaned and dressed by Dot, and he was under strict instructions to rest, a command that, for once, he showed no signs of resisting. Lilly thought he looked tired, leaning back against the cushions, Dot's head on his shoulder. It was as if they'd all slipped through time to the world before the shift. A time when pain, fear, injury and even just plain old weariness could bring them low. It felt all at once alien and horribly familiar.

No one had had the heart to tell Storm that for three long hours, everyone had believed them to be dead. Lilly watched her friend now, sitting on the couch, Isaac lying stretched out beside her with his head in her lap. On her other side sat Hope, who was as close to Storm as she could possibly get. Isaac, too, looked somehow defeated. Maybe it was the bandage over his head and eye, but she had never known him so quiet. Storm might have been the First, but as her partner and fellow witch, he was powerful in his own right. They had always looked to him for guidance, and yet he'd been so subdued since the attack.

Lilly felt Jack's arm squeeze around her, and when she looked up at him, he planted a kiss on her forehead. 'They'll be alright,' he whispered, reading her mind. 'I think it's the shock. We're none of us used to being vulnerable these days.'

Lilly nodded, but wasn't entirely convinced. Then she cursed herself for doubting her friends and losing hope so soon. She was about to speak when Veronica and Michael came into the room carrying trays laden with breakfast things.

There was a murmured groan around the room, to which Veronica replied, 'No moaning and groaning, my lovelies. We have work to do, and we can't do that on empty stomachs. I'm just going to get the tea, and when I come back I want to see everyone tucking in like you're at an all-you-can-eat buffet on your hollibobs. Okay?' She fixed them each with her raised-brow stare before leaving the room.

The groan was replaced by a collective giggle. 'Would Vee tell me off if I told her how sweet she looked when she was being all assertive?' Lilly whispered to Jack.

'She'd probably threaten to tan your arse,' Jack said, levering himself up so he could obey the breakfast-eating orders.

The last thing Lilly felt like doing was eating, but Vee was right, she thought. They needed to break out of this malaise if they were to have any chance at all of holding on to this world. Maybe if they started with food, everything else would fall into place.

Ten minutes later everyone except Asim, who was still doing something with the security system, was tucking into a breakfast of fruit, pastries and nut breads. It had had the desired effect, the energy in the room now markedly higher. Isaac had just about stopped himself from spitting a mouthful of coffee over the cream carpet when Hope confided that their first plan to get the humans' attention had been for Logan to pee on Isaac's leg. He'd apparently agreed only after a lot of persuading, but being new to such things, had found the balancing tricky, at which point Anchor had stepped in to volunteer. Even though nobody else in the room was party to the story, the laughing had started even before Isaac recovered himself enough to recount it. Lilly watched as Hope, her story told, went back to snoozing, her head on Storm's lap. She was a clever soul, that dog.

Once the hilarity had died down and Logan had been commended for his team spirit, the conversation had slipped into one of practicalities. Food supplies, security measures, calls to the other global co-ordinators and how best to notify the other Pont Nefoedd residents of the threat in their midst. Lilly felt the tension levels in the room creep up as everyone skirted around the question that, to her mind at least, was the most important. When she could stand it no more, she asked tentatively, 'Stormy, how long do we have? Before they realise you're not dead?'

'I doubt we have very long, darling. As the world didn't begin to unravel when they' – she mimed air quotes – 'shot me, I'm guessing they'll either assume that there's some sort of lag at play or they'll begin to worry that I'm still alive and go looking downstream for bodies. If they do have a witch in their number, then they'll likely be advising them of all the options.'

'But they might cotton on sooner,' Veronica chimed in. 'That lot were always crossing each other, let alone their enemies, so I doubt deception is ever very far from their minds.'

'Indeed. I know that's not answering your question, Lil, but I think we need to be prepared for what's coming,' Storm said.

Lilly turned to look at Jack sitting behind her. She didn't need to form the question for him to answer. He nodded, his lips set into a determined line. Lilly looked at Michael, who was sitting on the floor, Logan sprawled on his lap. She wasn't used to seeing him without Tim, and he seemed somehow unmoored. When he met her eyes, he nodded too, then said to the room, 'Then we need to leave now. To find Margot, I mean.'

Isaac made to speak, no doubt to protest, but Storm stopped him with a hand on his arm. 'They're right, my love,' she said. 'They will find us soon enough, and I fear for life itself when they do.'

CHAPTER 36

*I*saac found Storm in the sunroom. She was looking out over the gardens, Hope sitting at her side. Those at the back of the house had been untouched by the explosion, and from here, it was almost possible to forget that there was a crater big enough to bury a bus in just out of sight. He stood beside her and reached for her hand, following her gaze out towards the kitchen garden, the meadow, and the orchard beyond. 'When we were building this room, Asim told me that all this had once been laid to lawn,' Isaac said ruefully. 'Six acres. It was like he was confessing a crime, poor man. He said he'd always wanted one of those mowers you sit on to drive. So, when the architect asked, lawn it was.'

Storm laughed. 'I know for a fact that he never once even started the thing. There was a photo of him sitting on it, but that was it.' After a few moments she added, 'We were all of us guilty in so many ways. There were so many ways we could have helped the Earth, but everyone was just so busy. It's so like Asim, though, to take the wound to his heart. He's such a good soul.'

'That he is. And he's certainly done his bit to make good,' Isaac said. He was stalling for time, and he knew that Storm knew it.

'You think they should go corporeally.' It was a statement, not a question. She didn't turn to face him, and he was glad of it. Now was not the time to lose himself in her eyes. If he did, he wondered if his courage would leave him completely.

'Yes,' he said. 'If they go astrally and we have to move locations, we'll have three soulless bodies to protect.' He paused and licked his lips, trying to choose the right words. 'Plus, we don't know what the Very might do with a soulless body, and I'm not about to leave three of our friends lying around for them to find, just in case.'

'Plus, if we fail here and everything falls, then maybe it will be easier on them to be in spirit when it happens,' she added, reaching for his hand.

'That too,' Isaac said after clearing his throat.

Storm turned to him and touched his face, tracing her thumb lightly across the brow above his still bandaged eye. 'Does it still hurt?'

'Only a bit now. Tim took a look at it over video call earlier. It's healing, but not as fast as it should. Stormy, what if ...'

She touched a finger to his lips, holding his gaze as she shook her head slowly. 'The time for doubt and fear is gone, my love. We have to be strong now, stronger than we want to be, and stronger than we think ourselves capable. I have no intention of letting go of this world that has been fashioned by love, but if it is to be taken from us all, then they will need to rip it out of my cold, dead hands.'

Isaac hadn't seen that look on her face since London. It was the look, he remembered, that she'd had right before she pushed all her friends to safety and brought the entire house down upon herself with the Very locked inside. He felt his throat constrict as his heart hammered in his chest. Her expression was unreadable now, but when he made to speak, she leaned up and kissed him.

'There's no time to lose,' she said, then turned for the door, Hope at her heels.

CHAPTER 37

'Wait, so we're actually going into spirit and taking our bodies,' Jack stated. 'I mean, I used to do that when I was a guide, but is it really necessary now? Can't we just spirit walk like you and Henri used to do?'

They had chosen the library as their departure and return point, and Isaac was leaning against the large reading table. Since the shift, it was no longer the preserve of the keeper, and an assortment of old armchairs had been added to accommodate the various visitors who came to consult the ancient texts.

'We get it,' Lilly said, jumping in to interrupt. 'Jack, the others don't want to have to worry about hauling our bodies around when all hell might be breaking loose too. It makes total sense. Are we ready now?' she asked, hands on hips, but Jack didn't take the hint.

'Can I just double-check how we get back and how we decide where we'll return to?' he asked. Lilly groaned and put her head in her hands.

'Jack, please, we've been over this. Plus, you spent how many lifetimes flitting between the worlds?'

Jack shot her a hurt look. 'That was different. We weren't all Ethereal then, and we didn't have the fate of the world resting on our shoulders either.'

Michael stood up and rubbed his palms together as he spoke. 'As I understand it, it's all intention led. So when we're ready, we just hold hands, visualise a doorway or some sort of opening into the spirit world, and when it appears, we step through it. Most importantly, we all need to be focusing on Margot as we go through, as that will help us land as close to her as possible.' He looked in turn to Isaac, Storm and Henri for confirmation.

'Bravo, young Michael,' Henri said, giving him a double thumbs up.

'And to come back we just repeat the process, visualising the library,' Lilly said, hoping against hope that this last run-through would be enough to satisfy Jack. 'If we get separated in spirit, we can find each other by focusing on each other's energy, and if it all goes a bit Pete Tong, we can come back here separately.' She said the last part with a frown, adding, 'But that's not our intention, of course – that's only for emergencies.'

'Perfect,' Isaac said. 'Jack?'

Jack sighed and grabbed the arms of the chair he was sitting in. After a moment's hesitation, he pulled himself to standing. 'I'm ready,' he said, not looking at anyone.

Lilly sighed with relief. Jack was never usually this cautious – that had always been her job – and, irritation and impatience aside, it worried her. Pushing the thoughts to the back of her mind, she too stood up and walked to the wall they'd chosen as their departure point. She focused on calming her breathing. They had to do this. There was no other way. She wiped her palms down the front of her jeans before holding them out to her sides and looking pointedly at Jack and then Michael.

Michael winked at her before taking her hand. They had been together for only a brief time a decade and, it seemed to Lilly, a lifetime ago. They had both gone on to find the loves of their lives, she with Jack and Michael with Tim, and now he was her best friend. Aside from Jack and Storm, she could think of nobody else she'd rather have at her side.

Jack took her other hand, but before she could say a word, he dropped it again and said, 'Wait, what happens if things go wrong here? If the library is compromised?'

Lilly wanted to laugh, but the look Isaac and Storm exchanged told her she'd been missing something all along.

'If for any reason you can't sense me here, don't come home,' Storm replied. She said it so simply, as if she were saying, 'If my car's not outside then I'm likely out walking with Hope.' She added, 'I can't cloak my energy again, that was a one-time deal – they won't fall for it now. So if it happens, it'll be for real this time.'

'No!' Lilly didn't intend to shout but her voice echoed around the library, causing some of the fussier books to flutter off the shelves in complaint.

Storm crossed the room and cupped Lilly's face in her hands. 'I'll do everything in my power to be here, little one, you know that, but if I'm not, then you're not to return.' When Lilly made to shake her head in defiance, Storm only nodded. 'To return once I've gone will be to walk into hell, and I know you wouldn't do that to me. Would you?'

Lilly felt her throat constrict, but she refused to give in to tears this time. She hugged Storm instead and tried, without much success, to contain her misery.

'The library is our most heavily fortified sanctuary,' Storm said, 'but it's not beyond threat. Look through the portal before you return, just to be sure. Check for my energy signal. Also, look to see if this picture is still on that table.' She turned and pointed behind them. 'If it is, then it's safe to come home, but if it's not, you need to find another location. Understand?' Storm now sounded every inch the leader of souls. 'If you can't sense my energy at all, then under no circumstances are you to return.'

'Spirit will fall too, though, without you. Won't it, Storm?' Michael asked.

'That's our assumption, yes,' she replied gently.

Lilly didn't trust her voice so just nodded miserably. Was it only minutes ago that she'd been raring to go? Why hadn't she thought about this? No wonder Jack was asking so many questions. He was worried that they were on a one-way ticket to spirit – or worse. She felt like an idiot.

'Okay, enough with the glum faces, you three,' Isaac said, stepping in next to Storm. 'You have your mission, you knew it came with risk. Don't let the risk of what may or may not happen here distract you from what you're there to do. You need to find Margot and find out what spell she used to protect the Very post-shift. Most importantly of all, you need to persuade her to undo it.'

Michael said, 'Got it,' in a tone that suggested to Lilly that he'd already put the 'what ifs' out of his mind.

Jack too seemed back on track now he had all the facts. 'Let's get on with it,' he said, huffing out a long breath and hopping up and down on the spot as if he was about to run a race.

Lilly simply couldn't find the words, so she just said, 'Okay,' as she stared at the floor, the conversation around her rising in volume as Jack, Isaac and Michael began talking.

Storm stepped forward and placed her hands lightly on

Lilly's upper arms, and squeezed them as she planted a kiss on the crown of her head. Lilly gasped as what felt like a minor electric shock surged through her body.

Storm shook her head, fending off Lilly's question. 'If you can't come back safely to Pont Nefoedd, then follow the energy here,' she said, pressing a small flat grey pebble into Lilly's hand.

Lilly opened her mouth to speak, but Storm shook her head again.

'We ready then?' Jack said, coming to join them.

Lilly felt her head nodding as if it didn't need her conscious permission. After giving Storm a final hug, she mutely held her arms out at her sides. Jack and Michael took a hand each. She closed her eyes and pictured Margot in the photograph that Storm had given them earlier, then squeezed the hands holding on to hers. When they squeezed back, she opened her eyes, and the plain white wall had been replaced by a long country road flanked by lavender fields. Lilly stared, breathing in the sweet scent of the flowers, already feeling the warm summer sun on her face and the tickle of her hair against her cheeks, stirred by the breeze. She looked to Jack, who appeared equally taken aback. Then she turned to Michael.

'Shall we?' Michael said.

Lilly took a deep breath, and then the three friends stepped out of the Ethereal world and into that of spirit.

CHAPTER 38

*S*torm watched as the portal closed behind Lilly, Jack and Michael. For a split second she had actually contemplated jumping through after them. She only realised that she had been holding her breath when Isaac stepped behind her and wrapped his arms around her waist.

'You okay?' he asked.

She tore her eyes away from the now blank wall that, just seconds ago, had been the doorway to Margot's afterlife. She felt far from okay. Fear for Lilly writhed around in her gut together with the fear of what might happen to them all if they failed. Yet again, all life hung in the balance, and yet again, she was at the middle of it. At least the first time she'd been blissfully unaware of her part in things. Mixed in with the fear was another emotion. Longing.

Storm had not seen Margot since the day she died. She'd played their last conversation in her head more times than she could reliably count. She often thought that the full spectrum of emotions she felt for Margot had played themselves out in the mere minutes they had together in the basement of the

Holland Park house where she'd been killed. It had been Storm's fury that had awoken the full extent of her magic, the magic that, in the end, had saved them all. It had taken her a while to realise that it had come not just from the knowledge that Margot had been the one to bind her magic and sever her connection with spirit but from the fact that she'd abandoned her in the first place to go to America all those years ago.

Margot's relocation to the States had been expected, but it had still come as a heavy blow. Storm had half expected Margot to suggest she join her and transfer to a US university. She had held on to that hope until she met Nick and began to feel the roots quicken under her feet. Then the hope was that Margot would simply tire of the US and come home, but that never happened either. They were in regular contact at first, but even that had dwindled, and over time Storm felt the ties that bound them loosen and stretch until they were just two ribbons, fluttering in the wind.

Storm's fury had turned on a sixpence when the true extent of Margot's plight had been revealed. That she had lived enslaved to the Very for so long, all to protect her. That Margot had all but lost her mind in the process wasn't in doubt. The woman she had known and loved would never have contemplated giving up on the world so that a monied elite could ride out the apocalypse in luxury and reclaim it as their own when most of the population had been annihilated. But who knew what two decades of forced servitude could do? Cutting herself off from those she loved was, Storm realised, just another way of trying to protect them. She had locked herself away in her gilded cage. Maybe anyone would lose themselves eventually, surrounded by crazies and plans for visions of the apocalypse.

Margot had sacrificed so much and had almost lost her humanity in the process. Standing in the basement of the

Holland Park house, Storm couldn't have imagined doing anything differently if she had been in Margot's place and it was Lilly who had been threatened. Of course, she hadn't had the chance to say that to Margot, and in her darkest moments, she wondered whether her friend and mentor had intended to die that day. As a seer, had she foreseen what happened? Chosen death as her release from the grip of the Very? Storm still couldn't quite believe that Margot wouldn't have shielded herself from the gunmen who killed her. Spells like that were child's play to a witch so powerful.

Storm had so much she wanted to ask her old friend. Often it was just the mundane – the white T-shirt or the orange? Would an enrichment spell help on the top meadow? Other times, she just longed for the reassurance. Was she doing this right? Was there a handbook somewhere on how to be the First? Now, she longed to know whether Margot had foreseen this. Did she know how this would end? She sighed, feeling the emptiness in her gut that even the great shift had done nothing to fill. She had no anger left for Margot, only a deep, enduring love with nowhere to go. She wondered whether Margot knew that. She hoped she did.

In the decade since her death, she'd thought often about seeking Margot out in spirit, but as the First, she was bound to the Earth, just as it was bound to her. If there was any visiting to be done, then it would have to be Margot's choice. She reminded herself that every soul needs time to heal, and so she had waited for Margot to come to her. That she'd chosen not to visit was a sadness Storm carried like a small cold stone in her heart.

'Hon?' Isaac repeated.

'Not really,' she murmured as she laid her head back to rest on his shoulder, enjoying the presence of him and feeling, as she always did around Isaac, that despite everything, she was exactly where she needed to be. If home was a person, then he was hers.

'Thinking about Margot or worrying about Lil?' he asked as he swayed gently back and forth.

'Bit of both,' she said with a sigh.

'Wishing we could have gone instead.' It was a statement rather than a question, and as ever, he was spot on.

Not trusting herself to reply, she just nodded.

Stepping around her, Isaac had just pulled her into his arms when the house shook so violently, her first thought was of an earthquake. The lights in the library flicked off for a second and were replaced by the red glow Storm associated with submarine war films. A woman's voice from the security system calmly announced, 'Attention. Security breach detected. Lockdown procedures activated.'

Hundreds of books took flight, flapping around like startled birds. Storm ducked, pulling Isaac with her to escape being struck by a panicking hardback tome with lethal-looking metal bindings. As she straightened, a small volume thumped into her shoulder then fell to the floor, where it writhed around, seemingly unable to take off again. Storm picked it up and held it her chest. 'Come on, you're alright,' she cooed as she stroked it.

'You're going to do yourselves an injury,' Veronica implored, raising her head from under the reading table where she, Henri and Dot had taken refuge. 'We're safe – Asim just confirmed it,' she added, tapping the earpiece she wore. 'Now back to your places at once,' she commanded, obviously channelling her inner schoolmarm, because even the little book Storm was soothing obeyed.

Before the last of the books were back on the shelves, the lights flicked back on and the security announcement was cut off midway through another eerily calm warning. As Storm and Isaac joined the others at the reading table, Asim hurried into the library, tablet in one hand, Anchor in the other and the dogs at his heels.

'You sure you're all okay?' he asked, looking at each of them in turn, his brow furrowed.

'Everyone's fine, my love,' Veronica said. 'You lot were the only ones upstairs when it hit, so I think it's you we should all be worried about.'

'Hit?' Dot asked. 'Hit by what?' Her voice betrayed the merest hint of a wobble.

Asim took a deep breath and laid the tablet on the table, propping it on its stand so that they could all see. Anchor hopped onto the table and sat next to the screen, his fat ginger tail swishing irritably.

'It appears that they have more short-range missiles,' he said, shaking his head. He sounded slightly incredulous. 'Luckily for us, their guidance system isn't all that, because it wasn't a direct hit, but I think it's fair to say they've realised that you're still alive and well,' he added, looking at Storm.

'Or maybe the plan is to frighten us half to death,' Henri said, leaning down to rub Ludo's ears affectionately.

'Or that,' conceded Asim as he touched the screen to set the video to play. 'They did succeed in taking out the big green-house, though, and the back of the house has extensive shrapnel and blast damage.' He looked at Isaac and added, 'Sorry, mate.'

Storm felt Isaac freeze beside her at the mention of the greenhouse, the home for so many of the rare and endangered plants he'd been cultivating over the years. She laid her hand on his back as he leaned forward to view the smoking crater and debris that had once been his haven. Hope whined from where she sat between Isaac and Storm.

'Thanks, sweetheart. At least none of you are hurt,' Isaac said to her.

'I've managed to activate some of the old satellite defences, so' – Asim started counting off the points by holding up his fingers – 'one, we'll get an early warning of any further attacks, two, we'll be able to play intercept, and three, we'll be able to monitor the rest of the area to see where they might be heading next. Bloody annoying though, because had it been operational a few minutes earlier ...' He sighed and dragged his fingers through his hair.

'What does "play intercept" mean, exactly?' Storm asked, her tone sharper than she'd intended.

'I've commandeered the old Air Shield defence system. It was a joint European project back in the day, used mainly for monitoring and drone deployment, but what Joe Public didn't know at the time was that the satellites could be used to launch air attacks and protect assets using new wave-deflection technology.' Asim held up his hands as he added, 'And that's what I mean on the intercept. If they launch another attack on us here, the system will deflect and disarm any missiles. Even Ethereals are allowed to defend ourselves, surely?'

Storm didn't think it was a question, but when, after a few seconds of silence, she looked up from the screen, Dot was holding on to Henri's sleeve as if bracing for bad news, Veronica seemed not to be blinking, and all eyes were fixed expectantly on her.

'Yes. And no,' she conceded. She pulled out a chair, intending to sit down, but changed her mind. Feeling the need to move, she prowled around the table, chewing at a piece of loose skin at the side of her thumb. 'Any violence, even in defence, will lower the energy. Remember, there's no court of law when it comes to energy – it just responds, it doesn't judge. We can't plead mitigating circumstances – we may as well be pleading to gravity.'

Storm felt her own energy reserves flag, and she slumped down heavily in the armchair at the end of the room. She put her head in her hands, her long hair falling like a curtain either side of her face. She took a deep breath. She could practically smell the fear on her friends, and it all but broke her heart. Hauling herself out of what she scolded herself for being a selfish moment, she forced herself to stand up, but the effort made her head swim.

'Right. No point getting maudlin,' she said brightly. 'We all have to watch our energy levels now. Keep the negativity at bay as far as is Ethereally possible, okay? And that goes for any murderous intent towards our bunker buddies out there with the heavy artillery. I know it's hard, but we all have to try.'

'Stormy's right,' Veronica chipped in. 'We need to keep our energy up physically too. Come on, there are scones in the kitchen that need eating.' Dot and Henri groaned at the mention of more food, and Storm saw Isaac and Asim share a smirk.

Catching Veronica's eye, Storm pointed to Isaac and mouthed, 'We'll be up in a minute.'

Veronica said, 'Okey doke,' and turned to leave. At the door, she looked back, her brow furrowed. The others filed past her up the stairs, already lost in conversation. Veronica shook her head and gave Storm a sad, fleeting smile. That was the thing about best friends, Storm thought. It was so hard to keep anything from them.

CHAPTER 39

Storm and Isaac waited until everyone had left the library before making their way to the stairs. She paused halfway. Her head swam and her legs were leaden. Her magic, once charged by the life and the love of the world, felt thin and weary. Isaac rounded on her and cupped her face tenderly in his hands.

'You're weakening,' he said.

Storm could never lie to him, even for his own protection. Besides, some truths were inescapable no matter how much she wished them otherwise. She wanted so badly to scream. To wail her anguish and her fury into the ether and then to rid the universe, once and for all, of the evil that walked among them. What frightened her most was that, in that moment, she doubted she could even find the strength to scream.

In London, she had been faced with a choice. The human part of her had so longed for rest, but she had chosen duty. She stayed so that she could love the Earth and all its broken souls back to life. As life and love had flourished, so had she.

Not wanting to say the words aloud, she held his gaze and nodded slowly.

The tears came instantly to his eyes, and the sight of them all but cleaved her heart in two. She grabbed him, holding him tightly as she fought back her own tears. She felt his body shudder as he wrestled with the weight of the knowledge they alone shared. Guiding him to a nearby sofa, she pulled him down to sitting and held him until he was calm. He pulled up the bottom of his T-shirt and wiped his eyes.

'Can't actually remember the last time I did that,' he said, not meeting her eye.

Storm thumbed away a fresh tear that was tracking its way down Isaac's cheek and bit her lip to stop herself from joining in.

'Margot used to say that a chilly day in August was infinitely more miserable than a true winter's day,' she said.

'The cold of summer,' Isaac said wryly. 'I get it. To have worked so hard. To have put right nearly all of the wrongs we had done to her, only to ...' He shook his head, unable to finish. There was no need; she felt it too. To think of the world slipping back to what it had been, a piggy bank for the rich to be plundered and abused, was bad enough, but there was no going back. The shift had changed everything, and if the Very returned, magical amulets or not, everything would fall, spirit included.

Isaac lifted his face and studied her. His expression was one of such pure love that her own tears responded without her permission. She bit her lip to stem them. Everything depended on her now.

'You know there's a chance that they'll still be able to—' Isaac began, his voice thick with emotion.

She pressed her finger to his lips before he could finish the sentence and closed her eyes. 'I know, my love. It won't buy us much time, but if they take us together then it will be all the easier for them.'

Isaac slapped his hands on his knees as he exhaled. 'To think that just a few days ago our biggest concern was having to eat leftover party food for six months.' He gave a wry laugh.

'You'll persuade the fur kids?' Storm asked.

'They won't want to leave you, but you know that. I'll tell them that staying would play into the Very's hands and endanger you. They'll see the logic in that.'

Storm nodded, and almost smiled as she imagined the long and likely protracted conversation Isaac would probably need to have with the animals, Logan especially. Having lived in a world made up almost entirely of old souls, they had all forgotten the innocence of the newly incarnated. Logan's arrival had been a joyful reminder of that. The first new soul to join them in the Ethereal world and live their life entirely untainted by the old world – or so they had thought.

Storm made to stand but felt a weakness in her legs which made her doubt their ability to hold her upright. Things were progressing much faster than she'd feared. They didn't have long. Isaac helped her to the stairs.

'There's not much time, my love,' she said. 'You need to go now.' Had she had the strength, she would have conjured a glamour to steady her voice, but she had to make do with force of will alone.

Isaac sucked in a deep breath, held it and blew it out slowly through his mouth. Standing, he lifted her gently to her feet and stood looking down into her eyes as he stroked his thumbs lightly across her face. Sometimes not even words were enough, she thought as she rested her palm against his cheek. He turned and kissed it.

'Are you ready?' she asked.

'Of course I'm not,' he said, swallowing hard. 'But there is no other way, I know that.'

Lifting herself onto her tiptoes, she placed her hands either side of his face, and then, as he leaned forward, she kissed him on the crown of his head. It was but a moment, but it was all she needed.

'It's done,' she whispered, resting her forehead against his and wrapping her arms around him as if doing so might keep him safe.

The skitter of paws on tiles followed by a soft thump and a disgruntled whine heralded the arrival of Logan. Storm and Isaac managed to smile and roll their eyes. 'He'll figure out one day that stopping is easier if he doesn't take everything at a charge,' Storm said, glad of the distraction.

'Take your time, mate,' Isaac said kindly, jogging halfway up the stairs to pick up the puppy. Anchor, Hope and Ludo appeared silently a few steps behind Logan, who was now jumping up, excited that he'd heard Isaac's call and enjoying the head rub he was getting as his reward. Storm saw Anchor narrow his eyes at the puppy, before turning his attention to her. He flicked his fat ginger tail.

'Please do as I ask. There's no other way. Isaac will explain it all,' Storm said, bending down to stroke each of them in turn as she tried to swallow the lump in her throat. She couldn't give them reason to refuse. The animals were always the inno-cents. That she had believed that they were all finally free of human torment … She squeezed her eyes closed to banish the thought.

'I love you, my darlings,' she said, and then rose quickly. After kissing Isaac briefly on the lips, she mustered all of her strength to climb the stairs.

At the top, she looked back. Hope was still standing at the bottom of the steps. Her limp tail flicked into a little wag as they made eye contact. Storm felt her heart twist in her chest but managed the smallest of smiles as she raised her hand to wave. Hope's tail fell still, and after a few beats, Isaac reappeared to shepherd her back into the library and the secret tunnels that would take them to safety – at least for now.

CHAPTER 40

*S*torm found the others in the kitchen. Dot was cleaning the already spotless surfaces, and Henri was sat at the island, bent over a book. Asim was next to him, similarly hunched, but over a large screen. Only Veronica noticed her as she appeared from the back stairs. She bit her lip and hurried over to enfold Storm in a hug.

'I know, sweetie, I know,' she said as she rubbed her back.

Storm took a deep breath, drinking in the scent and strength of her friend and marvelling at how Veronica had always held a kind of magic of her own. It was as if the wisdom of the library were somehow inked into her cells. She was from a long line of women who had kept and defended the library for centuries, and Storm imagined that their strength had been gifted to Vee along with the books themselves. While she had no knowledge of Storm and Isaac's plan, partly for her own protection, she could read Storm as clearly as any of her charges on the shelves below them.

Storm centred herself and squared her shoulders. There were no words, so she just gave Veronica a final squeeze before joining the others at the kitchen island. Asim's and Henri's heads snapped up as she approached, and Dot stopped midway through scrubbing the sink. Before either of them could give voice to the obvious question, Storm asked, 'Where are we, Asim?'

Storm saw him swallow and rake his teeth over his top lip before he spoke, something she'd not seen him do in years. It was strange, she thought, those little tics and tells that had been lost since the shift. Another unwelcome reminder of the world as it was before, full of stress and enough worry to sink ships.

'So far as I can tell, everything is holding up. Remarkable, really, given how old it is. I'm talking to friends in Canada and Japan who helped build the system back in the day. They've added some patches for me and reinstated some of the fire-walls. I'm just waiting on confirmation from my contact in Turkey that she's been able to fix a bug I spotted earlier. It took a while to track her down as she's been on a boat in the Black Sea, apparently. Anyway. That's too much detail. She's on the case now,' Asim said, his eyes flicking back and forth between Storm and the screen in front of him.

Henri looked up, sensing that it was his turn. 'I thought maybe my old scribblings might yield something,' he said with a sigh as he leaned back in his chair. 'But no. Bugger all so far, I'm afraid,' he added gruffly, sounding like an old headmaster.

'He even tried having a nap,' Dot said, looking lovingly at her husband, 'in the hope that he could do his automatic-writing trick again and get some sort of message.'

Henri huffed. 'It wasn't a trick, my dear,' he said testily. 'Something or someone was trying to tell me something back then, and I just thought that maybe it might work again. Anything is worth a try, isn't it? I mean, it worked rather well the last time, if you'll recall.'

'Don't be so sensitive, Hen,' Dot said, wringing out the cloth she'd been using with unnecessary force. 'I was only filling Stormy in on what we've been trying and—'

Storm held up her hands. 'Please,' she said in a tone that stopped Dot in her tracks and caused Henri to bite back whatever he had been about to say. 'This is not us. We don't bicker like this. We need to keep our energies strong.' Even as she said the words, she felt like a liar, given the fragile state of her own energy levels.

'Got it,' Asim exclaimed. Veronica went to stand behind him and peered over his shoulder at the screen. 'Email just received from Elif, which hopefully means ...' He paused as he clicked on the message, glanced up and smiled, letting out a long breath. 'That she's fixed the—' He looked back to the screen, and Storm watched as the smile slipped from Asim's face. 'Oh,' was all he had time to say, because just then, the back of the house exploded.

CHAPTER 41

$\mathcal{J}$ saac had just reached the first blast door when he felt the impact. The tunnel lights flickered once before darkness surrounded them. The dogs whined and Isaac felt two soft, familiar paws against his thigh. He leaned down and scooped Anchor into his arms, and the cat wasted no time in settling himself around his neck.

'She's okay,' Isaac said, finding it hard to force out the words. He had wanted to say, 'She's still alive,' but the words wouldn't come. When the emergency lamps blinked into life, he saw Hope, Ludo and Logan standing shoulder to shoulder, heads and tails hung in despondent unison. Catching his eye, Hope looked pointedly behind her. Isaac shook his head. 'We can't go back,' he said. Hope growled and sent a stream of images flying into his mind. He held up his hands. 'Hope. Come on, you know this wasn't my choice, but as ever, Stormy's right – this is the only chance we have.' Anchor rubbed his head encouragingly against Isaac's chin and chirruped his support. Hope held Isaac's gaze for another second and then seemed to deflate.

'Come on, quickly. We don't have much time,' Isaac said, turning the wheel on the iron blast door before heaving it open. He held it ajar while the dogs hopped over the rim. Once safely on the other side, he locked it and muttered a spell to seal it, hoping that whatever sensitivity the Very had for detecting magic, it wouldn't extend to underground tunnels designed for concealment.

As Hope passed him, she licked his hand. A single word appeared clearly in his mind: *Sorry.*

'You don't need to be sorry, darling. She's our world, after all,' Isaac said, his voice so thick he feared it might choke him. 'Come on, the further we are from her at the moment, the safer she'll be.' He picked up the pace, one hand steadying Anchor, who was still wrapped tightly around his shoulders, the dogs at his heels.

The lights in the tunnel clicked on ahead of them as they ran. He almost missed the graffiti, illuminated as it was, just before they reached it. He didn't slow to read it. He didn't need to, as he had written it, almost a decade ago.

Storm had teased him when he'd shown her. 'Getting all posh now that we're Ethereal, are we?' she had said, laughing.

He had stepped back from the wall to admire his work, which he had magically carved into the stone in a looping script. 'How do you know I wasn't posh all along?' he asked, feigning offence, as he pulled her into his arms. 'I did Latin in school, you know. Granted, only for two terms before I dropped it like a hot brick, but I remember that much.'

Storm had reached out to trace the script with her fingers. 'Amor Omnia Vincit,' she said, before turning back to Isaac and fixing him with a wistful look. 'I always hoped, you know, that love really could conquer all, but I doubted it too. Sometimes I felt silly for even wanting to believe it. Like it was a fairy tale I should have grown out of. I'm glad we know for sure now that it does.'

'So, remind me again why we're magically creating a secret tunnel that we can't even tell our closest friends about?' Isaac had asked, already knowing the answer but still feeling far from convinced about Storm's plan.

He'd watched as her beautiful face had shadowed, a cloud over a bright, sunny day, even as she tried to maintain her smile. They had no secrets from each other, or so he had thought. They were, after all, two halves of the same whole, but he knew there were some truths that only she could carry.

'Because to be the First is also to be the Last. To sustain life, I had to bring death.' Her eyes had filled with tears, and Isaac had wiped them gently away, wishing that he could take her pain away at the same time. 'I want to believe that the sacrifices we made will protect us forever. Believe me, I want nothing more, but we have to have a back-up plan, just in case.'

Isaac had made to reply – they had had this debate so many times in the days since she had confided her plan that his argument was well practised – but instead he said, 'You are as wise as you are beautiful, my love, which means you're pretty much Einstein on his best day.'

She had laughed then, and the sadness had taken flight, like a huge black butterfly in her wake, no longer settled on her shoulder. 'Maybe we should invite him for tea now that the hereafter is an open door,' she said, laughing, and from there the conversation had drifted on to who else from history might make the guest list.

Isaac's thoughts returned reluctantly to the present as three identical doors were illuminated ahead of them. He slowed to walking. This too, of course, had been Storm's idea. Behind each door would be the choice of three more, then

another three, and on it would go until the probability of
anyone being able to guess where the other had emerged
would be close to impossible. He had gone along with it, of
course. As they were creating the tunnels, weaving their magic
together to hollow through not just rock and soil but time,
place and dimension, he had pictured them together, holding
hands as they fled, choosing doors at random to evade whatever horror pursued them. The realisation forced a sigh from
his lips, and he stopped, bending forward to brace his hand
against the middle door. The First could never leave. Would
never run. This plan had always been intended for him, and
him alone.

CHAPTER 42

'*J* don't think—' began Jack as they stepped out of the portal and into the country lane.

'If you're about to finish that sentence by saying we're not in Kansas anymore, mate, I might have to punch you,' Michael cut in, with a nervous-sounding laugh.

'Hey, I'm nothing if not comfortingly predictable,' Jack replied good-humouredly.

'Wow,' Michael exclaimed after turning around, 'the library is gone already.'

They all turned to look behind them but saw nothing but the single-track road, hedgerows and the lavender fields beyond. The smell was incredible, and Lilly wondered if it had the same soporific effect in spirit as it did on Earth. The last thing they needed to do was nod off. They had to find Margot as quickly as possible and then get home before anything bad happened.

They walked straight ahead in silence for a few moments. If she didn't think about it too closely, they could be on a day out back at home. The sun was warm on their backs. Bees buzzed contentedly in the fields, and the lavender-scented air smelled pure and clean. Then again, hadn't the Earth's ascension taken it closer to a kind of paradise state? How different could the spirit world be now that so many of the Earth's problems had been fixed?

'I have to say, it wasn't what I was expecting,' Michael said, breaking the silence. 'In life, Margot was a big TV star, as you know. She had the city penthouse and the weekend beach house in the Hamptons and all that, so I was expecting us to be in a version of New York, or some other big, swanky city, not rolling countryside.'

'Maybe this is what she always yearned for?' Jack suggested. 'Either that or we're about to round the next bend and find a humongous chateau with a few hundred staff waiting on her hand and foot.' They all laughed at that, but Lilly couldn't help feeling apprehensive about meeting Margot. She had, after all, been the one who had allowed the Very to believe that it was Lilly who was the First Ethereal. She had been there on the street the day that Lilly had been snatched, and in the ballroom on the day slated for her execution. Her reasons had become clear only after her death. For all of her power, fame and riches, she was enslaved to the Very because of her love for Storm. They had ruthlessly exploited Margot's weak spot, and to protect Storm, she had done some terrible things. Almost burning Lilly alive being one of them. Lilly pitied Margot and could well imagine her suffering. Exactly how she'd feel when face to face with her, though, was another matter.

They walked on, chatting about everything and nothing. Lilly kept her thoughts about Margot to herself. They didn't have time for analysis. When they rounded a bend and came to a crossroads, Jack cursed under his breath and said, 'Do you think it would have been too much to ask if we'd arrived in her living room, perhaps? What's with the journey of a thousand bloody steps?'

Lilly rolled her eyes. 'We've only been walking for about twenty minutes, Jack, and it's hardly like we're trekking through a rainforest or scaling a mountain. You should be grateful Margot's afterlife is so sedate.'

Jack pulled a face until she giggled. 'So which way, Sherlock?' he asked, casting around. Every direction looked to contain more of the same. Road. Hedge. Lavender fields. Lilly closed her eyes, bringing Margot's image to mind. As she did, she felt her energy pulling her backwards. 'But we've just come from there,' she said aloud, turning around.

Before she could respond to Jack and Michael's collective 'What?', they heard a distant car horn, swiftly followed by the unmistakable roar of a raspy old engine. They turned around in the middle of the crossroads, trying to see which direction the car was approaching from. Before it came into sight, they heard singing. '... It's a long way to go. It's a long way to Tipperary, to the sweetest girl I know ...' The voices sounded young, almost childlike. All became clear when the car, travelling from the direction they'd just come, screeched to a halt next to them. At the wheel of the old convertible was Margot. She didn't look much like the picture Storm had given them. Gone were her trademark glossy, bobbed ebony hair and red lips. Her hair was mid-brown, and despite being pinned in a loose bun at the nape of her neck, long strands had escaped and were flying around her make-up-free face. She wore a simple white cotton sundress, and perhaps most disconcerting of all, the car was full of children.

'Why darlings,' she purred when she saw Lilly, Jack and Michael. 'I suppose you've come to see me, have you?' She beamed at them and, without waiting for a reply, said, 'Of course you have. How completely delightful. Look, children, we've got friends come to stay.'

Lilly counted five children in the car. Two teenage girls, a little girl of around ten and two boys who looked to be around four and six. They all waved and said hello, but Lilly found that she couldn't speak. To her relief, Jack stepped in and started to introduce them all. 'I know who you are, darlings,' Margot said. 'Especially you, sweetheart,' she said to Lilly, her face flushing. 'I owe you both an apology and an explanation, but let's get home first.'

Lilly smiled, warming to Margot despite herself. There was something about her energy that just felt genuine.

'Bunch up, kids. Little ones on laps, please, so we can make room for our guests,' Margot said, turning in her seat to address the back.

A few minutes later they were all barrelling along the country roads, Lilly, Jack and Michael coaxed into song by the children, who had looked crestfallen when at first they didn't join in. 'Louder,' Margot shouted. 'You know how this works, darlings – the louder you sing, the faster the car will go.' The children giggled and cranked up the volume, adding in a complicated-looking set of arm actions to accompany the song. The little boy sitting on Lilly's lap guided her hands so that she could join in with the actions too.

Lilly exchanged a puzzled look with Jack and Michael as they roared along seemingly endless narrow roads, the sun on their backs, the summer breeze in their hair and all of them singing at the top of their lungs.

CHAPTER 43

*M*argot's home was nothing like the grand country pile Lilly had been imagining. After the lanes, they had turned down an unmade road that wound through a broadleaved wood and eventually emerged into a clearing. A small thatched, whitewashed cottage, half covered with wisteria, sat at the top of a winding pathway that was flanked by the most glorious garden Lilly had ever seen. Foxgloves, lupins and delphiniums swayed in the breeze. Lemon and pale pink roses in full and glorious bloom rambled over the old stone walls, tangling themselves with honeysuckle and jasmine. Lilly felt half drunk on the scent even before stepping out of the car. There were tulips, daffodils and dahlias, geraniums and sunflowers and dozens more Lilly couldn't even guess at. While she would never claim to be an expert, she had spent much of the last decade restoring the wild spaces and gardens around Pont Nefoedd and had learned to identify most plants, but the sheer variety here was almost overwhelming.

The children had already gone into the house. The two

little boys had towed Michael by the hand, chatting excitedly about how much he was going to like the toy they had been building. Lilly had been following but found herself almost rooted to the spot by the glory of the garden. Butterflies, bees and dragonflies fluttered and danced in the air around them. She spotted a hare and two leverets sunning themselves on a patch of clover. Above them, in a large pale pink wicker chair, a slinky coal-black cat slept. She half expected Snow White to step out of the front door surrounded by bluebirds.

'Pretty, isn't it?' Jack said, draping his arm lightly around her shoulders. The master of understatement, Lilly thought. She suddenly didn't trust herself to speak, so just nodded.

'Looks a bit like back home,' Jack said quietly. 'You know, before.' And Lilly heard the slight catch in his voice. They rarely spoke about their lives before this one or their time in the Eternal Forest, which was not too dissimilar to the one they'd just driven through. Their home had been a treehouse, but Lilly could imagine herself living here. Her last life had changed her, as had all her lives, but now, looking at the cottage, she decided that if they ever returned to spirit for good, then she'd like to live somewhere just like this.

'Fancy this as a forever home someday?' Jack said, moving to stand behind her. He wrapped both arms around her shoulders.

'You read my mind,' she said, leaning back against him. 'It's not a million miles different to our place in Pont Nefoedd, but everything here is in full bloom. It took me a minute to realise what it was. I'd forgotten that here things can be exactly as you imagine them.'

'Well, it looks like Margot likes the summertime.'

'Indeed I do,' said Margot from behind them. 'The weather on the east coast of the States was horribly unpredictable towards the end. Snowstorms and freezing rain for so much of the year, which I suppose is why I now so enjoy my eternal summer.' Her voice had a smile in it, but Lilly could sense a note of something else too. Nerves, perhaps.

'You have a beautiful home,' Jack said courteously.

'And a magical garden,' Lilly added, forcing herself to speak to burst whatever bubble it was that sat between them.

Margot looked genuinely thrilled at the compliments and smiled broadly. 'It's very much my little piece of heaven,' she said. 'Come on in and I'll make us some tea.'

They followed her into the cottage, Jack ducking his head to clear the low door. To Lilly's initial surprise, they stood in a spacious but modestly decorated hallway with high ceilings and a sweeping wooden staircase. Margot had disappeared from view, so they followed the sound of voices through the open door to the left and found her, Michael and the children in a large open-plan kitchen/living area that looked like it had stepped fully formed from the pages of a seriously posh home decor magazine. Dark navy cabinets topped with white marble lined the longest wall and a huge central island completed the look. The room was flooded with light, too much light to be emanating from the wall of glass doors at the end of the room, Lilly thought. She looked up to see a huge lantern skylight above the island unit. She glanced back to the hallway, mentally pictured the front of the house and its two floors, then frowned.

Margot caught her eye and gave a little shrug. 'You have to love the afterlife for the flexibility it gives on the decorating front,' she said with a smile. 'Paint can work wonders, but bending the laws of physics, well, that comes in very handy indeed.'

'Neat,' Jack said, then wandered off to join Michael and the children.

Margot seemed to be at a loss for what to do or say next.

Without Jack, the tension was back, sitting between them like a thunder cloud on a summer's day. Margot picked up some mugs and put them on a tray, then seemed to forget what came next.

Lilly was about to speak – not that she had a clue what to say; she just couldn't bear the tension or the other woman's disquiet – but Margot beat her to it. 'I'll ask Mireille and Odette if they wouldn't mind getting tea started while we three have a chat. We can walk in the garden,' she added.

Lilly was dreading this conversation even more than the one they needed to have after it. That Margot needed to get what she assumed would be an apology off her chest first was screamingly obvious, though. Gesturing for Jack and Michael to join them as they passed, they walked out onto the terrace and picked up the path through the garden to walk along the wide tree-lined riverbank beyond.

Lilly thought back to the day that she had been taken. The village fete. The afternoon watching films with Michael, and then their walk along the river as the perfect day slipped into the perfect summer evening. That's what she had been thinking as they ambled back up the hill – how everything had been absolutely perfect. But then the nightmare had started.

'Sorry doesn't seem enough,' Margot said, pulling Lilly out of her memories.

She instinctively opened her mouth to reply, but Jack put a hand on her arm to stop her.

Margot was walking slightly ahead of them, her eyes on the lazy river, which looked like it had nowhere to go and all day to get there. She stopped and smiled as a mother duck swam past followed by a line of seven fluffy ducklings. Then she turned to face Lilly. 'Sorry isn't enough, I know that, but it's all I have,' she said, her eyes bright with tears. 'There were reasons, of course. I wanted to keep Storm safe. They murdered Nick, you know, when I tried to leave. He was the most adorable man you'd ever want to meet. But they murdered him to teach me a lesson. Me. I as good as killed him.' Margot screwed her eyes closed. When she opened them again her gaze strayed to the water, but Lilly imagined that she was seeing a different scene altogether.

Margot cleared her throat and began to walk again, picking up her story. 'I had my suspicions about Storm. She was always a talented medium – that was clear from the first time I laid eyes on her – and once she had some guidance, she proved to be an incredibly powerful witch, but there was always something I couldn't put my finger on. Something that seemed to hide itself, even from me – and, I sensed, from her too.' Margot lapsed into silence again, and nobody rushed to fill it.

'Storm was going off to uni, and I'd be a bad liar if I said I wasn't beginning to worry about my empty nest. I know she wasn't mine, but she might as well have been. It felt like mere moments between her opening the door to me that afternoon, this leggy, frightened little fawn so desperately needing someone to love her, and then all at once she was a woman, itching to get out into the world. To be her own person. Not a mini version of me. I told myself it would be best to give her some space. Let her spread her wings.' Margot laughed. 'Well, I didn't know then that it would one day be literal.'

They walked on in silence for a few more moments, until Margot picked up the story again. 'I went to the States, and my career took off so quickly I barely had time to process it all. That was when they first stepped out of the shadows. The first time I realised that perhaps hard work and talent had bugger all to do with my rise to fame and fortune.'

Margot stopped and sucked in a deep breath before turning to look at them. 'Ironically, it was the High Council that alerted me to the story about the Ethereal. It was one of the first meetings I'd been encouraged to attend. The snivelling Martin Flynn-Rivers was giving a tedious presentation on the mitigation of magical risks. I was almost asleep it was so dull, but then he mentioned the prophecy about the Ethereal and my blood ran cold.' She snorted a half-laugh. 'I had to scramble to get a glamour in place before anyone noticed that I'd gone as white as a sheet. But I felt it. Do you follow? Something resonated within me as soon as I heard the name – as if it had been waiting for me to remember.'

'When did you know for sure?' Lilly asked, falling back into step beside Margot.

Margot wrapped her long tanned arms around herself before answering, as if protecting herself from a chill breeze nobody else could feel. 'It was just after Nick became ill. They told me what they'd done, of course. Crowed about it. Made damn sure that I knew it was my punishment for wanting to leave. I was out of my mind. I tried reason first, but even if they'd been minded to forgive me, the bloody fools had created an untraceable poison with no known cure or antidote. I used the sight to check, of course, but they were telling the truth. Magic wouldn't work on issues of life and death, not back then in the old world, at least. They never quite understood the full extent of my sight. I never told them about the reach I had in time and space, and because none of their other seers had my ability, I was able to hide it. That's how I found out that they were planning on taking Storm anyway – hence, I had to do something to protect her.'

'Hence the binding and severing,' Lilly offered, working hard to keep her tone neutral.

Margot froze as if the words themselves had immobilised her. After a few beats she said, 'Yes. But it was an almost impossible spell, even for me. And I don't mean to sound immodest about it, but I poured everything I had into developing my powers while keeping the true extent of them a secret from the High Council. I had hoped it would be a way out for us. After Martin's presentation I had started trawling through the recorded energy spikes in the area, then using the sight to go back and view what might have caused them. It took me months, but then one day, I found I was looking at a young Henri. He was a handsome young chap, you know – very dashing. Anyway, he was sound asleep with his head on his desk. There was a pencil still in his hand and an exquisite sketch of Storm in his journal above the title—'

'*The First Ethereal,*' Lilly said quietly, wondering if Storm herself had put all of these pieces of the puzzle together. 'We assumed it had been you who swapped the journals, but nobody knew for sure.'

'By that point I had no choice – or so I thought. I should have trusted in her strength, in her goodness, but I suppose I still thought of her as the little lost lamb who needed me. Either way,' Margot said, turning to Lilly and looking directly into her eyes, 'I had no right to endanger you, darling girl. For that I am deeply ashamed and sorry beyond measure.' She looked down, strands of her long waves escaping to swirl around her face as she shook her head. When she glanced up, she addressed Jack and Michael. 'And I owe you both apologies too. For the part that I played in taking and endangering the woman you love, and all that that entailed. I am so very, very sorry.'

Margot pressed her hands over her face and turned away.

Lilly looked at the woman in front of her and focused hard on how she felt. She would not lie, even to soothe or comfort, because to do so would not come from love. She was quiet for a long minute, but then came to a decision. Stepping closer to Margot, she reached forward and took the other woman's hands in hers. Margot's head snapped up in surprise, already shaking in confusion, the seed of a question on her lips. Lilly opened her mouth to speak, but what came out was 'Oh, come here' as she pulled Margot into a hug. She felt the other woman's body shake as she cried, and they stood like that for what might have been minutes or hours; Lilly couldn't tell. When the worst of the shaking had subsided, Jack joined in too.

When they eventually stepped apart, Michael said, 'I seem to remember someone promising us tea. Can we assume it comes with cake?' Lilly beamed at him, grateful for his attempt to lighten the mood.

'I did indeed, didn't I?' Margot said, giving Lilly's hand a final squeeze before releasing it. 'The children will have baked enough for the five thousand by the time we get back.'

When the other three looked confused, she clarified, 'I've been teaching them to how to bake magically – it's so easy here, after all, so I often get up to find that the house resembles a patisserie. Not that I'm in any way complaining, of course,' she added quickly.

'Are all of the children yours?' Lilly asked as they strolled back towards the house.

'Depends how you define "yours", I suppose. Are children ever ours?' she said, sounding as if the question was one that she was genuinely curious about. She looked a lot more relaxed, Lilly noticed, than when they'd first arrived, and there was a real light in her eyes at the mention of the children.

'I'm being facetious, of course, darling. Ignore me. Odette and Mireille were born to me in previous lives, so I suppose you could say they were at one time mine. The other three just sort of gravitated here. Dax is enjoying being a toddler, so I suppose he will stay for as long as he finds it necessary. Jeremiah shows up and stays for a while, then disappears again, and Aaliyah is like the wind, one moment here, the next off on another adventure. I certainly enjoy having them around. There have been others, of course. They come and go as they please.'

When they reached the garden gate, Jack held it open for them. He raised his eyebrows to Lilly, and she nodded. She was grateful, though, when Michael asked the question.

'Margot,' he said, chewing at his bottom lip, 'we need to talk to you about the real reason we're here. We have to ask you about the amulets.'

Margot turned, looking confused. 'Sorry, sweetie, you've completely lost me.'

Michael's eyes darted between Lilly and Jack before returning to Margot. He chewed his lip, then said hesitantly, 'Er, the protective amulets that the Very are now using to survive the shift?'

'What?' Margot all but screamed the word, her face ashen.

Lilly leapt forward and caught her elbow, just as Jack had the same idea. Margot remained on her feet but looked visibly shaken. They steered her to a nearby bench so that she could sit down.

'They're back?' she asked, her voice plaintive and her face a study in anguish. 'That's not possible. It can't be. No! It can't be!'

Lilly knelt down and took Margot's hands in hers. 'I'm sorry we're the bearers of bad news, I really am. But it is true.'

Margot held her head in her hands. When at last she spoke, she said, 'They asked for protection, of course they did. I gave them protective rings, but they were fakes. In fact, anyone wearing one post-shift would have been ushered into the lower realms at top speed.' She shook her head vigorously. 'You know, one of my last thoughts, just as I died, was, "Well at least I did something right in making sure that these bastards are never coming back.'" She let out an anguished sob. Lilly rubbed her back, trying to find something that might help, but resorted to 'Just let it all out' and 'It'll be okay, you'll see'.

When Margot appeared to be over the worst of the shock, Jack said carefully, 'It sounds as if they either knew about the deception or decided on an insurance policy. Storm said that that kind of magic wouldn't have been easy to come by. Do you know who else might have been powerful enough to have done something like that?'

Margot was already shaking her head. 'Magic like that? No, it's rarer than hen's teeth, and I was the only witch of calibre they had managed to trap, bloody idiot that I was.' She stared at the ground, frowning, lost for a long moment in her thoughts. 'Oh no,' she gasped, clasping her hands to her lips. 'Oh goddess, please no.'

'What?' Lilly asked, her sense of panic rising. Margot seemed to be ageing in front of her eyes.

'Doreen.'

'Storm talks about her. She was one of her magic teachers, wasn't she? Back when she was in school. Didn't she pass away just before the shift?' Lilly asked, trying to keep her voice calm and level, a defence against her escalating heartbeat. Something told her that whatever was coming next, it wouldn't be good news.

Margot nodded. 'There was nobody else powerful enough. Wait,' she said. Then she became very still, her eyes fixed and unblinking on a point in the distance. Lilly cast an anxious look at Jack.

'Trance,' he mouthed.

After a few moments, Margot gasped, making them all jump, but then she was sobbing uncontrollably again. 'Oh, my darling friend. How could they? How could they?' she screamed.

Thunderous black clouds appeared in a sky that only seconds ago had been the palest of watercolour blues. A bitter wind raced across the lawn to whip around them, lashing Lilly's long hair around her face and buffeting the already fragile-looking Margot. A streak of black caught Lilly's eye. The cat from the front garden sprinted across the lawn towards the house as if all the devils of hell were upon her. A boom of thunder sounded overhead, just as the first icy rain-drops landed.

'What the hell?' Jack asked, casting around to take in the ominously sudden change in the weather.

'Let's get her indoors quickly,' Michael said, raising his voice above the howl of the wind. Then he scooped Margot up as if she weighed nothing, and they all hurried for the house.

CHAPTER 44

'*M*argot!' Mireille and Odette cried in unison as Michael burst into the kitchen. The rain had chased them the last hundred yards and they were already soaked to the skin. The girls rushed over as Michael lowered Margot gently onto the sofa furthest from the open bifold doors. Half of the living end of the room was already dotted with puddles, and a dark wet stain was creeping across the antique rug by the coffee table.

Lilly and Jack pulled closed the huge glass doors just as a fork of lightning lit up the steel-grey sky. It was swiftly followed by a clap of thunder loud enough to wake the dead. Lilly cast a confused look at Jack but saw only the same confusion reflected in his own eyes. She let out a shriek as the rain turned to hail and machine-gunned itself at the doors. It was only then that the penny dropped.

'What did you do to her?' Odette asked accusingly, her eyes flicking between Jack and Lilly. Michael, it seemed, was off the hook as he'd carried Margot in.

Lilly ignored the question, reasoning that time was likely of the essence. 'The weather is linked to Margot, isn't it?'

Odette rolled her eyes and muttered something in French that Lilly didn't completely catch. 'Of course it is. You are not babies, you should know these things,' she said irritably. 'This is Margot's world we're visiting, and—'

Lilly cut her off. 'And if we don't calm her down soon—'

'It'll fall apart,' Mireille said flatly as she crossed to the kitchen. 'We need to find Lilith.'

'Odette, I swear we didn't mean to upset Margot. We assumed that she had been forced to help the Very return to Earth and …'

'Oh my,' Odette said, looking visibly pale. 'I see.'

'I found her searching the third floor,' Mireille said from the kitchen door. Lilly dimly registered the inconsistency in the building's layout before a black flash dived from the girl's arms and all but flew to where Margot sat quietly sobbing into Michael's shoulder.

'I'll go check on the others, Maman. Lilith is here now,' Odette said, a noticeable tremor in her voice. She leaned down to plant a kiss on Margot's forehead before hurrying out of the room.

The cat wound herself around Margot as if she were fashioned from smoke. She bumped her head into Margot's chin, and Lilly had a sudden urge to hold Anchor and have him head-bop her in the same way.

To Lilly's surprise, Margot straightened up so that she could wrap her arms around the worried feline. She shushed her gently, even though Lilly couldn't hear Lilith make a sound. 'I'm okay, darling girl. It was just the shock, you see. I thought these lovely friends were here answering my wish to make my apologies, but they brought other news too.' Fresh tears streamed from Margot's eyes, but she continued speaking to the cat as if there was no one else in the room. 'News of the very worst kind. Yes. They're back, my darling, and worse, they must have damned our dear Doreen in the process.'

'When you say damned ...?' Michael asked carefully, turning on the sofa so that he could face Margot.

Margot sat forward, focusing all of her attention on the cat, who was now perched four-square on her lap having her ears rubbed. Michael looked from Jack to Lilly, then to Mireille, who was perched on the arm of the sofa nearest to Margot. Michael shrugged, and after a moment, Mireille said to Margot, 'Do you want me to explain it to them? I think I know the gist of what this must mean.'

Margot smiled sadly up at her, then patted Mireille's hand. 'You always were such an angel,' she said, 'but I think I should probably do it. I can try and make sense of what might have happened as I do. Maybe you could fill the others in on the situation? Reassure them?' When Mireille showed no sign of rising from her place on the arm, Margot said, 'I'll be fine, darling. Really, I will.'

Mireille pressed her lips into a smile and got up slowly. Like Odette had done a few moments before, she bent to kiss Margot before she left the room. Lilly was glad that Margot was obviously so loved.

Lilly joined Jack on the sofa opposite Margot and Michael. The air felt charged. The silence was almost total now that the hail had stopped pounding against the glass doors. The skies outside, Lilly noticed, were still leaden, but she hoped that perhaps the worst of the storm might have passed. The beautiful garden, though, looked to have been savaged. Margot's voice startled her back to attention.

'As you can see,' she began, gesturing with her hand to the garden, 'this has been something of a shock for me. We used to say that things "rocked your world" – well, unless you've not worked it out yet, it's quite literal here. Anyway, I'll do my best to explain it as I go, but just to be clear, what I'm about to say is my best guess – it's not strictly fact.'

'Got it,' Jack said.

Margot took a deep breath and Lilith took that as a cue to curl up on her lap, her tail arranged carefully across her eyes, reminding Lilly of the vixen at Ascension Day. Margot resumed stroking the cat and continued, 'As I said, there is – was – only one witch alive powerful enough to have given the High Council the means to survive the shift. Doreen was a dear friend of mine. She tutored me in magic when I was a young girl, and then, years later, I took Stormy to her too. She was an incredible woman. Not just magically either. PhD in something mind-boggling like chemistry, I think, a whole host of degrees in other things that took her fancy, art history, languages, you name it – she did degrees like other people took evening classes in knitting.' Margot smiled at the memory, and Lilly noticed a pale shaft of light break through the clouds outside.

'She had a son, too, and a no-good husband who left her when the child was still very young, seven or eight maybe, but she never complained. She just worked and studied and raised her boy and taught mind-blowing magic to little lost witches in the evenings. She was never interested in organised witch-craft, preferring to do her own thing and let those who needed her find her. I'm telling you all this because you need to know the woman as well as the witch. She was a woman of principle and, I'm ashamed to say, that's why we drifted apart. She didn't approve of my mediumship career. She felt very strongly about such a sacred practice being turned into enter-tainment, and she counselled me against taking that path. But I was young and ambitious and I wanted to be loved and adored. I probably said some unkind things to her while trying to defend my decision. She was right, of course, but not wanting to hear that, I simply cut her out of my life. Just before the shift, Storm told me that she'd passed. I wasn't surprised – she must have been in her eighties by then – but …' Margot faltered and cleared her throat.

'I'll get you some water,' Michael said, getting up.

'Thank you,' she replied, but pressed on, raising her voice a little so that Michael could still hear. 'Just before the shift, they, the High Council, started murdering magical people.'

Lilly gasped, and was grateful when Jack reached for her hand.

'I'm sorry, darling, but that's the truth of it. I played no part in it – in fact, I didn't know for many months, but when I did find out, I didn't stop it either, which makes me just as guilty. To have tried would have sealed Storm's fate, but you know that part of the story already. Until today, I assumed that Doreen's death had been the accident it was claimed to be. If I'd given it proper consideration, I might have put two and two together, but sometimes we only believe what we want to believe. There's great comfort in lies, especially when the truth is too hard to bear,' she said, reaching up to take the glass of water from Michael.

'The thing is,' she continued after taking a few sips, 'Doreen is the only witch capable of a spell that powerful, but she would never have done it willingly.' Margot shook her head vehemently, and Lilly saw fresh tears pool in her eyes. In the distance, a low rumble of thunder accompanied a fresh volley of rain against the glass.

Margot shot a disapproving glance at the garden and seemed to take a long minute to collect herself. When the rain stopped, Margot continued, her voice stronger. 'They tortured Doreen,' she said matter-of-factly. 'The vision in the garden was crystal clear. Some things hide in time and space, even from seers of my experience, but it was like this memory was just there, waiting for me to go and look for it.' Margot took a deep, shuddering breath.

'Memory? Wait, you mean you were there?' Jack asked. If he had been trying to keep the judgement out of his tone, he'd well and truly failed, Lilly thought.

'Good goddess, no!' Margot snapped, just as a flash of lightning lit up the room. 'I did some terrible, wicked things in my last life, Jack, but even I wasn't capable of what they did to her. The universe has a memory just as we do. As a seer, it's the memory of the universe that I connect with.'

Jack held up his hands in apology, and after a few long, painful moments, Margot continued, 'I'll spare you the details – believe me, you wouldn't want those pictures in your mind. There are ways of taking magic by force – none of them good. The bottom line is that they kidnapped, tortured and then murdered Doreen after they'd taken what they wanted. They even tortured and killed her little dog.'

Lilly wiped her eyes on her sleeve. To imagine how anyone could be capable of doing such a horrific thing to anyone was unthinkable, but to a lady in her eighties? It was obscene.

They were all silent for a few moments. It was Michael who spoke first, addressing Margot. 'So it looks like we need to be in Doreen's afterlife and not yours,' he said. 'Can we do that from here or do we need to go back to the library first?'

Margot frowned and looked at each of them in turn. Then she tipped back her head and closed her eyes. When she straightened up, she said, 'It's my fault. I didn't explain this all very well. I'm sorry, darlings. The thing is, Doreen isn't here. In the afterlife, I mean. If she were, then, well, it would be easy, wouldn't it.'

'I don't understand,' Lilly said. 'Where else could she

possibly be?' But she knew the answer the moment the words had left her lips. 'Oh.'

Margot wiped away fresh tears with the heel of her hand as she nodded morosely. 'She's in the lower realm. The brightest, kindest witch who ever lived has been damned to hell.'

CHAPTER 45

$\mathcal{F}$or a split second, Storm was back in London, lying under the rubble waiting to die and hoping that she had been wrong about the afterlife. Oblivion would suit her fine. She didn't want an eternity to contemplate her murderous actions. How could she exist anywhere knowing she had used her magic to kill people? Margot's voice had sounded in her head, loud and defiant. 'That's the wrong question, darling girl. What you need to be asking yourself is how many did you save?'

Storm snapped painfully back to the present as the pointed toe of a shoe slammed into her ribs. She let out an involuntary scream as the air flew from her lungs. She lurched forward and braced herself on her hands, trying to take a breath.

'Aww, sorry, did that hurt, bunny?' came a sing-song voice from somewhere behind her. Before Storm could turn, she felt someone grab her hair, whiplashing her backwards. She scrabbled to find purchase on the tiled kitchen floor, covered now with the dust and debris of what had just seconds ago been the back wall of Veronica and Asim's beautiful home. She winced as her palm found not cool marble but broken glass. The blood pooled at once under her sliced hand and she slipped back, landing heavily on her elbow.

The face that leered into her line of sight was a surprise. For a moment, Storm thought it was a mask. The skin was unnaturally taut and had the sheen of a freshly painted door. The eyes, small, pale blue and unblinking, were decorated with unnaturally long lashes and heavy make-up. The face tilted to the side and fat pink lips moved upward to reveal perfectly even white teeth. Her breath when she spoke, however, reminded Storm of old drains and dog sick, but as someone still held her hair, she wasn't able to avoid it. She tried a quick shielding spell, but nothing materialised.

'Got you now, witch bitch,' the woman crowed, and Storm felt her spittle land on her cheek. She tried the spell again, her sense of panic growing. She had lived so long severed from her magic and she had sworn on everything sacred that it would never, ever happen again, but why then wasn't it working? Her energy was depleted, yes, but not to this degree. She took a deep breath to calm herself and felt her ribs protest.

The woman with the big eyelashes straightened up. She smoothed down her pale pink skirt suit before adjusting the Alice band that held back her long ash-blonde hair. Storm pictured her with the curling iron, twisting her hair like a good little Insta clone and then spraying it into submission before posting a dozen pouting selfies. If she hadn't been so terrified, she might have laughed that their world could be toppled by this throwback to vanity writ large.

'Up!' commanded a man's voice at the same time she was yanked by her hair. Storm tried to stand, but obviously wasn't quick enough because rough, impatient hands grabbed her beneath her armpits and hauled her to her feet. It was only then that she felt the white-hot pain in her leg. Storm had never broken a bone in her life, but she was pretty sure she had now. She called to mind a healing spell, something that just twenty-four hours ago would have been the work of seconds, but nothing happened. In her mind, Storm raced around a great mansion, flinging open doors, calling frantically, only to find nothing but her own voice echoing back at her. Her magic was nowhere to be found.

'Her leg's busted,' the man said irritably, tightening his grip on her upper arms and giving her a shake. Storm bit her lip against the pain, which now seemed to be coming not just from her broken leg but from everywhere. She tasted hot bile in her throat and willed herself not to be sick. Her hand was still bleeding, and she watched as small globules of scarlet dripped steadily onto the tiled floor, mixing with the dust into dirty black puddles. Tearing her eyes away, she scanned the room, looking for the others, but they were nowhere to be seen. She thought of Isaac and the animals and squeezed her eyes closed. She would not succumb to tears.

Getting no reply from the pink-suited woman, who was busy giving instructions to another man dressed in black combat fatigues, the man holding Storm said tersely, 'Imelda. I said, her leg is busted.'

Imelda's head snapped up like a cobra spotting its prey. 'What did you call me?' she said, every word punctuated with venom.

Storm felt the hands on her arms stiffen. 'Sorry, ma'am. I mean, Mrs Benedict-Hatman.'

So that was it, Storm thought. The madman's widow back to seek her revenge. She thought back to that day in London. She hadn't been able to put a name to him until afterwards, of course. She had spent hours poring through Veronica's files on the Very to understand more about the men and women she had killed. The Very's leader, advertising man Charles

Benedict-Hatman, had led the proceedings that were to end
with Lilly's ritual execution by burning. They had all gathered
in the basement ballroom of the Holland Park mansion,
dressed in their finest clothes, champagne flutes in hand,
waiting to bear witness to a murder that would, in their sick
and twisted minds, secure their right of dominion over the
Earth. If those assembled were the foot soldiers, then Charles
was the general pulling their strings. Storm had caught him
trying to escape while ordering his guards to kill her. A
coward and a murderer. She had suspended him high above
the ballroom, and then, with a thought, she had bolted all the
doors. Next, she let loose her magic and brought the house
down upon them all.

Imelda ran her tongue around the inside of her cheek and
twisted her mouth as she glared at the man behind Storm.
With a sigh she said sharply, 'Better. Ma'am will do fine. You'll
have to carry her. We're going to set up here.'

'But shouldn't we take her back to the bunker? I mean—'
he began, but Imelda cut him off.

'But nothing. You're not paid to think, Tate. Let's just enjoy
the sun on our faces again, shall we? Once we get this little
business' – she flicked a dismissive finger at Storm – 'out of
the way, we can get busy looking for more suitable accom-
modation.'

'If you kill me, everything will end,' Storm said, her voice
coming out as a raspy whisper as fear and dust conspired to
close her throat. 'The world isn't how you left it.'

'Oh, please. Spare me the chosen one bollocks, sweetie.
You lot perpetuated the myth in order to take what didn't
belong to you. The shift was a natural phenomenon, you just
manipulated the situation, pretending that you were this
Ethereal and that your choice was what saved the world.'
Imelda mimed sticking her fingers down her throat and made

a gagging noise. 'All utter crap. Just lies so that you could set yourself up as queen of the world.'

'No!' Fuelled by indignation, Storm's voice was stronger now. 'It's nothing like that. We're on a completely different vibration now, but just by being here you're lowering it to the—'

'Gag her.' Imelda sighed dismissively, then turned and picked her way through the debris and out of sight.

Storm turned her attention to Tate. She tried twisting on her good leg to face him, but he tightened his grip. 'You have to listen to me,' she said urgently over her shoulder as she heard the sound of tape being torn from a reel somewhere behind her. 'There is nobody in charge here – it's all about energy and we all live in peace. The world is perfect again, no pollution, the climate is stable, everyone is free and well fed, but unless you ascend too, unless you join us, then we'll bring the whole world and the afterlife down to the frequency of the lower realm, and that's—'

At that moment, a tall slim woman in black fatigues who might have been a sports model in another life stepped into Storm's line of sight, a length of silver tape between her hands. The thought of being gagged was terrifying enough, but something even more chilling struck Storm as she met the other woman's eyes – she looked amused.

CHAPTER 46

*L*illy felt like a fish as her brain and her mouth refused to coordinate a response to Margot's revelation about Doreen. Beside her, Jack stared at some point on the rug in front of him. Michael sat next to Margot, his elbows on his knees and his hands clasped behind his bowed head. Margot stroked Lilith while staring out onto the garden as soft, fat raindrops fell methodically onto the already sodden ground.

The thought of this elderly woman trapped in the lower realms for the past decade was hideous, but even more vile was the idea of the Very torturing her, and her little dog, for her magic. Lilly pushed herself to standing, suddenly needing to do something, even if that something was only moving.

'What I don't understand, Margot, is why such a strong and principled witch would have ended up … there,' Jack said, hesitating slightly over the last word.

'Oh, she fought them with everything she had,' Margot said, a sad smile playing at the edges of her lips. 'Octogenarian or not, Doreen was a force to be reckoned with.' She paused as

Lilith stood up, tail swishing. 'That's why they used the ripping spell.' Her voice was barely more than a whisper.

Lilly was about to ask what that meant, but Margot held up her hand and took a few deep breaths. Lilly dreaded what might come next. Lilith seemed to be on high alert, and you didn't need to be any kind of empath to read the tension in Margot's expression.

Lilith tapped at Margot's jaw with a soft paw and was scooped into the woman's arms, where she proceeded to purr loudly. Lilly was once again reminded of Anchor and his uncanny ability, even before the shift, to know when she needed comfort or strength.

When Margot spoke, her voice was high and tight, her words clipped. 'The ripping spell was outlawed in magical communities a thousand years before the shift. The ancients were fond of it, but then again, they were partial to sacrificing babies at the time too. The thing is, it was considered too barbaric for modern times. I doubt even the magical libraries had record of it, so where they found it is anyone's guess.' She shrugged.

There was a long pause before she picked up the story. 'The spell does what it says on the tin. It rips the magic out of a witch by magical force. The ancients also called it the flaying spell, because it's the magical equivalent of skinning someone alive and just as unthinkably agonising.'

Lilly didn't want to hear the details – she could already taste bile in her mouth – but there was no time. Margot pressed on, still gazing out of the window as she cradled the purring cat.

'They need the witch alive while the magic is removed. Once separated, another witch can use that power to whatever end they desire. In this case, the amulets. Whether it was intention or incompetence is hard to say – I couldn't bear to linger in the vision – but it took them many, many hours. By which time ...'

She didn't finish the sentence, but she didn't need to. Lilly couldn't imagine what that sort of agony would do to a soul. She thought of the factory-farmed animals and the stories from the shepherds about their madness at the end making them turn away from the light.

'Who was the other witch?' Jack asked, ever practical, Lilly thought.

Margot snorted. 'Wang. Another of the High Council seers. He wasn't a witch by blood, at least I didn't think so, but it would be just like him to think himself capable of anything. Even so, it must have taken him years to learn how to control a spell that powerful. That's probably why it took so long, come to think of it.' She fell silent, then after a few moments said, 'Serves him right.'

'What do you mean?' Michael asked, visibly confused.

Margot turned to look at them for the first time since starting her story. 'They killed him too,' she said flatly. 'Once they had the amulets and Doreen was gone, he was next. Probably too much of a risk to have a bona fide psychopath in your bunker. That said, they spared Tanya, and she was just as sick as Wang. Then again, she was better looking, and Charles always liked a pretty face.'

Lilly felt increasingly queasy at all the talk of killing and flaying and torture. It was hard to believe that just a few hours ago they'd come here expecting to simply find Margot and ... what? What had they expected? Margot to scribble down a counter-spell on the back of a cereal box like she was sharing her grandma's muffin recipe? That they'd all just head back to the library together so that she could battle the Very and send them all packing? She suddenly felt hopelessly naive, but worse, she felt horribly out of her depth. How on earth were they going to break the amulets now? Storm, Isaac, Henri, everyone was depending on them. Hell, the whole world was depending on them. Was this how Storm felt? She often caught sight of a strange look on her friend's face. A weariness, red-tipped with sadness that felt leagues deep. It was always quickly shuttered behind her warm smile, her easy laugh and her desire to help everyone. Maybe this was what it was like to have the weight of the world on your shoulders.

Just when Lilly thought things couldn't get any worse, Jack stood up. 'Well, it looks like we're off to the lower realms to save Doreen. Margot, you're going to need to teach us everything we might need to know – and fast.'

*B*y the time Lilly's brain had processed the words, the other three were on their feet and congregating around the island unit. Margot still had Lilith in her arms, but the cat hopped onto the worktop as soon as they were close enough, leaving Margot free to pull mugs and plates from a cupboard.

'You'll need to eat well before you go,' she said, moving with surprising speed around the vast kitchen as she took bowls and platters of food from the fridge that would have had to have been a Tardis to have accommodated it all. Michael fell into step with her and soon the island looked like the set of a wedding banquet. 'You're here corporeally so you'll need to fill up. The lower realm will sap your energy quickly, and it'll be all the worse on an empty stomach.'

Lilly's stomach gave a loud rumble, and she realised that she was actually ravenous. It felt like a comfort to know that even in the midst of all this horror, her body was still her own and still intent on survival. She pitched in, handing out cutlery and pulling yet more dishes from the bottomless pit of a fridge, while Margot went to update the children.

An hour later, their stomachs full and ration packs filled up with leftovers, they turned their attention to the small matter of their trip to the lower realm. Margot briefed them, telling them pretty much what Isaac and Henri had already shared. In short, they didn't have long; the energies would start to bring them down vibrationally the moment they arrived, and there was a very real danger that they'd soon give up trying to leave, such would be the lure of the low energy.

'The thing I don't understand, though,' Jack said, picking up another pastry and pointing it to punctuate his question, 'is how we're even going to find Doreen. I mean, none of us even met her when she was alive.'

'Don't worry about that,' Margot replied. 'Hold out your hands.'

The three shared a questioning look, but obliged. As they did, a photograph of an elderly woman appeared in each of their palms.

'Now look closely,' Margot said.

'Wow! Is that a hologram?' Jack asked in amazement, peering at the foot-tall figure that had materialised on the counter.

Lilly thought Margot looked quite pleased with herself, or maybe it was nostalgia in seeing her old friend, for there in front of them, looking to all the world like a human in miniature, was the woman in the photograph. Her grey hair was cropped short and neatly styled around a surprisingly unlined face. She wore smart fawn trousers and a cream short-sleeved jumper. There was a string of pearls around her neck and two dainty pearl studs in her ears. In her right hand was a cane, which she leaned on lightly as she walked across the counter-top. The mini Doreen seemed to spot someone in the distance, and she smiled, waving her free hand and crinkling the laughter lines at the corners of her eyes in the process.

'No, just a conjured likeness so that you'll recognise her when you see her,' Margot said. Her eyes, looking rather misty to Lilly, were trained on the image of her old friend.

'How do we get from here to there? And, most importantly, how do we get back?' Michael asked, seemingly mesmerised by the likeness of Doreen, who was still walking to and fro in miniature in front of them.

'Getting there is easy enough. You need to intend it. Focus on Doreen and ...' Margot snapped her fingers, and Lilly jumped.

'Sorry, darling girl,' she said, laying a hand on Lilly's arm. 'Intend it, just like you did at the library to come here. Then it's just a question of keeping your vibration up for as long as it takes to find Doreen.'

'These will help us with that though, won't they?' Jack said, holding up his arm and pointing to the braided bracelet around his wrist. 'Storm woo-wooed them to protect our energy levels.'

Margot held out her finger. 'May I?'

When Jack nodded, she touched the bracelet. 'Where's yours?' she asked, turning to Lilly and then Michael. She repeated the procedure with Lilly's silver ring and Michael's necklace.

When Margot didn't speak, Michael said, 'Is something wrong?'

Margot bit her lip, clearly in two minds about what to say.

'The animals didn't get one,' Lilly said, resting her head in her hands. 'Of course.'

'What?' Michael and Jack said together.

When Lilly looked up, Margot was staring at the counter.

'They're placebos. Storm needed us to keep our vibration

levels high, so she gave us the equivalent of Dumbo's feather. The animals didn't get anything though, which was something I noticed but didn't properly process at the time.'

'Because placebos don't work with animals,' Michael said. 'Makes sense. They're way too smart for that.'

'But I got a real head rush when she did mine,' Jack countered.

Lilly raised her eyebrows at him.

'Yeah, you're right. Could have been just a little energy zap to make the point,' he conceded.

'Please don't think badly of Stormy, my darlings,' Margot said. 'She can do many things, but interfering with free will is beyond both her desire and capability. Maintaining your energy levels was always something that you, and you alone, could do. She just gave you a boost of belief to help keep you safe.'

Walking to a cupboard, Margot pulled out a small backpack and placed it on the counter. 'Time to pack up the supplies. I sincerely hope you won't be there long enough to need them, but food will help maintain your energy levels.'

Lilly pulled the backpack towards her. She flipped back the top and then pulled on the toggle to undo the drawstring, but it snagged on a large knot. She pulled and pinched at the cord with her nails, but the knot didn't budge. She was about to suggest that they may have to cut it off, or find another bag, when in her mind flashed a picture of the knot loosening under her fingertips. She tried again and the knot yielded without complaint.

Lilly frowned and looked at Margot. The other woman's brow was creased too, her eyes still trained on the backpack. When she met Lilly's eyes, she shook her head, answering the question Lilly had been about to ask. If Margot hadn't used magic to help, then it must have just been loosening so slowly she'd not realised, she reasoned. There was something in Margot's expression that gave her pause, though. The frown had been replaced by something else, and Lilly couldn't help feeling like she was being appraised in some way.

'Okay, so now what?' Michael asked, all business.

'Time is, of course, of the essence, so I don't want you to delay. To get there, you open the portal just as you did to get here. Focus on Doreen, then step through once all three of you can see her. When you find her, she's likely to be confused, apathetic and even a little hostile to your suggestion that she leave that god-awful place. She's been there a long time now, and we can assume that she wasn't entirely well from the start, given what they did to her.' Margot stopped herself, pursing her lips together and taking a deep, deliberate breath. 'Once you have her attention, I want you to show her this.'

Margot handed Lilly a small black photograph album. Lilly opened it and flicked through the pages, confusion mounting. 'But it's empty.'

Jack took it gently from Lilly's hands. 'But I'm guessing it won't be to Doreen?'

'Precisely. To Doreen, it will be filled with everything she held most dear. It will help her remember herself. Plus, there's a picture of me in it. She'll need that,' Margot explained, a sad smile tugging at the corner of her mouth.

'You must get her to agree to come back here. She'll need time to heal and get over the confusion, and there's no better place to do that than the afterlife. That may, I think, be your greatest challenge. Once she's here, we can talk to her properly, understand the spell and then hatch a plan to undo it,' Margot said.

'That sounds like a hell of a long process,' Jack said.

'All the more reason we get going now,' said Lilly. 'What

about coming back, Margot? Do we just focus on a part of the room like we need to do to get back to the library?'

Margot nodded slowly. 'Focus on Lilith. If for any reason you can't see her, then go home instead. You're less likely to get stuck here.'

'What do you mean by stuck?' Michael said, his expression darkening.

Margot gave a slightly impatient sigh. 'This is my afterlife. It doesn't exist without me, and so there's a risk that ...' She paused and changed tack. 'But it's also Lilith's afterlife, so it's safer to focus on her just in case ...'

It took a moment for Lilly to catch up. 'No. They wouldn't, would they?'

'Who wouldn't what?' Michael snapped.

'You found me easily enough,' Margot said with a sad sigh. 'There are, after all, no gates on the afterlife. We have to assume there's a possibility that they'll come looking for me too. If they have the means to survive the shift, they may also have the means to come here. Settle old scores or ...' She shrugged and held up her hands. Lilly noticed how the bright summer sunshine that had been streaming into the kitchen through the lantern skylight just moments ago had now flattened and dimmed. Glancing up, she saw that the pale blue sky had been replaced by iron-grey cloud.

Jack leaned over and squeezed Margot's hand. 'It's a risk, but let's hope they're too preoccupied with us for the time being. Please, keep yourself safe. We'll be back as soon as we can. Now, is there anything else we need to know?'

Margot shook her head slowly. 'Just be quick and don't be distracted. As hard as it is, you need to focus on Doreen and Doreen alone. You can't save anyone else, and if you try, you'll all be lost. Do you understand?'

'We understand,' Lilly said quickly, pulling on the backpack. 'Let's just go.' She worried that if they didn't do this soon, her courage might actually fail her entirely.

As they stood shoulder to shoulder in front of the counter, Lilly held out her hands to Jack and Michael. Jack held up the photo album to signal that he had it before slipping it into the back pocket of his jeans.

'When you're ready, I'll project the image of Doreen again. Focus on her and the intention to meet her where she is. That will open the portal. Don't delay – we can't risk keeping it open for long,' Margot said, and Lilly noticed just the hint of a tremor in her voice.

Lilly looked from Jack to Michael. They nodded solemnly in turn, and Lilly said, 'Ready,' her own voice high-pitched and tight even to her own ears.

The projection of the tiny Doreen appeared on a low table directly ahead of them. She seemed so real, smiling and waving as if she were in some sort of home movie, signalling to whoever was behind the camera. Lilly felt an almost physical pull from the centre of her chest towards her, and just like that, the portal opened and they were looking at an empty city street at twilight.

Lilly felt her legs weaken as the adrenalin coursed through her. 'Let's go,' she said, and, still holding hands, they stepped into the underworld.

CHAPTER 48

*T*he first thing Lilly noticed was the cold. While it wasn't depths-of-winter freezing, there was a cutting wind that seemed to be coming from multiple directions all at once. Her long hair was flying like startled snakes around her face, all but blinding her.

'Everyone okay?' Jack asked cautiously. He was still holding tightly to her hand, which made trying to tame her hair even more difficult. She wiggled her fingers free, tugged the elastic tie from her wrist and pulled her hair into a tight ponytail.

'Better now,' she said, slightly breathless from the exertion. What she was about to say next withered on her lips as she took in the scene. The city street was deserted, save for the litter that scuttled past them, propelled by the wind which, as Lilly turned in a circle to get her bearings, seemed always to be blowing directly into her face. Everything was grey. As if some filter had fallen over the world and put a moratorium on colour. Then she noticed the smell. A mix of blocked drains and something that, though she couldn't name it, made her feel sick to her stomach.

'Cheapside,' Michael announced, reading the street sign. 'London. We're in the City.' He laughed wryly. 'Doreen wasn't far wrong when she conjured her version of hell.'

'Can't be,' Jack said, walking out into the deserted road and standing on tiptoes, craning his neck. 'Where's St Paul's?'

'I'd put money on there not being anything beautiful in this version of reality. No Postman's Park, no Guild Hall, no green spaces at all come to think of it,' Michael said, warming to his own theory.

Jack didn't entirely agree, but Lilly tuned out his and Michael's good-natured debate. A flickering light caught her eye in the distance. The iconic red-and-blue London Underground sign seemed to be the only colour in sight, but even that couldn't decide on whether shining was actually worth it. It seemed so sad, Lilly thought. The poor, sad little light in a grey world.

'Lil! Wait!' Jack yelled over the noise of the moaning wind.

Lilly stopped, amazed to find that she'd walked so far away from the others without really realising.

'We've been here minutes and already this place is messing with us. We need to stick close together, okay,' Jack said when he reached her. 'Let's focus on Doreen and get out of here,' he added, glancing anxiously around, his jaw set and his eyes watchful.

'Look!' Michael stage-whispered. He pointed in the direction of the Tube sign, which had given up its attempts to stay lit.

At first Lilly couldn't make out what he was pointing at, but then she saw what she'd taken to be just another shadow separate itself from the wall. It was another few moments before she could make out what looked to be someone pushing a shopping trolley. She sucked in her breath and instantly regretted it as the stench of the city hit her. 'Do you think that's her?' she whispered, trying to ignore the fact that her stomach was doing cartwheels, but whether down to revulsion at the smell or just plain old fear, she couldn't tell.

'Must be,' Jack said. 'Margot said we'd be drawn to her, and there's nobody else around.'

'What do we do? Just walk up to her?' Michael asked. 'We didn't get that far in terms of the game plan.'

'I don't see what other option we have,' Lilly said, all at once feeling horribly exposed on the abandoned street. She wanted to look around but daren't take her eyes off Doreen, if indeed it was her. Lilly had no sense of whether the sun was rising or setting, but some things appeared to be harder to see than others.

'No time to waste,' Jack said. 'Come on.'

As the three friends strode forward, the distant figure picked up speed, hurrying past the long-abandoned coffee shops and sandwich bar chains that lined the street. A few still had their plate-glass windows intact, while others stood open to the elements, their voids like the missing teeth in a bleached skull. As they followed, the figure burst into a run.

'Shit,' Jack snapped. They all broke into a run. Jack and Michael could easily outrun Lilly – hell, Michael's legs were almost twice the length of hers – but they kept pace with her, and she was glad of it. Getting separated here just didn't bear thinking about. Lilly desperately wanted to turn around, to reassure herself that they were the pursuers, not the pursued, but fear propelled her forward. Could this really be Doreen? For an octogenarian, she moved liked an athlete.

The running figure disappeared from sight, shielded from view by a thick tangle of thorn bushes that were this reality's version of cityscape gardening. It reappeared near the Tube station. They quickened their pace, and Lilly forced her legs to find another gear. There was no way this could be Doreen, but whoever it was, they'd been drawn to them for a reason.

The piercing shriek all but stopped them in their tracks. Lilly felt as if her insides had just melted. She had never heard a banshee's cry, but in that moment decided that, should such things exist, that would definitely be the sound they made. When the shriek came again, just seconds later, it was already noticeably closer.

'Don't look,' Lilly panted as she willed her weakening legs to keep running.

'This way!' The voice from the shadows of the Tube entrance was strong and urgent.

The shriek sounded again, closer, and though it might have been her imagination, Lilly thought it sounded excited. A hunting hound closing in on the kill.

They all turned and sprinted for the gaping black mouth of the Tube entrance. Whoever it was, in that moment she would have agreed to afternoon tea with Attila the Hun rather than meet what was behind them.

There was just enough light to see the figure scoop up a bundle of blankets from the trolley before it disappeared down the steps into a blackness so dense it looked almost solid. While the thought of plunging headfirst into darkness was far from appealing, staying above ground was no longer an option.

Feeling their way down the steps, they had just reached the bottom when a piercing, furious shriek filled the space. The noise was as sickening as it was deafening, reverberating around the tiles and seeming to shake the very life out of her cells. She held her breath and, even though it was pitch black, screwed her eyes shut, waiting to die. It was only when Jack touched her arm that she felt her senses return. She gasped, disoriented by the fact that, aside from their heavy breathing, there was silence. The banshee, or whatever the hell it was, had gone. Or had it? She clung to Jack and groped her free hand in the darkness for Michael, too afraid to call his name. Her breathing began to hitch in her chest as the panic settled over her.

The light began as a soft glow a few metres away, but seemed to Lilly to grow brighter as her eyes adjusted. It wasn't a bulb but an orb. A witch light that she'd seen Storm and Isaac conjure thousands of times over the years. The ramifications of that seemed to hover but not settle, because with the light came a wave of reassurance as she saw Michael standing just beyond arm's length.

In her terror, Lilly had almost forgotten why they were here, so the polite cough made her jump. Spinning around, she saw a woman in her thirties dressed in black combat trousers, boots and a high-necked utility jacket. Her hair was cropped short and, save for a shock of silver above her right eye, was a flat dark brown. She was trying to smile at them, but her face was etched with barely suppressed tension.

There was something familiar about her though. The shape of her face. Her bright, clever eyes. Lilly gasped. 'Doreen?'

'One and the same. I assume you're my rescue party, correct?'

Lilly, Jack and Michael exchanged incredulous looks. They had been briefed to expect an octogenarian in a twinset and pearls, long past the edges of her own sanity, not GI Jane with a shopping trolley.

When nobody answered, Doreen pursed her lips in impatience. The blanket in her arms moved and a tiny Yorkshire Terrier popped its head out. Lilly felt as if the world had recentred itself.

'Yes,' Lilly said quickly. 'I'm sorry, but we were told we were looking for someone in their eighties. But …' She trailed off, her thoughts becoming muddled. 'And that thing. What was that? Nobody told us about that. Or that you have a sweet little dog.' She clamped her lips together, conscious that she was on the verge of babbling.

Doreen sucked in her cheeks, seeming to chew over the options before, at last, she said, 'Look, we don't have a lot of time. That you're here at all means the bastards have finally used the spell they took from me. Don't think I'm not grateful, I am, but we don't have time now for a Scooby-Doo flashback. That thing out there is hunting you, same as it's hunted me and Pip here for the last ten years.'

'I don't understand,' Michael said, staring open-mouthed at Doreen. 'How have you survived a decade without losing your mind? We've been here less than half an hour and it's already messing with our heads.'

The suspicion in his voice was hard to miss, and while Lilly understood where he was coming from – this could, of course, be a trap – some instinct told her that Doreen was no threat to them.

Doreen cocked her head in a 'Didn't I just say we didn't have time?' gesture, but answered anyway as she ushered them towards the escalators, the witch light hovering above them. When she spoke, her voice was flat and emotionless.

'As you're here, you'll already know that they …' She paused, as if selecting the right word from a selection in front of her. 'Extracted a protection spell from me so powerful it made them immune to the shift. I knew they'd kill me, so I kept one of the spells for myself, plus a few extras, just in case.' She stopped at the top of the escalator and faced them. Holding Pip in one hand, she unzipped her jacket and pulled down the neck of her T-shirt to reveal a complex mosaic of densely packed symbols and words tattooed on her chest.

Doreen let go of the fabric, tucked Pip into her jacket and zipped it back up, leaving only his head to protrude. Setting off at a trot down the escalator, she continued, 'I was indeed half mad by the time they killed me. It was what they did to little Pip that took me over the edge, but we don't dwell on that, do we, Pip,' she said, glancing down at the dog. 'We might have gone to our afterlife scarred but sound, but thanks to one of their nasty little spells, we ended up here. Torture and death weren't enough for them, apparently – they threw in a little extra.'

Lilly felt tears well in her eyes and willed herself not to sniff. She was glad of Jack's hand on her shoulder.

'Why didn't you—' Michael began.

'Leave?' Doreen snorted. Then after a beat, she said, 'Sorry, it's a fair question. By the time I'd recovered my senses and helped Pip, the shift had happened and I had no reference point. The world I knew had gone, energetically speaking, so the only way I'd ever be getting out of here was if some kind soul turned up with the right frequency in their vibration to show me the way home. And I knew that wouldn't happen until some clever bugger put all the pieces together and worked out that it was me who sent the devil himself marauding into paradise. I really am sorry about that.'

'Where are we going?' Michael asked.

'Just a few stations down,' Doreen said. 'The vamp – that's what I call that thing out there – it can't track energy signals underground, but neither can we open the portal from down here, which is a bit of a bitch. So we need to put some distance between us and it before we go back up top and attempt to get out of Dodge.'

Lilly felt Jack's hand squeeze her shoulder as they reached

the bottom of the escalator. She turned and saw his face pinched with the same anxiety she felt. Michael, though, looked on the verge of an outright challenge. Noticing it too, Jack stepped in front of him and put his hand on the other man's chest. Michael stared, hard-eyed, after Doreen as she strode along the platform, heading for the train tunnel, his jaw set. When at last he softened slightly, Jack stepped back.

'Keep up, kids, I'm not joking about the time thing. The longer you're here, the crazier you get, and we have a world to save, remember?' Doreen said, speaking without breaking stride or turning around. As she disappeared into the mouth of the tunnel, two new witch lights flew out behind her and hovered at the entrance, waiting for them. After a moment's pause, they followed her into the darkness.

CHAPTER 49

*T*hey walked in silence along the edge of the tracks, the witch lights floating above their heads. Lilly, who had never considered herself to be claustrophobic, found that she had to concentrate hard on her breathing to keep her sense of panic at bay. The thought of the city above the tunnel roof seemed to be squeezing the fetid air from her lungs. Her heart felt like a cantering mustang on the brink of an all-out gallop. Just when she thought she could stand it no longer, a station came into view.

'Lil?' Jack's voice was full of concern as he turned to look at her, and she realised she must have sighed particularly heavily.

'You alright, Lillykins?' Michael asked, putting his hand on her shoulder from behind.

She found her throat had gone dry, and her tongue seemed to get stuck around the words. After one mumbled attempt, she managed to say, 'Yeah. Fine. Just glad to be out of there, that's all.'

Doreen was already standing on the platform, one hand on

her hip, while with the other, she stroked Pip's ears. The little dog was gazing up at her with wide, frightened eyes. Maybe someone else got claustrophobic, Lilly thought.

'Quick as you can,' Doreen said, motioning with her head along the platform. 'With any luck the vamp will have continued east, but we won't have long once we're back up top,' she added, shifting her weight impatiently as she waited for Lilly, Jack and Michael to clamber up from track level. Once they were all back on their feet, she strode off towards the exit at the end of the platform. Lilly had to jog to keep up.

As before, Doreen spoke without turning. 'This is Chancery Lane Station. When we get to street level, we're going to need to get off the main road as quickly as possible. The vamp seems to do better in straight lines and open spaces. I've no idea why, maybe the buildings interfere with its sight – who knows. We're going to exit and double back on ourselves to take the first side street. It's called Staple Inn Buildings. Got it? There's an old coffee shop on the corner. The first bit is the riskiest part as it's a narrow pedestrian lane with buildings on either side, but going around would take too long – we'd be too exposed. We're going to run down Staple Inn Buildings and through some wrought-iron gates which are always open. The lane is a dead end, so we're all turning right into a street called Southampton Buildings. The first building on the opposite side of the road is the London Silver Vaults. That's where we're headed.' Doreen spun around and Lilly jumped at the sudden move. 'If we get separated, that's where we're going to meet, okay?'

'Got it. But why there?' Jack asked.

'I can't be sure. To tell you the truth, I've been loath to test the theory scientifically, but the vamp seems to have some level of aversion to silver. Either that or it messes with the energy signal. Whatever the reason, I've taken refuge there a few times and, well,' she said, running her hand through her hair, 'it's the best chance we've got.'

'And what happens when we get there?' Lilly asked. 'Do we go home straight away?'

'Hell yes. As soon as we close the door behind us, we get out of this nightmare,' Doreen said, and Lilly thought she could hear the merest hint of emotion in her voice.

'Isn't this all a bit pointless?' Michael asked, the last word mangled by a drawn-out yawn. Lilly turned around in time to see him stretch out his arms, looking for all the world as if he'd just woken from a refreshing afternoon nap.

Doreen stopped in her tracks and spun around so quickly Jack had to take a swift step backwards to avoid a collision.

'What did you say?' Doreen said, her face just inches away from Michael's. If he was perturbed, he was showing no sign of it.

'All this running around like we're in a comic or something. This place isn't so bad. I vote we take a chill pill and relax for a bit. Get to know the place before we jump to any big decisions, you know?' Michael shrugged and made to step around Doreen. As he did, she grabbed a handful of his shirt and pushed him hard into the wall. Lilly heard the thud of Michael's head against the tiles and cried out as if it had been her skull taking the knock.

'Ow! Why'd you do that?' Michael moaned, rubbing the back of his head.

Doreen didn't release him. She continued staring into his face. 'Tell me again what you just said.'

Lilly saw Michael's eyes dart away from Doreen's. His brow creased in concentration and he screwed up his face. 'I ... I don't know what I just said,' he said hesitantly. 'You were telling us about the route and the silver place, but then ...' He frowned again, but after a few long moments, shook his head and met Doreen's eyes. Lilly saw first confusion and then anxiety in his face. Doreen stepped back and let him go.

'That's how it starts, Michael,' she said, pronouncing his name like a schoolteacher gearing up to issue a detention. 'This place gets to you quietly. Insidiously. Its first job is just to cast doubt on the horror of it all, and once we doubt, we're an open door for the demons. You were suggesting that this place wasn't so bad after all.'

'What?' Michael said, his eyes wide as he cast a panicked look at Lilly and Jack.

They nodded.

'You're wrong, Michael. This is the very worst place in existence, and we need to leave as soon as possible. Do you agree?' Doreen slapped her hand on his shoulder and peered into his eyes. 'Do you?' she prompted when he only nodded.

'I do. I agree. We need to get home. Now,' Michael said, his voice unusually strained. 'This place is awful.'

'Good man.' Doreen patted him on the shoulder again. 'Let's go. Remember the plan. Staple Inn Buildings. Turn right at the end. Then you look for the Silver Vaults on the right-hand side of the street. If you get to Chancery Lane, you've missed it. Don't hesitate.'

As they approached the escalators, Doreen turned and gave Lilly and Jack a hard stare. She didn't have to say a word and Lilly knew exactly what she was thinking. Michael had suddenly become the weak link in their armour. *If only it had been me*, Lilly thought. *They could have picked me up and carried me like a roll of carpet if need be, but there'll be no such plan B for Michael.*

CHAPTER 50

The ticket hall was full of shadows as they crested the top of the escalators. One overhead light flicked on and off with no apparent rhythm, making the space feel like an abandoned disco. Litter swirled and eddied at the foot of the stairs leading to the street, propelled by a chill wind that made Lilly shiver.

Michael hopped over one of the barriers and turned, presumably to help the next one in line, but looked somewhat crestfallen as he saw Doreen holding open the swing gate near the wall and Jack and Lilly already on the other side. He shrugged and his lips made an attempt at a smile, but Lilly could feel the tension coming off him in waves. His energy felt all wrong, suddenly, and she chided herself for not noticing before. She'd been too wrapped up in her own claustrophobia to realise. When she looked at him in the flickering light, his edges seemed to be less solid than they had been. Was she imagining it, given what had happened down on the platform? She stared at him. The side of his mouth twitched and then twisted into a smile that wasn't at all like his. She crossed the space between them and hugged him.

'We've not all got crazy, crane-long legs like you, you know,' she teased. 'Some of us have to use gates instead of hopping over barriers.'

He didn't hug her back for what seemed like minutes but what must have been mere seconds. When he did, his muscles felt drum tight. Then at last he squeezed her and said, 'I'll have you know that these long legs won me a medal in the hurdles at a prestigious sporting event once.'

She stepped away and batted him. 'I think Pont Nefoedd Junior School when you were eight is stretching it a bit, don't you?'

He laughed and feigned offence. Lilly breathed a silent sigh of relief. Still Michael. All they needed to do was to get through the next ten minutes and they'd all be home safe.

Doreen motioned for them to join her at the foot of the steps.

'Follow me and move on my signal. Run, don't walk. Don't look back, don't stop and – sorry to sound like a complete bitch, but this isn't the Marines. What matters now is that we get back to our world in time to stop the Very destroying it and the afterlife. I only need one of you to do that, so if anyone goes walkies, that's on them.' She didn't look at Michael, but she didn't need to.

Lilly and Jack started to protest, but Doreen cut them off with a look. 'Don't you even dare. I've spent a decade in hell, and unless you want all of the worlds looking like this one, you'll listen to me. Hard as that is to stomach.'

'Wait,' Michael said, smiling. 'The afterlife isn't going to be affected by all this.' He waved his arms around absent-mindedly and spoke as one might to a slightly dim child.

Doreen threw her head back and muttered, 'Goddess save me.' When she looked back, she said through gritted teeth, 'What did you think, child? That the Earth could exist outside of universal law? As above, so below, remember? If the Earth falls, it falls into this.' She gestured around them with her hands. 'There would be nothing to anchor the afterlife to except this hell dimension, so yes, the whole shit and shaboodle would fall to the lowest of the low. And mark my words, matey, once it does, there is no going back. So yes, Michael, all life, including the afterlife, will turn to a version of this if you don't get your shit together right now!'

Michael continued smiling, his eyes unfocused. Before Lilly could move, Jack stepped in and slapped him on the back. 'You with us, mate?' he asked.

Michael startled at the contact. He looked around, licked his lips and began wringing his hands. When his eyes found Lilly's, his expression was close to pleading. She wanted to reassure him but had no idea what to say.

Lilly opened her mouth to speak anyway, but Doreen pressed a finger to her lips. She was standing on the steps, her head cocked, listening. All Lilly could hear was the thump of her heart and the blood pumping through her veins. Her legs felt weak, too weak to hold her, although she knew they'd have to. Pip was shaking like a leaf, his tiny head just visible as it poked out the top of Doreen's jacket. Lilly wondered how much more terrifying it must be for a tiny dog in such a hideous world.

Michael moved towards the stairs. When he glanced back at them, Lilly was relieved to see that he looked calmer and much more like himself.

Feeling her resolve return, Lilly didn't hesitate when Doreen gave the signal. She took the steps two at a time, bursting into the cold twilight and pausing only long enough for Doreen to do a three-sixty-degree scan. 'Go!' she hissed, and they were running.

CHAPTER 51

*L*illy kept her eyes trained on Michael as they sprinted down the side street. Despite Doreen's warning, there wasn't a world in which she could even entertain the possibility of leaving her friend behind in this hell hole. Unlike Doreen, he had no magic to protect him and would soon become prey to the vamp or just the ravages of his own mind.

The alley was shrouded in the same semi-darkness as the rest of this world, but the shadows loomed larger in the narrow space. The tall, ornate gates up ahead were at first a reassuring sight – at least they were on the right road – but it took Lilly just a moment more to realise they were closed. She prayed with every pounding step that closed wouldn't also mean locked.

Doreen reached them first, and after failing to budge them, began looking for a foothold. She reached up with one hand, the other making sure that Pip was secure in her jacket. Michael was there a second later, and Lilly saw him hold out his hands to Doreen, but she shook her head. Michael scaled the gate with ease, paused at the top and helped Lilly up and over. After a moment's hesitation, Doreen unzipped her jacket and handed the trembling Pip to Jack. She all but vaulted the gate and then reached through the bars to retrieve the little dog.

'Run!' she mouthed to Michael and Lilly. Michael took off and Lilly waited only until Jack's feet hit the ground on their side of the gate before she broke into a sprint too. It was then that they heard it. A piercing screech that seemed to suck all of the light out of her. She couldn't tell which direction it was coming from; it seemed to be everywhere. Remembering Doreen's words, she pumped her legs and kept on running. Jack was at her side, and with relief she watched as Michael turned right at the end of the alley in front of them. It was only a few hundred yards to the Silver Vaults, and she watched him cover the ground like an athlete. He sprinted to the entrance and threw his weight against the heavy-looking wooden door, which yielded without complaint.

The screech came again, closer this time – too close. Lilly felt the relief wash through her as they reached the door and burst through it to join Michael, who was stood, hands braced on his knees, catching his breath. Lilly swung around, looking for Doreen. She was running with Pip clutched to her chest, her free arm pumping as she sprinted. They were just yards away from the safety of the Silver Vaults when an old black street bin careered into her, knocking her to the floor. Pip flew out of her arms, hit the ground with a pitiful yelp and rolled into the gutter.

Lilly watched in horror as the vamp appeared around the corner. It looked to be nothing more than shadow and oily smoke, but the energy emanating from it was pure hell. Jack and Michael rushed past Lilly, moving together. The vamp threw back what might have been its head and screeched, obviously relishing the idea of five souls instead of one. As Jack and Michael hauled Doreen to her feet, Lilly sprinted past them, ignoring their collective screams of protest. A piercing gust of wind took her breath and almost toppled her. Instinctively she ducked, just as something sailed above her head. The uprooted lamp post landed with the deafening clatter of metal on stone a few yards away, narrowly missing Pip. Fury suddenly burned in her gut. Lilly had always despised bullies, and as she scooped up the lifeless-looking little dog, she was all but blinded by the injustice of it all. What light there was dimmed, and she knew without looking that the vamp had covered the ground separating them. Turning, she saw it towering above her. Through it she saw the others about to burst out of the Silver Vaults – intent on saving her. Her mind flicked, quick as a knife, to the day in London when Storm had used her magic to contain her friends, Lilly among them, in a protective bubble while she brought the mansion down upon the Very.

The fire in Lilly's belly flared and then she heard the music. It swirled around her like a melodious tornado, the sing-song voice of two children singing made-up songs. They weren't just any songs, though – or indeed any two children, Lilly realised. Jack's voice aged about six, singing their bubble song. Lilly, sounding even younger, sang back to him, word perfect, giggling joyously. He had taught her various ways of protecting her energy over the years, but of course, it had started with this song.

The vamp threw back its head as if to scream, but hesitated. Through it, Lilly could see the others pounding on an invisible shield. She didn't allow herself the time to think about it. As the volume of the song ratcheted up, she ducked past the vamp and hurled herself through the door, hoping the other three would move out of the way in time and that

Doreen would take down the shield before she and Pip bounced off it and landed in the vamp's lap.

The precise details of what happened next were a bit of a blur, but the sound of the heavy oak door slamming shut coincided with the furious screeching of the creature outside, which seemed to have recovered from its confusion a nanosecond too late to intercept her.

'Can it get in?' Jack asked frantically as he crawled over to where Lilly was crouched, her back against the front door.

'Hey,' Lilly said as she felt Pip move for the first time. The little dog lifted his head to look at her and then gave a tentative wag of his wispy tail.

'Pip!' Doreen cried as she skidded to her knees next to Lilly. Pip's tail all but beat a tattoo in reply as he stretched out of Lilly's arms to reach Doreen.

'Doreen!' Jack snapped. 'Can it get in?'

'No,' she snapped back, tearing her attention away from the little dog. 'I told you, it doesn't like this place for some reason – but we've seriously pissed it off, so let's not hang around and test the idea.'

Doreen jumped to her feet and, after kissing Pip on the top of his head, tucked him carefully back into her jacket. She offered her hand to Lilly. When Lilly was on her feet, Doreen held on to her hand and looked her in the eye as she said, 'Thank you.'

'I should be thanking you,' Lilly said, feeling embarrassed and reaching for a distraction. 'If you'd not done the dome, the thing with the protective bubble, we might all be—'

Doreen cut her off. 'That wasn't my magic, Lilly.'

Lilly frowned and managed a confused 'Eh?', but Doreen interrupted her again. 'Where's Michael?' she asked urgently.

Lilly scanned the foyer, her pulse quickening.

Jack jumped up. 'He was right here just a moment ago,' he said, jogging to the corridor. 'Michael!'

The door at Lilly's back strained as another furious scream from the vamp outside pierced the air. When it screeched again, the sound was further away. She leapt to her feet.

'It'll look for another way in,' Doreen said. 'It always does. Come on, we can't waste any more time.'

Lilly ignored her. She didn't want to have this conversation, and the only way to avoid it was to find their friend – and fast.

'Hey, dude, chill.'

Lilly froze, then raced back to the door. Ignoring Jack and Doreen, she slid back the bolt and cracked it open to peer out. To her horror, she saw Michael on the pavement opposite. He was lying on his back, propped up on his elbows as if he was sunbathing in Hyde Park, his feet keeping time to music only he seemed able to hear.

'Honestly, mate, you need to stop with all that screeching and just relax a bit. This place really isn't so bad when you get used to it,' Michael said, tipping his head backwards to look up towards the roof.

Lilly's flesh went cold as a shadow fell across him. The vamp must be up there, ready to pounce.

'How the fucking hell did he get out there?' Doreen spat. 'Stupid, stupid bloody boy!'

Another furious screech tore through the building, and everything shook with the force of it. The vamp was getting ready to strike. Lilly could feel the excitement emanating from it. She made a grab for the door handle, but Doreen was too quick, jamming her foot to stop it opening. Lilly made to protest, but Doreen said, 'We've got one chance to grab him, but you need to use your magic, Lilly.'

'I don't have magic,' Lilly wailed. If this was what Doreen was relying on, then Michael was as good as lost.

'Oh yes you do. It's curled up tight as a new kitten, but it's there,' Doreen said, peering into Lilly's face. 'Just trust me that's it there, okay, and stay close to me.'

Lilly felt her head nod on her behalf.

Doreen shook Lilly's forearms until she made eye contact. 'When I say go, we're going to make a run for it, grab his lordship and get back here as fast as we can.'

'But—' stammered Lilly.

'Don't think. Trust!' yelled Doreen. 'Ready. Go!'

The vamp was indeed on the roof of the building. Lilly didn't trust herself to look around, but she could feel its presence. It screeched when it saw them, its obvious delight whipped up in the icy wind that still seemed to be coming from all directions at once. Michael was still lying on the pavement. He was singing to himself quietly, all of his earlier bonhomie gone. He waved them away as they tried to pull him up. 'Leave me be. I'm comfy,' he slurred.

Doreen and Jack grabbed an arm each. Michael resisted, leaning away and slapping at their hands like a sulky toddler. 'Get off me,' he shouted.

As Lilly watched, the vamp slid down from the roof and hovered between them and the door to the Silver Vaults. She felt her legs turn to jelly at the sight of it. She hadn't been thinking first time around, her anger and desire to save Pip propelling her on, but now, staring at it up close, feeling the strength of its intent, she was truly terrified.

'Ow!' Michael shouted.

Lilly glanced down to see him rubbing his neck and glaring at Doreen. 'Why did you do that?' he whined, sounding, thankfully, like his usual self. Before anyone could reply, he said, 'Oh shit!' as he caught sight of the vamp rearing above them.

'It's up to you now, Lilly,' Doreen said. 'You used your magic when you saved Pip. Time to do it again.'

Lilly felt the panic rise in her chest. Doreen was wrong to think she had any power save being oversensitive to other people's emotions. She couldn't do this! Doreen was the witch, not her. She turned to say as much when the vamp struck, bearing down upon her friends. Jack was managing to hold it with an energy shield that looked to Lilly's eyes to be as thin as an eggshell and just as fragile. She'd never seen his energy shields before. He'd had no reason to use one since the shift, but there was no way this one was a match for the vamp. The moment it broke, they'd all be consumed.

'No,' she said under her breath, feeling her fear overlaid with a new determination.

As Jack's shield dimmed and cracked, Doreen shouted, 'Catch!'

Lilly instinctively held up her hand and caught a small, glowing silver orb. It looked to be filled with writing. Words, letters and symbols swam around inside it. She cast a confused glance at Doreen, who opened her mouth and pointed at it. Lilly put the orb in her mouth.

The explosion of light knocked Lilly onto her bum, but it propelled the vamp back towards the Staple Inn Buildings side of the road. Like smoke, it looked to have been blown into a hundred plumes, but even as she watched, she saw it was already regrouping. Jack and Michael lifted her off her feet, a hand under each armpit, barely breaking stride as they sprinted for the door of the Silver Vaults.

Slamming the heavy wooden door home and bolting it again, Doreen headed towards the corridor.

'I'm so sorry,' Michael stuttered.

'No time,' Doreen called over her shoulder. She stopped as soon as they were out of sight of the foyer. 'We're going to leave right here.' She pointed to the blank wall in front of them. 'Whatever your anchor point in Pont Nefoedd is, think of it now.'

'But what about Margot?' Jack asked. 'She said we needed to take you to her first.'

'I'm guessing that was when you thought I'd be a doolally old dear in need of a rest. As I'm clearly not, let's cut to the chase,' Doreen said.

'Agreed,' Lilly said, once Jack and Michael had nodded their approval.

Lilly took Jack's and Michael's outstretched hands. She focused hard on the library. There had been too much to contend with here to even wonder about what might have happened back home. Storm's warning ricocheted around her head. 'If the picture isn't here, or you can't sense my energy, don't come back.'

'Lil!' Jack's voice was urgent at her side. She snapped open her eyes, fearing the worst, but saw to her eternal relief the Ascension Day picture sitting on the table on the other side of the portal. Her relief was short-lived, however, because at that moment the sound of splintering wood preceded what felt like an earth tremor. The screech told them all they needed to know. The vamp had finally overcome its aversion to silver.

They leapt through the portal, the welcoming aroma of old books replacing the cold, vile stench of the underworld. The vamp's furious shriek was cut off as the aperture snapped closed behind them.

CHAPTER 52

Isaac hadn't bothered to count the number of doors. There was no point. The way back would be different anyway. That's just how magic worked. This plan in particular was designed to evade any pursuer, so who knew where they might end up.

He had lost all track of time, but when he heard one of the dogs' stomachs emit a loud gurgle, he guessed they must be nearing dinner time. He turned and crouched down. They had been remarkably quiet since entering the tunnels. He had expected Logan to start asking if they were there yet after just a few minutes, but he'd not heard a peep out of them. 'You all okay?' The jumble of pictures that appeared in his mind as the three dogs and Anchor answered all at once had a common theme. They were scared, but also frustrated that they had to leave Storm and the others to face the Very alone.

Isaac slumped to the floor and leaned back against the wall. Anchor climbed down from his shoulder to perch instead on his lap. They felt as he did. 'I can't say I'm pleased about it either, but she was right. At least this way they can't use you as leverage – because of course they would. They still live in a time defined by the idea of species, where anything that isn't human is for human use, abuse and consumption.' He shuddered, remembering the long years he'd spent as a shepherd, guiding the souls of slaughtered animals to the afterlife. He'd worked night after night to the point of almost complete exhaustion, then, during the day, worked to recruit, train and mentor others to do the most heartbreaking work. There had never been enough of them to help all those in such desperate need.

'At least this way, there is hope should the worst—' Isaac bit off the rest of the sentence. They had enough to deal with without being burdened with this new truth, too. Plus, Storm had made him promise.

Anchor chirruped as he cocked his head in question. 'Ah, nothing, mate. Ignore me, okay. I'm tired and worried like you. Let's get you somewhere safe and then we can reassess.'

Ludo, usually such a stoical dog, surprised him by leaning his head against Isaac's shoulder. He reached up and stroked the dog's head while trying to sound as comforting as he could. Logan too took advantage of the pit stop, waiting until Ludo had stepped back before taking his place. Hope merely gave Isaac a small wag before walking on a few paces, pausing and woofing softly at them. Isaac smiled. She was never one to waste time with pictures when her body language already spoke volumes.

They walked on in silence until Isaac noticed a change in the air temperature. As the light flicked on ahead of them, a door appeared. It was different from the others, not just because it was a single door this time but because this one didn't look like it was protecting a bank vault. It was just an old wooden door. The ironwork was black and rusted in places. The lock was a boxy brass affair, with a round, well-worn knob and a long barrel key sticking out of the keyhole, a red tassel attached to its top. Anchor jumped down at once and wasted no time in batting the end.

'Old habits die hard, eh, old friend?' Isaac teased.

Anchor startled, as if remembering himself, but then carried on regardless.

The breeze that blew in around the door was warm, and Isaac could smell the earthy scent of a forest beyond. He turned to the others and said, 'Well, it looks like we've arrived. Shall we?'

He turned the key and pulled the door open to reveal the front porch of a smart wooden cabin. Looking around, he saw it was on the shore of a shimmering blue lake and flanked by a thick broadleaf forest stretching as far as the eye could see. The breeze that ruffled his hair was warm on his skin. He turned around to see that the tunnel had already vanished. The front door of the cabin stood open, revealing a very comfortable-looking country home with timber-clad walls the colour of honey.

A blackbird landed on the porch rail outside. Isaac asked where they were, and in reply, the bird shared a picture of a vast forest with this the only cabin for what must be a hundred miles. Even the nearest road looked to be at least a few miles away. After thanking the bird, he sighed. 'Guess that's mission accomplished then, folks. We are, officially, off the grid.'

CHAPTER 53

The library was in semi-darkness, lit only by the reading lamps and soft-glow wall lights.

'Where is everyone?' Lilly whispered, feeling a weight of disappointment settle over her sense of relief. If disappointment was indeed the right word. Just minutes ago they'd been running for their souls in a hell-like underworld, and now they were home, mission accomplished. What was she expecting? Bunting and a marching band? Lilly chided herself, but knew even as she did so that something wasn't right.

'Maybe it's really late and everyone's in bed,' Michael offered. 'It's not like that place had clocks, right?'

Lilly felt a prickle across her back. Doreen must have felt it too because she spun, and in one swift movement, she unzipped her jacket and handed Pip to Lilly, making a shush gesture with her finger as she did.

'Welcome home, kittens.' The woman's voice from the darkness was both plummy and patronising.

Lilly's heart hammered in her chest, and even as she hoped against hope that Storm would appear and introduce the newcomer, she knew it wasn't going to happen. They all cast round, looking for who had spoken. Pip whimpered in Lilly's arms and trembled. It was only the second time she'd heard him make any sound at all, and it felt strangely portentous.

The woman stepped out of the stacks, an old book wriggling frantically in her grip. Lilly felt her legs turn to lead. She was certainly older now and dressed more for a girls' lunch at Selfridges than the ritual execution of the Ethereal, which had necessitated a cocktail dress and a real-life tiara, but she would have recognised Imelda Benedict-Hatman anywhere.

The memory came unbidden. Lilly had been lying, exhausted, on the wire floor of her cell when the cover was slowly removed. The light seared her eyes, and she shrank back.

'I just want a peek, Charlie-warley,' the woman had said, affecting the tone of a cajoling child. 'If you can't describe a dress beyond telling me it's white, then how am I to choose what to wear myself?'

The man had thrown back his head and laughed. 'Only the great Imelda Benedict-Hatman herself could fret about her outfit clashing with the soon-to-be executed. I knew I married a good'un.'

Lilly's eyes had adjusted to the light just in time to see them kissing, which even in that moment had felt like poor timing given the slobber-mouthed technique of Imelda's rubber-lipped husband. When he'd marched off to shout at a minion, Imelda had stood inches away from the glass cage, her unnaturally plump lips pursed as she raked her narrowed eyes over the girl. After a few moments, she had given a short snort. 'Wasted on the young,' she muttered before turning on her six-inch heels and stalking away, her long ash-blonde curls bouncing against her back.

'Oh look. It's the girl we very nearly burned back from Oz,'

Imelda said, snapping Lilly back to the present moment. 'That Toto?' She laughed at her own version of a joke.

Lilly made to reply, but Doreen touched her elbow, so she bit back the retort.

'And you're the hapless boyfriend who couldn't save her.' Imelda pointed a long pink nail at Michael, her sing-song tone more fitting to a toddler's bedtime story.

'And you ...' She narrowed her eyes at Jack, but the rest of her face seemed strangely immobile. 'You were there too, as I recall. Did the whole *Officer and a Gentleman* thing, carrying Miss Madam out of the building?' She jerked her head in Lilly's direction. 'It was very impressive.' She stepped closer and looked Jack slowly up and down, the edges of her shiny lips turning up at the sides. 'Hired help, maybe. Or just a handsome nobody. Or maybe ...' She tapped her hideously long nail on her bottom lip as she gazed upwards. 'Oh!' she exclaimed. 'Or maybe the ex-boyfriend.' She tilted her chin triumphantly and looked from Jack to Lilly to Michael. 'Oh yes, I think that's it. Oh, you've got to love a juicy love triangle.' Imelda grinned, baring her Tipp-Ex-white teeth.

Lilly felt her stomach twist. She longed to reach out and hold Jack, but they all seemed to be frozen by some unspoken agreement that to say or do anything would give ground that they couldn't afford to lose. She stroked Pip instead.

'You, though, I don't know.' Imelda stood in front of Doreen. The smile had vanished, her tone now all business as she stared at the other woman.

'Yes, you do,' Doreen said, sounding bored and a little exasperated.

Imelda obviously didn't. Anyone else might have raised an eyebrow in question, but she cocked her entire head, giving her the appearance of a slightly unstable china doll.

'Melly, it's me. Margot,' Doreen said with an exaggerated

sigh. 'We get to choose how we look now, remember? Here and in the afterlife, so I went for a rebrand.'

Imelda pursed her lips and twisted her head to look at Doreen side-on. Lilly didn't think she looked convinced.

'Do you need me to prove it by telling everyone what we got up to in Grand Cayman?'

Imelda all but flinched. After a beat she looked Doreen up and down, her nose wrinkled, and said, 'Dear god, M, you can choose anything you want to. This is what you pick?'

Doreen gave a sarcastic titter. 'Well, I can't say ten years underground has done you any favours either, darling.'

Imelda pulled back her lips in a sneer that made Lilly think of the vampires in old black-and-white horror films. If talking their way out of this had been the plan, it was heading south at a rate of knots.

'You always were a complete bitch,' Imelda said, glaring at Doreen. 'I see death hasn't mellowed you. Maybe we'll have more luck this time round,' she added. The book in her hands tried to wriggle free again, and she hurled it in temper across the room.

'Oh, do shut up, Melly,' Doreen huffed. 'You always did love the sound of your own whining voice. Just take us to our friends, will you, and let's get on with whatever silly little plan you've cooked up this time.'

Imelda sucked in her cheeks, obviously torn between her resistance to being told what to do and, if the nasty gleam in her eye at the mention of their friends was anything to go by, the desire to do just that. It took another few seconds of stand-off before she spoke again.

'Well, M, for old times' sake, I'll grant your little wish,' she said in the childlike voice she'd started with. 'It's only fair anyway, I suppose. I had to watch as that bitch murdered my Charlie, so now you can all watch her fry.'

Lilly felt acid at the back of her throat. The room swam around her, and she clutched Pip tightly, terrified that she might pass out and drop the little dog. In an instant, Jack's hands were around her waist, steadying her. 'Lover boy to the rescue again,' Imelda scoffed. 'Take them!' she screeched, as if her first instruction had been ignored. Guards, three men and a woman, all dressed in black fatigues and carrying machine guns, appeared from the shadows between the stacks.

While Jack's swift action had stopped Lilly from hitting the deck, there seemed to be nothing anyone could do to prevent the panic attack that followed. Maybe it was the sight of the guns, but whatever it was, she felt herself sliding towards the floor, her legs no longer willing to keep her standing. She felt Jack lift Pip from her arms and guide her gently until she was sitting. Her body seemed suddenly beyond her control. Her hands and legs shook as if someone else had hold of her bones and was intent on shaking the meat off them. Her lungs seemed to have been reduced to the size of matchboxes, for all the air they brought in. Little Pip whined frantically and licked her face, leaning out of Jack's arms to reach her, but she couldn't even form the words to reassure him.

She dimly realised that Michael and Doreen were being marched away, guns at their backs. Jack let out a yell as he was hauled to his feet by the collar of his jacket. Lilly didn't see if Pip had jumped or been dropped, but she saw him land on the floor and crouch.

'Bloody rat,' said one of the guards, and Lilly screamed in horror as the man aimed a polished black boot at the tiny dog. Had it made contact, she knew it would have been fatal, but thankfully Pip darted, quick as lightning, under a stack.

'Leave it,' snarled Imelda. 'Hardly a bloody threat, is it? Just shut the door when we leave and come back for it in a few days when it realises it can't eat books. We'll be long gone by then anyway,' she added, laughing.

Fury burned through Lilly like lava, and she knew her unwholesome thoughts were doing much to bring down the energy levels, but she was past caring. They had all worked so hard to rebuild the world for everyone, and now these monsters were about to destroy it. Realising that at least her panic had been subsumed by her fury, she was ready when the guard poked the muzzle of her gun into her back. Lilly, still sitting on the floor, snapped her head around and glared at the woman in black fatigues, then, in her own time, got to her feet. She only hoped that Pip would be able to find a way out, or at least, enough to eat and drink to sustain him until help arrived. Her heart sank at that last thought as she realised they were meant to be the help.

CHAPTER 54

$\mathcal{P}$ ip lay flattened to the library floor, trying to breathe as quietly as he could. He was shaking all over and desperately wanted to be tucked safely into Doreen's jacket. The other place had been hell, but at least they'd been together. The thought of what those terrible people might be doing to his friend made him feel sick. Here was meant to be better, but those people were as bad as the vamp. He had counted the sets of footsteps on the metal stairs and waited until the security door had swished shut and beeped before crawling forward to the edge of the bookcase he was hiding under. Their scents were diminishing, but although he was almost certain they had all gone, he was still too afraid to leave his hiding place.

A noise behind him made him jump. He spun around to see that it was just an old book. His relief was short-lived. Had it fallen? If it had, then something or someone had caused it to fall, which meant that ... He didn't finish the thought because at that moment, the book moved on its own. As he stared, it moved again, ruffling its pages at extraordinary speed. Then, without warning, it flew up into the air only to land on the opposite side of the bookcase. It repeated the movement twice more before Pip decided that the coast must be clear. He crept cautiously from his hiding place, his nose on high alert for any trace of the monsters and still half expecting a kick from the darkness, but none came.

The book hovered in front of him, then moved off towards the back of the library. Pip followed, still scanning the room for the scent of danger. The book stopped beside an open door to a small kitchen, pressed into what was no bigger than a broom cupboard. He smelled coffee and what might have been biscuits, but it had been such a long time since he'd smelled either that he doubted himself. High above him, a tap dripped, and he was reminded of the reality of having a corporeal body back on Earth. The monster had been right. Without food and water, he wouldn't live very long locked down here. He hung his head and sighed.

The smell of dust and ancient paper roused him, and he lifted his head just in time to see a line of old books file into the small space and, to his amazement, organise themselves into steps from floor to countertop. He stared, disbelieving, until the first book he'd met nudged him gently towards the first step. The books held firm as he scampered up them. The sink was empty save for a large washing-up bowl, which, with a nudge to the long-levered handles, he was able to fill with cold water. The little book did a somersault mid-air and the books below ruffled their pages in what Pip decided must be a sign of approval or celebration. He nosed off the water once the bowl was almost full and leaned in to take a long drink.

When he had quenched his thirst, he made to descend, but the little book whizzed around him and up to the top cupboard. Nudging open the door, it disappeared from sight. Pip heard a shuffling sound, and then, sailing through the air, came a paper bag. It landed with a dull thump and, the bag now split, some of its contents spilled onto the tiled floor. Pip wagged his tail – he hadn't been wrong about the smell of biscuits after all.

After eating a few and nosing the rest into a convenient hiding place behind a loose kick board, Pip thought back to their escape from the hell dimension. There had been something bothering him all along. He had been so scared that the thoughts had been all jumbled up in his mind, but they were clearing now. Someone had said that so long as the photograph of the first Ascension Day was next to the lamp, it was safe to come back. And it had been. He'd heard them checking before they crossed through the portal, but it wasn't safe. Maybe the monsters had surprised the others and they'd not had time to move it. He crept out into the library and stood looking at the wall the portal had come through. There in front of it was the small table, the silver-framed photograph sitting proudly in the middle of it. He knew nobody else would be coming through the portal, but it still niggled him. It was an unwitting trap, and one that they'd all fallen into. Allowing himself a rare growl, he trotted to the table and threw his weight against the delicate wooden legs. He retreated when he heard the frame rock – no sense dodging a monster's boot only to be accidentally brained by a falling object. Frustrated that the frame didn't fall, he was about to repeat the action when a large old book hovered past him, ruffling its pages. Backing up to get a better view, Pip saw the book open, clamp the frame between its covers and then glide off to the far corner of the room.

CHAPTER 55

*I*saac sat on the cabin's front steps, drinking coffee and watching the last rays of the day burnishing the surface of the lake. The wind had picked up, rippling the water's surface and rousing the leaves, still clinging to the trees but already surrendered to autumn, into a chorus of gentle, rustling song. A lament for summer, Isaac thought.

Ludo lay snoring at his side. The others had long since found comfortable spaces to retire to. Hope was curled tight as a squirrel in an armchair. Anchor was stretched across the back of the sofa, looking twice as long as normal, and Logan had claimed one of the double beds. They had said very little since they arrived. In the decade he'd had to refine his gift for conversing with animals, he had become accustomed to their taciturn ways. Animals had their own language, after all, and no longer needed humans in the Ethereal world. He considered it an honour that they chose to speak at all, but even by their usual standards, his companions' quietness spoke volumes about the depth of their sadness.

He tried and failed not to think about Storm for what felt

like the thousandth time since they had parted. He also tried to convince himself that the shock they had heard in the tunnels was one of Asim's defence systems blasting something dangerous to smithereens, but every time he tried, the image slid from his mind like oil in a hot pan.

No longer being able to sense Storm was the hardest part of all this. They had been bonded since that first day in London. Storm had made her choice that day, but so had he. While he knew this was the only way, the only insurance against the end of all things, he wanted so desperately for it to be otherwise. He had lost count over the years of how many times he had secretly wished Lilly had been the Ethereal after all. Every time he saw Storm put duty before her own needs or smile when he knew she wanted to cry, he had wished for a simpler life for her. A life just for living. Few knew of the burden carried by the First. No matter how many times she told him it was just the way it had to be, it didn't feel fair. But wishing the burden onto Lilly wasn't fair either, and for that, he felt guilty.

Isaac drained the last of his coffee and placed his hand on Ludo's side to rouse him. He stood up and took in the scene before him. It was almost dark now. The sky was the colour of freshly bottled ink. A waning moon lingered on the brow of the distant mountain, a thin sickle of light. If he waited, it would shine directly onto the lake as it rose, and once the stars came out, it would be a sight to behold. Storm would love it here. A sharp gust of wind made Isaac shiver. Ludo nosed his leg and looked up at him.

'Thanks for keeping me company, friend,' Isaac said, pulling open the door and holding it for the dog. Although he doubted his capacity for sleep, he needed to rest.

CHAPTER 56

*I*saac woke to the sound of claws on floorboards. He was surprised to find the cabin already bathed in bright sunlight. A large fluffy ginger tail landed on his face, and he smiled at the thought of Anchor creeping in to share his bed in the night.

'Morning, Anc,' he said hoarsely as he levered himself to sitting, but Anchor merely stretched and continued snoozing. Isaac hadn't expected to sleep. After locking up for the night, another hard-to-break habit from the old days, he had lain, fully clothed, on the bed, removing only his boots to spare the covers. He had wondered where Storm was sleeping. Tried to picture which of the numerous guest rooms in Veronica and Asim's house she might have chosen. Probably the one with the little balcony overlooking the greenhouse, he decided, but then he remembered that the greenhouse was no more, and the full horror of their situation returned in glorious techni-colour to torment him. He'd tried to distract himself by creating a mental list of everything in the greenhouse that would need to be replaced. He hadn't thought it would work, but if he'd slept, then it obviously had. Now he was fully awake, the fear returned. That there was a real possibility that he would never see Storm again was too much for him to even entertain. They would find a way out of this that meant they didn't need this plan of hers. It was a back-up. Insurance. Nothing more, he told himself. Perhaps if he said it enough times, he'd start to believe it.

After collecting his thoughts for a few moments, he put on his boots and went to find the others. Hope appeared at the front door, nosing through the dog flap and bringing with her a flurry of crisp, newly fallen leaves. She showed him a picture of food in the kitchen, from which Isaac discerned that she, Ludo and Logan had already eaten. Then she explained that they were off to explore the lake.

Isaac opened his mouth to tell her to be careful but thought better of it when he saw the look on her face. 'Okay, but we all need to talk when you get back.'

Hope woofed her acknowledgement and then disappeared back through the dog door, leaving only the scattered leaves on the mat and the sound of the flap swinging to and fro against its frame.

Isaac had just poured his much-needed first coffee of the day when he heard the thump, thump, thump of the dog door again. 'Did you three just run around the lake then?' he said, carrying his mug into the empty living room. The dog door was still swinging gently to and fro. He crossed to the front door and pulled it open, expecting to see one of the dogs in the distance, having returned for something and then raced off again. The last thing he expected was the young man who stood on the porch grinning at him.

'Riley?' Isaac said, his mind ricocheting between two equally implausible explanations.

'Miss me, teach?' Riley said, taking off his sunglasses and

revealing the stone-grey eyes that had always slightly unsettled Isaac, even when Riley was a teenager. They had a new flintiness to them now, and the man who had once been his star shepherd looked to have aged far more than the decade that separated their meetings should account for. He was still rake thin, but there was an added angularness to him now, a sharpness that made Isaac think of lemon juice on paper cuts. Gone was the round-shouldered slouch of the lanky kid he had once known. Riley stood in front of him with his shoulders square, a good head's height taller than Isaac and with no reason in the world to be there, bar one.

Isaac thought back to their last meeting. He had summoned Riley to attend the Council of Shepherds the next day. He would be charged with gross misconduct and dismissed from their service. The other Council members also wanted him handed over to the appropriate authorities, but on that matter, Isaac was determined not to move. Witches never fared well when they fell into the hands of those in power, and, his crimes aside, he would never sanction such a betrayal of their kind. It had been typical that, never one to obey the rules, Riley had appeared at his door twenty-four hours early to plead his case.

'There is nothing I can do for you, Riley. No one on the Council will vote in your favour, and nor should they!' Isaac had said through gritted teeth as they faced each other in front of the farmhouse. 'What you did was against everything we stand for!'

Riley had grabbed at his own head, taking rough handfuls of his unwashed hair, and screamed, kicking out at loose stones in the dust. Isaac had been glad he'd not invited him into the house.

'They were laughing at them as they slaughtered them, for fuck's sake. Taking it in turns to see how long they could draw

it out! How long the pigs would squeal for. By all that's holy
and good in this god-forsaken world, they deserved to feel
what those poor creatures felt, every last fucking ounce of it,'
Riley bellowed, spittle flying from his lips as his voice grew
hoarse with the pain of the memory.

Isaac took a deep breath and steadied himself. 'I know,
mate, I know,' he said, trying to banish from his own mind the
scene he had witnessed when called to help with the clean-up.
'What those people did, the suffering they caused, is uncon-
scionable. They are – or, I should say, they were – the very
worst of humanity, but they were sick. As Soul Shepherds we
swore an oath to harm none. And that includes the—'

'The torturers?' Riley screeched. 'The brutalisers? The sick,
twisted abusers of the innocents? We're just meant to stand by
and watch that, are we? Are we!' He screamed the words,
leaning into Isaac's face, his eyes wild and his cheeks flushed
red with fury.

Isaac refused to move. 'What we are not permitted to do is
use our witchcraft to channel the emotions of the animals into
the humans abusing them,' he said slowly. His own temper
was straining for release, and he worked hard to contain it.
'What you did led to the deaths of fourteen men and three
women.'

'I prefer to think of some of them as suicides,' Riley
retorted, pulling himself up to his full height, his lip curled.

'Enough!' Isaac bellowed, his patience finally spent. 'We are
not there to be judge, jury and executioner. We are there to
bring peace to the animals in their darkest hour. And you! You
just unleashed more darkness. You proved to them that even
shepherds are capable of unimaginable cruelty.'

Riley stared at him, his face a mask of hatred as if Isaac
himself had been the one wielding the butcher's knife. 'I used
to idolise you, you know. I wanted to be just like you. I took

your word for gospel and dedicated my life to this cause because of you.' He shook his head as he kicked at the dust. 'You're a sell-out. So, screw you and the Council. I don't regret doing what I did. Seventeen souls against how many billions of animals? Drop in the fucking ocean, pal. I'll find my own way to fight for them.'

The sound of a car making its way up the long drive caught their attention. Before Isaac could say any more, the young man had turned, sprinted across the yard and disappeared into the woods. There had, of course, been no Council of Shepherds the next day. Instead, Isaac was racing to London with his old friend Henri and the woman who, unbeknown to him then, would save the world.

Isaac had thought of Riley countless times over the years. He had found a family of sorts in the Council. He was a bright, angry, neglected kid from the wrong part of town. The youngest of six children, he had obviously learned to fight from a young age. He was always tight-lipped about his family, but bruises were hard to hide. When he also turned out to be the only child with magical ability, his situation had turned from precarious to downright dangerous. The Council of Shepherds had used their influence to find him first foster care and then a place of his own. All the while, Isaac had worked hard to train him in an attempt to channel his passion and contain his anger. But, Isaac reminded himself, he had failed him. That he was here, standing in front of him on the porch of a cabin in the middle of nowhere, did not bode well.

'So it was you I saw at the Ascension Day party,' Isaac said, keeping his tone steady.

'Just getting the lay of the land.'

It was only then that Isaac noticed the trail of blackened leaves on the trees closest to the cabin. A thick gold chain glinted in the gap between Riley's T-shirt and neck, and Isaac made to step back, already conjuring a defence spell, but the other man was too quick. He grabbed for Isaac and slapped a plastic ring around his wrist, which tightened on contact. Isaac fell to the ground as he felt his magic rear up like a terrified horse.

'Sorry, pal,' Riley said. 'Not the nicest thing to do to a fellow witch, I know, but needs must when the devil drives and all that.'

Isaac lay gasping on the porch. He felt as if his heart had been ripped from his chest. There was pain everywhere, and although it was diminishing, the sense of utter desolation settling over him was far worse. If this was what Storm had endured all those years after Margot had bound her magic, he had no idea how she had survived it.

A questioning meow from inside the cabin behind him brought him back to himself, and a new panic flooded through him.

'Well hello,' Riley said warmly, crouching down on his haunches and extending his hand.

Bad man. Run. Hide, Isaac thought, not expecting Anchor to have heard him given the binding.

The cat hissed and gave Riley's hand a swipe.

Riley pulled his hand away just in time. 'Feisty. I like that,' he said. 'I've missed having animals around.'

'Leave him alone,' Isaac said, his voice a raspy staccato.

Riley pulled a face. 'What? You really never knew me at all, did you?' he said, his expression bordering on hurt. 'As if I'd hurt a cat. What the fuck do you take me for, Isaac? Everything I've done, I've done for the animals. That didn't change when I went to work for them.'

Isaac snorted, unable to think why anyone would choose to side with the Very.

'I just went where the power was,' Riley said, leaning down

to peer into Isaac's face. 'We weren't helping. We were soothing our own consciences while bearing witness to atrocities. We were enablers of the worst kind. At least the High Council had the power to really change things. When we take over again, things will be different for the animals, you'll see. They've committed to that.'

Isaac shook his head and tried to speak, but the pain, while settling in numbness, was slowing him down.

From behind him, Anchor growled menacingly.

Please, Anc, hide and tell the others what's happened, Isaac pleaded, although he guessed it was useless. He felt a lump in his throat at the thought that this connection with animals that had been so unexpected at the shift, but so joyful, was now lost to him.

When Anchor's reply arrived in his mind, clear and true, Isaac could have wept with relief. With a final hiss, the cat turned on his heels and sprinted back into the cabin and, Isaac hoped, out of the back door into the woods.

'Shame,' Riley said, looking disappointed. 'Right, let's get you back to the party, shall we.'

Riley hauled Isaac to his feet and held him. Still reeling from whatever the bracelet had done to him, he was almost incapable of standing, let alone running anywhere. Isaac felt a change in air pressure, and then before them on the porch was a new door that wouldn't have looked out of place in a 1970s office block. He stared, unable to take it in.

Riley laughed. 'Oh, yes. You're not the only witch on the block, you know. Some of us have been honing our craft while waiting you out.' With that, he kicked open the door and pulled Isaac into the blackness beyond.

CHAPTER 57

*M*argot felt the pain as if it were her own. She lurched forward in the garden swing, her unread book falling to the ground, as she tried and failed to stifle a scream. Lilith was at her side in a heartbeat, wide-eyed and tense as a bowstring. The bright blue sky darkened at once, and then came the sound of thunder rolling in the distance. The pain ebbed away slowly and was replaced by a numbness that Margot associated with unconsciousness. So they had taken her girl but not yet killed her. For that tiny mercy, she was grateful.

Lilith cocked her head in question. 'They've taken Stormy. She's hurt, but still alive for now.'

A picture of Lilly, Jack and Michael appeared in Margot's mind.

'Maybe they just haven't found Doreen yet,' she said, not liking the doubt she heard in her own voice. She tried again. 'Or perhaps it's taking a while to persuade her to go back.'

Lilith twitched the end of her tail and looked at the ground. Margot saw her outline soften.

'We must stay hopeful, my friend,' she said, reaching out to stroke the cat. 'But I can't stay here now, you understand.'

Lilith sprang onto her lap, landing with the grace of a dancer and all the weight of a butterfly. She stretched up and put her paws on Margot's face. She looked deeply into Margot's eyes, then rubbed her head against her jaw in farewell.

When the cat jumped down, Margot rose. 'I'll go and tell the children,' she said as they walked back to the house. The wind had picked up and her long summer skirt caught around her legs. With a wave, she changed into leggings, T-shirt and boots she could sprint in. The spell had come so swiftly to her mind that she realised that her magic, at least, had been expecting this moment.

Mireille was waiting for her in the kitchen, her brow knitted into a deep frown. They both spoke at once. Margot waved for the younger woman to go first.

'I saw the sky. What's happened?' Mireille asked.

'What we feared,' Margot said, crossing the room to take Mireille's hands in hers. There were calluses on her palms, a reminder, she said, of the work of her last life that she had chosen to keep for now, while she reflected.

Mireille nodded sadly. 'You'll be going then,' she said, her eyes on their hands.

'Yes.'

'I'll look after the children, although I'm guessing they'll leave if you're not here,' Mireille said thoughtfully. She held up her hand as Margot made to reply.

'If we all survive this, if there is an afterlife to come back to, then Lilith and I will be here at the very least. Odette too, maybe. But you have to decide whether this is still where you need to be, M. There is, you know, a fine line between healing and hiding.' She raised her eyebrow and fixed Margot with her trademark stare.

With no defence to offer, Margot simply said, 'Have I ever told you that you are wise beyond your years?'

'Several times, but I enjoy hearing it,' Mireille replied, a hint of a smile pulling at her lips. She had always been the most serious of children, even in their first incarnation together.

'How will you get there?' Mireille asked. 'Have you been to this place before?'

Margot nodded. 'Yes. Many years ago now, obviously, but I can easily scry for the memory and locate the energy signal. My biggest worry is what I'll find when I get there.'

'No time to lose then,' Mireille said, getting purposefully to her feet. She hovered for a second, her arms seemingly undecided upon what to do, then quickly crossed the space between them and pulled Margot into an awkward embrace.

Mireille had never been a hugger, not even as an infant, and Margot had to resist the urge to cling to her. Instead, she accepted the brief contact for the gift it was.

'Until the next time, then,' Mireille said.

'Until the next time, my darling girl,' Margot replied, her voice trembling.

Margot watched her leave and, with a sinking heart, wondered if indeed there would be a next time for any of them.

Ten minutes later, Margot was sitting in her meditation chair. The memory of her first and last visit to the library had come easily. When reviewing her own timeline, Margot often just replayed the memories, but knowing what she was about to see, she chose to take the role of the observer. It would be hard enough without the sense of reliving the event entirely.

She was watching a much younger version of herself carrying a box of books down a winding flight of wrought-iron stairs. There were caged lights on the wall and on each tread, and Veronica, who was walking just ahead of her, was telling her about the debate she'd had with the electrician about the wattage.

'I could hardly tell him that I wanted a lower light level in order to transition from the real world to that of the magical, less jarring,' she explained, 'so I said something about my eyes needing to adjust to the light just to shut him up, and he just assumed there was something wrong with my eyes. I felt a bit deceitful, but we've had to tell so many half-truths over the last eighteen months of the build, just to keep the library a secret, that it just joined the list.'

Margot had been about to reply when they reached the library. It was an incredible space. A blend of old-world, polished wood charm and high-tech security. The double security doors had been left open to facilitate the swift transfer of books from the old library to the new, being trans-ported by what felt to be a small army of security personnel and magical people from all over the world. The stacks them-selves were from the old library. Asim had suggested new ones to go with the new house but had beaten a hasty retreat when Veronica and the books had a blue fit at the suggestion. Margot had come to the rescue when the challenge of manoeuvring long, antique shelves down a narrow, secret staircase had almost scuppered the plan entirely. Although she'd been out of the country, Margot had coached Storm to perform a translocation spell, and a few weeks later, the stacks had silently vanished from the old library and appeared in the new one. Storm was over the moon, Veronica and the books were delighted and Margot couldn't have been any prouder of her protégé. When her schedule put her in the UK the weekend of the library move, she had jumped at the chance of helping with the relocation of the books, as much to see the evidence of Storm's magic as to contribute to something so vitally important to the magical community.

In the memory, Veronica turned to speak as Margot carefully placed the box on the reading table. Margot muted the sound. Watching it was bad enough. She didn't need to hear the words too. She saw Veronica's bright smile slide from her face as, once the lid of the box was lifted, the books shot into the air. They flew around the table and then zeroed in on Margot, flying in tight circles just inches from her head. Next, they became an angry swarm, and Margot had no option but to run from the room. Magical books, like animals, she had long since mused, had a way of taking the measure of people. Her path was already set – and the books had known it.

The energy signal appeared, a fine blue-white gossamer thread floating on the current of space and time. Margot reached for it and held it fast, feeling at once the connection she needed. She opened her eyes, and there on the wall in front of her was the portal to the library. The lights were dim, but she could clearly see that the picture was missing. She hardly needed a coded sign to know that there was trouble, but maybe the library wasn't the safest access point after all. She was about to close the portal when she heard a high-pitched bark. Peering into the semi-darkness, she saw a tiny Yorkshire Terrier standing on their hind legs, trying to be seen.

'Pip?'

The little dog yipped in reply and turned in a circle, trembling slightly.

Margot pushed away the last image she had of the little dog, whom she had never met in life, Doreen screaming his name as that bastard Wang...

'Is it safe?' she asked quickly.

Yes. Hurry, came the immediate reply.

Margot stepped into the library and knelt down. No sooner had her knee connected with the floor than the tiny dog all but threw himself into her arms. 'Oh, darling Pip. You brave, brave soul,' Margot soothed as she instinctively tucked the trembling dog into her gilet. 'Tell me all about it so that we can get out of here and go save them.' She had almost forgotten her trepidation at the welcome the books might have lined up for her, but so far, all was quiet. Forgiveness it might not be, but tolerance was enough.

Pip wasted no time in explaining the sequence of events he'd witnessed since returning from the underworld with Doreen.

'Clever witch,' Margot said with genuine admiration for her old friend. 'If they'd known who she really was then they'd have murdered her on the spot. And to think I felt guilty at the time for blabbing to her about the Grand Cayman thing.' She shook her head. 'Okay, so now we need to plan. It felt as if Storm's magic has been bound.' She cleared her throat before she could add 'again' and face the reality of what she herself had done to Storm all those years ago. 'If Dor's not done the spell yet, then we have to assume that she's been bound too,' she added. 'We need to figure out how to undo the binding of two witches at the same time, which is basically breaking someone else's spell at lightning speed and at a distance without doing it astrally.' Margot exhaled, feeling like a novice again, daunted at the idea of floating a feather.

The sound of ruffling pages caught her attention. Turning to the reading table, she saw that a large, ancient-looking black book, its binding hanging by threads and its cover lettering faded beyond reading, had joined them. Standing upright, it ruffled its pages again. Somewhat impatiently, Margot thought.

'Oh, hello,' she said, her mouth suddenly dry as dust. She held Pip more closely, but relaxed slightly when she felt the dog's tail wagging within the confines of her gilet.

The book glided onto its back and looked to be waiting. It ruffled its pages again and Margot hurried to the chair, popping Pip on the table next to the book. As soon as she was seated, the old tome wasted no time. It snapped itself open, releasing a small cloud of dust that made Pip sneeze. Peering at the blank parchment pages, Margot held her breath as a spell revealed itself. The script was tiny and closely packed around the sigils and diagrams that were drawing and redrawing themselves repeatedly as she read. As she sat back, ready to test herself, the book gave an impatient shudder, and then, to Margot's horror, it flipped over the page. More script appeared. Then more sigils, so complex now that they made her head swim. She read on, trying to quell the creeping sense of defeat that was building in her gut. How on earth would she remember this? She had just read to the end of one page when text began appearing on the facing page. She sucked in a breath that was almost a cry. The script halted, waiting.

'No, please. Carry on. I'll figure out how to remember it all. I promise. Please,' she said, focusing hard on the words and trying desperately to commit them to memory.

There was a long pause. Margot stared at the unmoving page. Pip turned in a circle and whined. Then the book emitted a flash of brilliant blue light. When she looked back at the pages, in the bottom right-hand corner was a fingerprint surrounded by inward-facing arrows. Margot gasped and felt tears prick at her eyes. Only the purest of heart were ever allowed to absorb spells from the ancient books. With a shaking hand, she reached out and gently touched her index finger to the page. She watched, open-mouthed, as the ink slipped from the paper into her finger, the magic surging into her veins like the lifeblood that it was to every witch who walked this plane and the next. She closed her eyes and sent out a prayer of love and gratitude to the universe.

'Thank you,' she said to the book.

When she looked back at the page, a new image had appeared. It was a watercolour of a Yorkshire Terrier. Peeking out from behind his spotty bandana was a star-shaped tag. 'Pip?' Margot said.

The little dog wagged his tail and spun in a circle.

CHAPTER 58

The guard didn't so much carry as drag Storm through what was left of the kitchen and into the living room. After securing her hands with a plastic tie, he pushed her onto one of the cream sofas. Smacking her broken leg as she stumbled, she fell, face first, her scream muffled by the tape secured across her mouth. The pain was blinding. White hot, it rendered all other thought impossible. She felt sweat trickle down her back and forehead and struggled to catch her breath as pain and panic vied for supremacy.

She willed herself to think of Isaac – of the first time he'd kissed her in the tunnels below the farmhouse. She had known right there and then that he was the soul that completed her. She had been desperately in love with her husband, Nick, but in Isaac she had a connection that felt as old as time itself. Nick had said as much too, as she had lain there in the rubble, waiting to die. He had told her to remember, and as she had been hauled back to consciousness by her well-meaning friends, she had. She had remembered it all.

When at last the pain had eased enough for her vision to

clear, she saw that, aside from the guards, she was alone in the room. Her heart pounded again as she thought of her friends, the others in the village and what else might be happening in the world. Were there other cells like this? Had their re-emergence been coordinated? She thought of Isaac and the animals safe in the cabin and pictured them sitting on the porch, looking out over the water as the sun set. She had known instantly how much he'd love the place the moment she'd found it. Then her thoughts turned to Lilly. She had placed an impossible burden on her young friend's shoulders, but if anyone could persuade Margot to undo the spell, it would be her. She just prayed that they'd get back in time. Imelda didn't strike Storm as a woman who could delay gratification for long – even more so now that she'd had to endure a decade in an underground bunker.

Storm wanted to be brave, but there was nothing she could do to prevent the tears that welled in her eyes as she thought about her own death. She had been brave in London. In fact, she'd not expected to live out the day. Saving Lilly had been her priority, and her own life had felt like a small sacrifice by comparison. Why had her courage left her now? Storm bit her lip. If this was how it ended for her, then at least she had the comfort of knowing life would go on.

She had wanted to tell Lilly. Hell, she should have asked her permission, as she had with Isaac, but there had been so little time. She knew Lilly wouldn't even contemplate a scenario in which Storm didn't survive. Trying to move beyond her objections would have just taken too long, if indeed it was possible at all. No, this had been the only way. Besides, Lilly had accepted on a soul level. As she kissed Lilly goodbye, Storm had offered up part of the Ethereal spark and asked for its safekeeping. Lilly, although she didn't know it consciously, had said yes. If Storm was killed, then the spark would make itself known to Lilly consciously so that she could choose to either become the First or pass it on to another. Isaac would have the same choice to make should Lilly refuse. Painful as it was to admit, maybe that was the only way out of this – to allow this Imelda woman to have her revenge and then wait for Margot to undo the spell? But even as the thought formed in her mind, Storm felt her defiance rise. In London, she hadn't cared if she lived or died, but now, she wanted so desperately to live and be part of the world.

Storm contented herself with the knowledge that Isaac and the animals were safe. Lilly and the others would take Margot to the cabin when they realised the house had been compromised, and then, with Lilly safe, Isaac and Margot could return to undo the Very's protective spell. Hell, for all Storm knew, Margot might not even need to come back to Pont Nefoedd to cast it. That would be ideal, because keeping Lilly safe and out of the way would be one of the hardest challenges. Isaac had already decided that telling her she needed to protect the animals was probably the only way of keeping her away from trouble. With a sinking feeling in the pit of her stomach, Storm thought of the Ascension Day picture in the library. What if Isaac had forgotten to move it? What if … but she didn't finish the thought.

'On your feet,' said the guard who had dragged her in. 'Time for a show,' he added as he hauled her up.

Storm screamed as she felt the severed ends of her shin bone slide against each other.

The female guard joined him, tutting. 'Alright, love, keep it down, will you,' she said with a huff as she grabbed Storm under her other armpit and lifted her. Storm tried to hop, but they were walking so quickly towards the patio doors that her only option was to allow herself to be dragged. A guard

standing on the terrace opened the doors, and they pulled her
out into the September sunshine.

Storm couldn't believe what she was seeing. She felt like
she'd slipped through the centuries and had landed back in the
Middle Ages during the burning times as she gawked at the
three enormous stacks of wood piled around central stakes.
They really meant to burn her. Her vision blurred at the
thought, and she swallowed down the almost overwhelming
desire to throw up. But why three? The thought broke
through her consciousness and replaced her fear with panic
for her friends. Did they mean to murder Dot and Henri,
Veronica and Asim in the same way? There was nothing she
could do to settle her stomach this time, and she retched. The
male guard only just ripped the tape from her mouth before
she brought up the contents of her meagre breakfast.

'Bitch!' screamed the female guard as she glared at the
vomit on her boot.

'Language, Tara,' Imelda scolded from the garden. 'It's only
a bit of puke. You should be used to bodily fluids in your line
of work, anyway,' she said, laughing. 'Bring her closer.'

Storm only just had time to lift her injured leg before the
guards dragged her down the wide terrace steps to the garden
where Imelda was waiting.

'You're going to hate every minute of this, kitten, I absolutely promise,' Imelda said. 'We've got a warm-up act first,
though,' she added, beaming and looking expectantly at the
assembled guards. 'Get it? Warm-up? Fire?' It was met with a
round of forced laughter. Imelda scowled and shrieked, 'Bring
them out!'

Storm watched in horror as Veronica, Asim, Henri and Dot
were marched into view. Veronica was white with fear, her
face so frozen that Storm might have done a double take
under normal circumstances. When she caught sight of Storm,

however, she cried out and made to run towards her, until one of the guards grabbed her in a choke hold and hauled her back into line. She reached instinctively for Asim as she coughed and rubbed at her throat, but the guard slapped her hand away and shouted, 'No touching!'

Dot and Henri walked as close to each other as they dared, a look of such defeat on their faces that Storm felt a sob catch in her chest. Henri met her eye and gave an almost imperceptible shake of his head as a tear slid down his wrinkled cheek. Storm thought she might explode on the spot from grief, but then she felt the axis of her world slide entirely as Jack, Michael and Lilly were marched out, machine guns held at their backs. There was another woman with them too, who Storm vaguely recognised but couldn't place. She was staring at Storm intently while pulling at a black band around her wrist – a witch then, but Storm only really had eyes for Lilly. Despite herself, she tried to move forward, but the guards held her back, their fingers digging into her flesh.

'I'm sorry,' Lilly mouthed, and Storm felt the words splinter like glass in her heart. She could feel her magic trying to rise like a fatally wounded animal, desperately fighting the inevitable, but the binding held it firm. Storm shook her head, trying to tell Lilly never to be sorry. That whatever it was, it was never her fault – ever. She tried to step forward again, and this time Tara punched her full in the face, snapping her head back and, Storm knew with certainty, breaking her nose.

What happened next, Storm witnessed through streaming eyes as blood from her nose pooled onto the dead grass at her feet. With a look of abject fury on her delicate, freckled face, Lilly shot a pulse of energy from her hands so strong that even the guards holding Storm were knocked to the floor by the impact. Lilly stared, open-mouthed, at her own hands as if they didn't belong to her.

Unable to balance without the guards, Storm lowered herself awkwardly to her knees. Her broken leg complained loudly, but the hope that blossomed in her all but silenced it. How had she missed this? Lilly had magic? Maybe Ethereals were evolving in ways they'd not even considered before.

Storm's train of thought was interrupted by Imelda screaming from where she lay sprawled on the grass, 'Witch! Witch! Bind her! Bind her!'

The guards were struggling to their feet, but Jack was already standing. He raced to Lilly, and Storm saw him speaking frantically. Lilly turned, ready to direct another pulse, a mixture of fear and determination on her face.

Storm heard a strange noise. Then Lilly lowered her arms. Jack frowned, and Storm saw him open his mouth as he made to pull Lilly away, but then came the sound again.

Beside her, Tara said, 'Night, night,' her tone mocking.

Lilly fell first, sideways into Jack. He caught her but wasn't able to hold her. He stared, dumbfounded, as she slid limp as a rag doll down his body. Storm saw the blooming rosette of blood staining the front of his shirt, and then he was falling too. Her scream caught in her throat when, just as she thought the nightmare couldn't get any worse, she saw Isaac, his hands bound in front of him, round the corner and race to the side of his fallen friends.

$\mathcal{W}$hen Storm came around, the memory of what she'd witnessed took a few seconds to resettle itself in her mind. Like some demonic bird of prey that had taken flight, it landed, talons digging into their target with no intention of letting go. She felt the bile rise in her throat and levered herself up to vomit, but nothing came. Her stomach, it seemed, was as empty as the rest of her.

She was lying where she had fallen, on the steps of the terrace. Lilly and Jack were still where they had died. She stared at Lilly's body, unable and unwilling to process what had just happened.

Imelda and a guard were standing within feet of them, chatting and laughing as if they had not a care in the world. That part was accurate enough – whenever they turned their attention to killing her and Isaac, the world as they knew it and the afterlife beyond would come to an abrupt end. Her darling Lilly would be ripped from her peace and condemned with the rest of them to the lower realms. Two guards appeared to drag away the bodies. Storm retched again and wished she could cry, but a numbness seemed to settle over her. A cold blanket of desolation and defeat. Was it shock? She hoped it was because the alternative, that the First had surrendered all hope, was unthinkable. Unbearable. She had always feared that she was not up to the job, and now, here was the proof.

She had planned for this. In secret at first, not wanting to ruin the joy that had followed the ascension, and then with Isaac's help. So many souls had left Earth and explored the afterlife, revisiting their old incarnations and revelling in the full awareness of their role in creation. Those who had stayed had been so determined to heal the Earth, their conviction was infectious, their love and energy boundless. Ten years of hard graft and solid science later, they had created a paradise for all life. Love had prevailed and Storm watched it all with a hopeful heart, while also preparing to defend it should the need arise. She realised now that she had not read the portents. Not even the First, it seemed, was immune to wishful thinking when the truth was too painful to bear.

That all her efforts had come to nothing made her feel hollow to her core. She knew there was no reasoning with Imelda. Delusion was too powerful a foe to win over with logic and truth. Her truth now was that she had failed creation itself. For that crime, perhaps an eternity in the underworld was punishment enough.

'Look at your wrist.' The voice was so clear that she looked around to see who had spoken. The guard nearest her was leaning against the balustrade, puffing on an e-cigarette. Tara, the woman who had murdered Lilly and Jack, had sauntered over to join Imelda on the lawn.

'Heal yourself,' the voice said again, and Storm realised it was coming from inside her own head. Was she losing her mind, too? But no, there was something familiar about it. Her heart thudded in her chest. She was almost afraid to look, but when she did, she bit her lip to stop herself from crying out. The plastic tie around her wrist that had bound her magic was changing colour. No longer black, it was fading to grey. Fissures appeared on its surface, giving it the appearance of a drought-riven riverbed. As she watched, it turned from grey to white, and then, all at once, it was ash falling from her wrist.

She felt her magic at once. Like a sleeping dragon uncaged, it roared into her belly, furious and more powerful than she had ever known it. Storm steadied it, then directed it at her broken leg and nose. As it worked, she saw to her horror that the guards were rounding up the others. Isaac was now in the front of the line, his hands still bound before him. Even from this distance, she could see the black band around his wrist. Then came Michael, Henri, Dot, Asim, Veronica and, last, the witch she couldn't quite place.

'Quick as you can, darling,' came the voice again. Storm gasped. Margot!

'Thought we'd treat you to a nice show before it's your turn,' snarled the guard from behind her. 'You know, eye for an eye and all that. You can watch your little friends fry this time, seeing as you killed the guvnor's husband an' all.' He laughed.

'No!' Imelda yelled from the lawn. She was wearing high heels and had to keep changing position to stop herself from sinking into the turf. 'I want the old couple to burn first, then the fat woman and the Indian bloke, and *then* the witches.'

Storm didn't hear Tara's reply. Her eyes were on Isaac. He was staring directly at her, the hitch of a tiny smile on his lips. He glanced at his still bound hands and Storm allowed herself to hope as she saw a wisp of ash catch on the wind.

'Now,' Margot said.

CHAPTER 60

*S*torm sprang to her feet and blasted the surrounding guards with a pulse so ferocious Tara was knocked over the low balustrade of the terrace. Not trusting to luck, she sent a containment spell after her. Moments later, the semi-unconscious guard was held suspended in the air.

Storm cast around, looking for her friends. Isaac and the other witch were shepherding Henri, Dot, Veronica, Asim and Michael towards the house. Storm's eyes lingered for a moment on the spot where Lilly and Jack had fallen. The grass where their bodies had lain was the only patch of green amidst the sea of blackened earth.

The pulse caught her off guard, lurching her forward as it landed between her shoulder blades. It did nothing more than momentarily wind her, but she remembered too late their theory that the Very might have had a witch of their own. Logic told her that only a witch could have found Isaac. She tried not to think about what that might mean for the animals. What caused a person of magic to side with such evil she'd never fathom, but witch or not, she wouldn't be pulling any punches. Everyone had a choice.

The tall, rake-like young man smiled almost shyly as she turned to face him. Her shield was too quick for him, and his next pulse rebounded, making him duck to avoid it. Caught off balance, Storm took full advantage of the moment and sent him flying down the steps. He landed hard on the gravel, bouncing face first before coming to a shuddering halt. He lay unmoving. At least unconscious. He couldn't do any more harm, Storm thought.

As Isaac and the unknown witch reappeared from the side of the house, the pop of automatic gunfire rang out. They dived for cover behind one of the huge stone planters that lined the path up to the terrace steps. At least the others were safe inside.

Storm sent another pulse of energy in the lawn's direction, hoping to flush out whichever of the guards was still concealed enough to be firing as she focused on maintaining her own shield.

'Time to end this, darling,' Margot said as she stepped from the patio doors onto the terrace.

Relief flooded through Storm's veins, like cool water on a runaway fire. 'Do it,' Storm said. 'Undo the spell.' She didn't add 'and please do it quickly', but she wanted to, as she could feel her energy rapidly diminishing. As she spoke, Isaac and the witch broke cover and headed in their direction.

'Not me, darling. Doreen,' Margot said, sounding confused and pointing towards Isaac.

A fresh volley of automatic gunfire rang out.

Storm cursed as she felt her shield flicker. She threw herself behind the stone wall of the terrace. Margot had done the same on the other side.

Storm peered around the wall, searching frantically for

Isaac. He was crouched with the witch behind another of the planters a few hundred yards away. Storm stared at the woman.

'That's Doreen?' she mouthed at Margot.

Margot nodded emphatically.

'I'll take out their guns,' Margot said calmly, and Storm watched as her lips moved in silent casting. Why hadn't Storm thought to do that in the first place?

Storm's relief was short-lived. Margot's disarming spell bounced off the weapons like soap bubbles against cold glass. Still the shots rained down. Margot's face was a picture of horror as she tried again, and again. Storm tried too, but her energy was low and still falling.

Peering around the wall, she saw Isaac and Doreen talking frantically. Lying prone on the gravel, just feet away from the pair, the young witch stirred. If it was Doreen who had cast the protection spell on the amulets, why hadn't she reversed it yet? What was she waiting for?

As Storm's mind spun, a tiny flash of fur leapt from the confines of Margot's gilet and bolted down the steps.

Imelda's voice, shrill and close to hysterical, pierced the air. 'Riley! Riley! Kill it! Kill it!'

So Riley was the Very's witch. A memory tugged at the edges of Storm's mind. A story about a rogue shepherd that Isaac wasn't able to save. She couldn't think of it now. Riley pushed himself to his knees and looked up at Storm. She winced at the sight of his bloodied face, pieces of gravel still embedded in his flesh. He smiled sadly, and she pushed the last of her energy into shielding herself against an attack.

The dog, who looked no bigger than a coffee mug, slowed, obviously calculating his chances of dodging the huge human en route to Doreen.

'Riley!' Imelda spat. 'Kill the fucking dog!' Losing patience, she picked up one of the automatic weapons on the ground.

It was clear to Storm that Imelda had no idea of the dog's significance. That said, neither did she, but every sense she had told her that their last hope depended on the little guy reaching Doreen.

Riley looked at the dog and smiled, wincing slightly. Storm saw Isaac put his hand on Doreen's arm. He shook his head.

'Wait,' Storm said urgently to Margot, sensing her about to act.

Riley lifted his arms. One pointed at the dog in front of him, the other at Imelda behind him. As he flexed his hands, Imelda shot backwards into the unlit bonfire and a pale blue shield formed around the little dog. 'Run!' Riley yelled to him.

A fresh volley of bullets rang out, and Storm watched as Riley lurched forward, one hitting his shoulder. *Stupid boy!* she wanted to scream. Why hadn't he shielded himself? Or maybe he too was weakened. Still, he held the shield around the dog. The next bullet bounced away from Riley. Whichever witch was protecting him, she was grateful.

The little dog moved like lightning, flinching every time a bullet bounced off his shield. When he was still a good three feet away, he leapt into Doreen's arms.

CHAPTER 61

It seemed to Isaac that Pip was airborne for minutes, even though he knew that, rationally, it was no more than a second. All they'd been through, and whether they lived or died, now depended on a dog so small he'd be lost in a shoebox.

Isaac was still marvelling at the ingenuity of the witch beside him. In explaining her plan, she had told him of the counter-spell she had hidden in Pip's dog tag. Isaac had no idea how Doreen had had the presence of mind to even think of such a thing while the Very and their henchmen were torturing her and her dog. All the while she was also covering them both in protective spells in preparation for the hell she knew was waiting for them. Her strength and quick-wittedness were beyond amazing. Her magic of an intensity that was off the scale.

Doreen held Pip to her face and kissed him gently on the nose as something close to a sob escaped her. Isaac saw the ink now through the little dog's straggly hair, words and sigils in tiny script. Taking a deep breath, Doreen reached under his

bandana for the tag and held it between her thumb and forefinger. The reaction was immediate. The tag pulsed, a golden
light pouring from it into Doreen's hand. From there, it raced
up her arms, filling every molecule of her being as her lips
began to move in silent casting.

Isaac glanced up to see Riley grinning widely. He looked
like the kid he'd first met, all those years ago, so full of pain at
the injustice and cruelty in the world but also desperate to do
some good wherever he could. Isaac acted on instinct,
shielding himself as he broke cover and dragged the injured
young man to their hiding place.

Riley's eyes filled with tears as his face contorted. Shaking
his head, he said, 'I'm sorry ...'

Isaac clasped him around the back of the neck. 'I know. I'm
sorry too. Time to put it right, yeah?'

Riley dragged his sleeve across his nose and nodded.

'Would you mind,' Doreen said, handing Pip to Riley. If
Isaac had needed any more confirmation that his instincts
about the young man had been right, then this would have
been it.

Riley looked all at once amazed and thrilled. He took hold
of Pip as if he were made of glass. The little dog wagged his
tail enthusiastically.

'Of course,' Riley said to Pip, opening his jacket so that the
little dog could climb inside. And another animal communicator too, Isaac thought proudly.

Disarm them. Doreen's voice was clear in Isaac's mind.
While his spell had bounced off the Very just minutes ago,
something told him it would be second time lucky. He tried
again and then watched as the gun held by the nearest guard
crumbled into dust. The man didn't make a sound, just stared
open-mouthed at his empty hands. Seconds later, every guard
had been disarmed. Imelda screamed at them until, out of thin

air, a line of silver tape appeared across her mouth. Two of the guards broke ranks and tried to run for it but found themselves hovering in the air, twenty feet up. Storm's magic, for sure – he could almost smell her perfume on the tail of the spell.

Isaac saw Storm and Margot walking purposefully down the steps from the terrace. Storm's eyes were fixed on him, and when he met her gaze, her smile seemed to chase away every shadow in the world.

CHAPTER 62

*T*saac took his place next to Storm and she grabbed his hand, grateful just for the sight of him. He smiled at her, but she knew that he too was trying hard not to look at the spot where Lilly and Jack had fallen. Their grief would need to wait until they were all safe. While her energy levels were recovering, she was grateful of the contribution from Isaac and Margot. She would need all her strength for what came next.

'I don't mean to rush you, but do we have a plan from here?' Isaac asked, directing his question at Doreen.

'Well, my plan is pretty simple,' Doreen said. 'I reverse the protection spell on their amulets and watch them go pop.'

'No,' Storm said softly. 'Everyone gets a chance here, regardless of how they lived or ...' She looked up at Tara, who no doubt was fantasising about all the ways she might kill her, and added, 'Or who they've hurt.'

Doreen sighed. 'Oh, Stormy,' she said, turning to look at her. 'You always were the kindest, sweetest soul.'

'It's the Ethereal way—' Storm began.

Doreen put her hand on Storm's arm to interrupt her. 'You are right. Of course you are. I've just spent too long in the underworld.'

Storm felt her jaw drop, but Doreen waved away the question that was forming on her lips.

'It's no wonder the world has thrived under your example, my dear,' she said.

Storm felt her cheeks flush. Doreen may look younger than her these days, but it still felt like being praised by the headmistress.

'The blessing then?' Isaac asked.

Storm nodded. 'Will that work, Doreen? Can they choose while protected by the amulets?'

After a pause, Doreen nodded. 'With a little modification, yes, I don't see why not.'

Storm felt the crows approach even before she heard their caws. They had arrived in force. Storm guessed that there must be a few hundred at least. She didn't know whether that was a good omen or not. Were even the crows anticipating trouble? They circled overhead, casting long shadows across the lawn before they settled in the trees above Imelda and the suspended guards.

Doreen and Margot sent a questioning look Storm's way.

'Those who refuse to ascend receive the Blessing of Crows,' she said simply. 'Our friends' – she nodded to the birds – 'attune to the vibration of the individual soul and open up a portal for them so that they go where they want to.'

'The blessing it is, then,' Margot said.

Storm closed her eyes as the ascension dress took form around her. It was hard to believe that just three days ago she had worn it to welcome Jean. The world had turned on a sixpence since then, and now she intended to turn it back. The wings appeared all at once, eager for their work and, she guessed, as eager as she was to get this over with.

Imelda and the guards had been lowered gently to the ground. Only Imelda remained gagged, as she would not be silenced and Storm had grown tired of her increasingly hate-fuelled ranting. She appeared to hate everything and every-one. Storm reminded herself that some of the worst bullies were the most vulnerable underneath the vileness. Everyone, including Imelda, would get the same offer – ascend and become Ethereal or reject love and choose a lower realm. The blessing spoke directly to the soul, so it would cut through the noise and the bravado to reach the true essence of the person.

Veronica, Asim, Dot, Henri and Michael joined them, standing in a semi-circle behind the four witches. They all looked exhausted, but Veronica had some colour back in her cheeks at least. It was all Storm could do to stop herself from flinging her arms around them, but that would need to wait. Instead, she smiled at them and beamed a load of love their way.

Riley, who had been silent until now, lifted Pip carefully from his jacket. He held him at eye level and said, 'You did great today, pal.' Pip wagged his tail and licked Riley's nose. The young witch laughed. 'Cheers, bud. Maybe see you around,' he said as he handed the dog to Doreen with obvious reluctance.

Turning his attention to Storm and Isaac, he gestured to the line of guards behind him. 'I should probably go stand there then.'

Isaac made to reply, but Storm squeezed his hand to quieten him.

She nodded at Riley, and he turned. 'Riley,' she said. He turned back to face them. 'Thank you. Whatever your soul chooses, know that your actions today, your kindness, helped to save the world. For that, you should be immensely proud.'

Riley bowed his head, then took his place at the end of the line.

Storm considered making a speech, but she could not bear to. All life was precious to her, and that some of the souls standing in front of her now would be lost to darkness, even of their own choosing, pained her to her core. In the end, Isaac volunteered to say what she could not find the voice for.

The sun was setting, casting long shadows across the garden. Storm stood, Margot to her right and Doreen to her left. They linked hands as Isaac began.

'The world has ascended since you last walked in the sunshine,' he said, his voice clear and calm. 'This is no fairy story. There is no conspiracy. No grand plan to steal the world from you. That, if you remember, was your intention. The First Ethereal is real.' He gestured behind him to Storm. 'Her choice was real. She saw enough goodness left in humanity to save, and that choice allowed us to ascend to the Ethereal age. Had you succeeded in killing her, then all life, including the afterlife, would have ended.'

He paused, looking at the faces of those who stood in front of him. All bar a few hung their heads. Imelda was shouting against her gag and Tara was standing with her head high, her eyes closed.

'You will now be offered the blessing – a call to join the Ethereal world.'

All heads snapped up in surprise. Even Imelda fell silent for a few seconds.

'If you accept, then you have the choice to either stay here on Earth or return to the afterlife to an existence of your choosing. If you reject it ...' He cleared his throat before continuing, 'If you reject it, then by default, you choose a lower realm of your own making. Our friends the crows will shepherd you safely to your destination. But whatever you choose, know that you have the love of the Ethereal world with you.'

Isaac paused, then turned to look at Storm. She put her hand on his shoulder. They could say more, but they had done what they could to save the souls standing in front of them. Their salvation or damnation was now a matter of their own deciding. Storm hoped that they all chose the former.

Margot and Doreen let go of her hands and Storm stepped forward. She felt her wings tense, ready and eager. She had already committed every face to memory, but she took one last look before closing her eyes and releasing the blessing. Some cried out in awe, others laughed or cursed. She tuned them all out and focused only on the universal energy surging through her – inviting all who might listen to join the Ethereal world.

CHAPTER 63

$\mathcal{T}$he park looked just as it had on the day of the party. The wildflowers swayed in the warm sunshine. The picnic tables with their pretty tablecloths were still topped with jugs of bright flowers. The entrance to the huge circus tent was pinned open, and through it, Storm could see the twinkling of fairy lights. The sense of déjà vu was palpable. The only thing missing were the people.

Anchor chirruped loudly from where he lounged on Storm's shoulder. She reached up and tickled him under the chin.

Isaac laughed. 'Something about taking a chill pill,' he translated for Storm.

She grinned. 'Easy for you to say, clever clogs,' she said to the cat. 'It's not you who's got to do this.'

'We're all behind you, my dear. One hundred per cent,' Henri said, stepping in beside her.

Storm smiled at him. Then she turned to look at her friends. Veronica and Asim, Michael and Tim, Margot and Doreen. Hope, Ludo, Logan and Pip. Her breath caught at the absence of Lilly and Jack. She swallowed the restriction in her throat and tried to smile through misty eyes.

It had been Michael's idea. They had been sitting in Cordelia's, still shell-shocked from the course of events and each needing to tell and retell their parts of the story. That the plan to hide the Ethereal spark had failed pained Storm more than anything. Once that had been aired, it was impossible not to share the challenges that came with being the First. There had been tears, of course, cries of 'But why didn't you tell us?' And then Michael had made his suggestion. Henri had guffawed, declaring Michael's hat trick of world-saving ideas complete. So here they were.

'Ready?' Veronica asked.

Storm bit her lip and looked at Isaac. He shrugged and then nodded slowly.

'Hold up,' yelled a voice from behind them.

Storm grinned at the sight of Riley, his long legs making short work of the ground between them.

'Sorry,' he puffed when he reached them. 'Lost track of time.'

Isaac brightened at once. He pulled Riley into a hug. 'Just in time, mate. Come on.'

The whispered conversations ended abruptly as Storm entered the tent. The whole town seemed to exhale at once, and then they were on their feet, clapping, cheering and whistling. To Storm it felt like sinking into a hot bath after a cold day. The love and joy in the tent filled her almost to bursting.

Storm climbed the steps to the stage alone, Anchor having firmly declined the offer of accompanying her. She glanced at her friends in the front row, then out to the sea of faces that made up her community. The camera drones hovered into life around her, just as the huge screens around the sides of the tent connected to other countries around the world. How she loved these souls.

She waited until everyone had stilled before she began. Her voice was hoarse and a little shaky, but she resolved not to resort to glamours. She had hidden for too long. Now she needed to tell the whole story – the whole truth of what it meant to be the First.

'Friends. As you know, in these past days, we have come close to losing our world to darkness. I know you all felt it, and I am so sorry that I wasn't able to be here to help you.'

A rumbled of disagreement rose from the crowd.

She held her hands up to quieten them. 'You are, as always, very kind, but it is the responsibility of the First to protect the Earth and all her souls. In that duty, I failed.' She ploughed on quickly, speaking louder to drown out the protests. 'I tried to keep everyone and everything safe by hiding the Ethereal spark. I reasoned that should I be killed, life as we know it would be able to continue. That plan backfired spectacularly, and had it not been for our friends' – she gestured to the front row, then to the picture of Jack and Lilly that appeared on the screens around the tent – 'all might have been lost.'

Storm swallowed hard as she fixed her eyes on the screen. After taking a deep breath, she continued, 'Life, my friends, is always moving forward. We may no longer be subject to the rigours of time on our physical bodies or confined by our consciousness to just this single lifetime, but we are forever evolving.' She looked back to the picture of Lilly and remembered the shock on her friend's face as the magic neither of them knew she possessed burst from her hands.

'If this dark episode in our history has taught me anything, it is that we must all be willing to change and adapt for the greater good. And that includes me. To be the First is to carry not just the light but also the darkness in order that all things can be held in balance. It is a joy and an honour, but it is also, on occasion, a tremendous weight. That weight, that burden, if you will, is felt by all who carry the spark.' Storm paused and looked at the faces of the crowd. All eyes were upon her, and from the outpouring of love she was feeling, all hearts too.

'That is why I am here today. I never again want to risk our paradise. I never again want to come close to failing you or creation.' She stopped and looked down. Hope was standing, looking up at her, tail wagging. She smiled at her, and the dog wagged harder. 'I am here today to ask for volunteers. We need around a dozen, more if possible, spread throughout the world. Volunteers willing to carry a tiny part of the Ethereal spark so that we may keep it safe from anyone who may try to threaten our world in the future. As I said, this is a heavy burden to bear, so please know that this comes with a weight of responsibility—'

'I will,' said a voice from the crowd, cutting her off.

Storm looked up to see Ash from the newsagent's on his feet, his hand raised self-consciously at half-mast.

'Me an' all,' said Jean, waving at Storm enthusiastically from the back row.

Hope jumped onto a seat and barked.

'Me too,' said another voice, then another. Soon the tent was filled with a chorus of voices as everyone stood and raised their hands. On the screens she saw the same thing. Row after row of people, hands raised.

Choked and unable to speak, Storm looked at Isaac. He wasted no time in jumping out of his seat and joining her on the stage. 'And that, my love,' he said as he pulled her close, 'is how the next Ethereal age begins.'

EPILOGUE

*S*torm and Isaac walked hand in hand down the country lane. The summer sun hung low and lazy in the sky and the air was heavy with the scent of lavender from the fields beyond. In other circumstances it would have made the perfect stroll, but they had somewhere to be. When the cottage came into view, they both gasped.

'Wow,' they said in unison, and then grinned at each other.

'How on earth can so many species be in full bloom at the same time?' Isaac asked, incredulous, as he sank to his knees to inspect a plant that had caught his eye.

He looked up, and Storm raised her eyebrows at him and laughed.

'Doh!' he said with a snigger. 'Of course.'

Storm pushed open the low whitewashed gate that led up to the cottage. It was, beyond doubt, the most beautiful garden she had ever seen. Two cats, one black and white, the other all black save for one whisker, snoozed together on a folded blanket on a cream wrought-iron bench. The cats looked up as they approached, then jumped down to greet them. Isaac was still making the introductions when a Fox Red Labrador bounded out of the house, almost wagging herself in half.

Storm was still crouched on the floor tickling the dog when a familiar voice said, 'Hey.'

The dog sprang back and sat next to the cats, tail thumping.

Storm's head snapped up and her eyes filled at once with hot, happy tears. 'Hey,' she said, although it came out somewhere between a laugh, a hiccup and a sob. She tried again. 'Hey, Lil.'

They each crossed the space between them at a run, and then, there she was, in her arms, as real as she had ever known her. 'I have to stop losing you like this, you know,' Storm said, laughing.

'That was the last time. I promise,' Lilly said, squeezing her.

Storm stepped back but held on to Lilly's arms. 'It really is, darling girl. They can't threaten us again, ever.'

'But how can you even be here?' Lilly asked, her bright smile falling. 'I thought you couldn't walk in spirit because creation needs the frequency of the First.'

Storm had been looking forward to telling her this bit. She'd go into detail later and explain all about what happened after the blessing, but for now she said, 'It seems that being the First comes with many choices. One of which happens to be whether to keep or share the Ethereal spark.'

Lilly's eyes widened. 'What! So you've given up being the First?'

'No. I'll always technically be the First, but I no longer have to be the only Ethereal carrying the spark and keeping the energies in balance. Apparently, any Ethereal can help with that, and when I asked, pretty much all souls agreed to take a share!'

Lilly gasped and put her hand to her mouth. 'Oh, Stormy, I'm so happy for you!' she said as she hugged her.

Storm felt Isaac's arm around her shoulders, and while she knew she should step aside to let him hug Lilly too, she wasn't quite ready to relinquish her friend.

'You're a sight for sore eyes,' Isaac said to Lilly. 'For a moment there ...' He broke off, and Storm was glad he'd not finished. They would all need a long time to get over the events of the last few days.

Over Lilly's shoulder, Storm saw Jack appear. He leaned against the door-frame, his famous thousand-watt smile even brighter here. She grinned in reply.

'So, are you pair coming in for tea or are you planning on loitering out there all day?' he asked.

They made their way up the path to the house, Lilly's arm looped through Storm's, pinning her closely to her side.

'We sort of missed the last chapter of the story, so I'm assuming you'll be here a while,' Jack said as they approached, his arms already outstretched to greet Isaac. 'I made cake and everything, mate,' he said, laughing, as they embraced and did the back-slapping thing that always made Storm and Lilly roll their eyes.

'We're going to stay as long as you need us here,' Storm said, turning to Lilly.

'Wonderful. Well, fill us in, and then tell us what jobs need doing back home, aside from building a new greenhouse, so that we know what to pack,' she said, glancing sideways at Jack before turning her attention back to Storm.

Storm had been afraid to hope. Did she mean what she thought she meant? She realised that she must have looked stunned, because Lilly said, 'You didn't think we were done, did you? It's glorious here, but we're all agreed,' she continued, looking to Jack and then the animals, who had just walked past them into the hallway. 'We're all of us up for one more life.'

The End

ACKNOWLEDGEMENTS

Someone once asked me if being an independent author got a bit lonely. While the hours spent hunched over a keyboard are indeed spent in solitude, getting a book out into the world is very much a team effort.

As ever, I have my lovely husband Stuart to thank for his unwavering belief, encouragement and plot support, and my soul sister, Katie for always being there to cheer me on.

To my editor Toby Selwyn for his guidance and support and for making the process so much fun. Katherine Stephen for her eagle-eyed proofing skills, and Andrew Nickson for designing another beautiful cover.

Heartfelt thanks to my beta-readers for their thoughtful and constructive feedback: Stu; Judith Oak; Nicola Sparkes; Becci Fearnley; Anne Coffey; Kate Arbuckle, and Kate Nicholls.

Maintaining one's sanity while running a business and writing in your spare time is always a challenge, so thank you to the ladies of The Write Honourables, and the Freelance Business Lounge for their support, encouragement and good humour.

Last, but by no means least, I'd like to say a massive thank you to everyone who read Ethereal. Your reviews and feedback gave me the courage to write and publish this sequel and for that, I'm truly grateful.

ABOUT THE AUTHOR

E L Williams grew up in the Welsh Valleys in a tiny house full of books and stories of magic. She's passionate about animals, nature and all things spiritual and frequently combines all three in her writing.

As a sustainability advisor by profession, her work is influenced by her desire to protect and cherish the natural world.

Emma lives in Berkshire with her husband and Bear, their elderly Miniature Schnauzer. When she's not working, writing, or pandering to the needs of her demanding pooch, she's usually to be found gardening or coddling her dozens of house plants.

Thank you for reading The Cold of Summer. If you enjoyed it, please consider leaving a review and recommending it to a friend.

KEEP IN TOUCH

To be the first to hear news of the next book, please head over to the website and join the readers' club. No spam I promise, just a short monthly update, plus occasional giveaways, free short stories and interviews with inspiring people.

You can also find me online, usually blathering about books, dogs and the joys of writing fiction in stolen moments. I love a natter, so please stop by and say hello.

Website: www.elwilliamsauthor.com
Email: hello@elwilliamsauthor.com
Facebook: @ELWilliamsAuthor
Instagram: @el_williamsyoung

READER REVIEWS

The First Ethereal

"Like nothing I've ever read before. I can't recommend this book more highly. I absolutely loved it. An intelligent, generous and ambitious novel.'

— Z. ARDEN

"'A powerful and beautiful story of a passionate fight for the greater good and the earnest hope for a better future. I can't wait for the sequel!'

— M. WISH

'Eerily predictive following current world events! Not only an exciting read but thought provoking and magical at the same time.'

— S. ANGEL

READER REVIEWS

'A beautifully told modern fairy story.'

— LYNNE H

'With the looming backdrop of climate change, strong characters are drawn together; forced to tackle something bigger than all of us, forged together for the greater good. Beautifully told, The First Ethereal will stay with you for a long time.

— WOSSY

'I'm struggling to put into words how much I loved this book and why. It's so relevant and rooted in reality while still being full of real magic, with a sprinkle of hocus-pocus for good measure!'

— MRS. T

READER REVIEWS

'An amazing story filled with love! I could not put it down! I fell in love with the story, and oh my, the plot twist!'

— K. ARBUCKLE

'Beautifully written story with engaging and relatable characters that'll keep you turning the pages till the very end. Timeless in its message but particularly relevant to society today, but also fun and easy to read.'

— DAVID

'Wow...what an imagination....I just loved this book. It keeps you guessing right up to the end.'

— J.KINNAIRD